Marth   rs with her
master   come alive.
She's r   Ann Mills

AUTHOR, *Firewall* AND *The Survivor*
CHRISTY AWARD WINNER

In *Love Never Fails* Martha Rogers once again delivers a strong historical romance with engaging, multi-layered characters. I found myself transported to the 1880s and caught up in the lives of the heroine's family, as well as her struggles with her own personal beliefs and how those might impact her future and chance for love. I very much recommend   o enjoys a sweet hi

Lee Ferrell
AUTHOR OF
THE LOVE BLOSSOMS IN OREGON SERIES

I have loved Martha Rogers' stories ever since we shared the pages of the Southern romance novella collection Sugar and Grits together. In *Love Never Fails* Rogers has once again penned a tale of two completely unlikely characters who find love, despite the odds that are stacked against them. From the first page until the last, the story of Molly Delaney and her Stefan will be one I won't soon forget.

—KATHLEEN Y'BARBO
A ROMANTIC TIMES CAREER ACHIEVEMENT NOMINEE
AND BEST-SELLING AUTHOR OF
THE SECRET LIVES OF WILL TUCKER SERIES

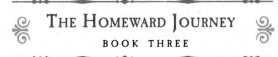

Love Never Fails

THE HOMEWARD JOURNEY

BOOK THREE

Love Never Fails

THE HOMEWARD JOURNEY
BOOK THREE

MARTHA ROGERS

REALMS

Most CHARISMA HOUSE BOOK GROUP products are available at special quantity discounts for bulk purchase for sales promotions, premiums, fund-raising, and educational needs. For details, write Charisma House Book Group, 600 Rinehart Road, Lake Mary, Florida 32746, or telephone (407) 333-0600.

LOVE NEVER FAILS by Martha Rogers
Published by Realms
Charisma Media/Charisma House Book Group
600 Rinehart Road
Lake Mary, Florida 32746
www.charismahouse.com

Unless otherwise noted, all Scripture quotations are from the King James Version of the Bible.

Cover design by Justin Evans

Visit the author's website at www.marthawrogers.com.

Library of Congress Cataloging-in-Publication Data:
Rogers, Martha, 1936-
  Love never fails / by Martha Rogers. -- First edition.
      pages cm. -- (The homeward journey ; book 3)
  Summary: "At odds over their beliefs and separated by the war, Molly and Stefan must learn to depend of God. In book three of the Homeward Journey series, Daniel and Sallie Delaney's daughter Molly finishes school and returns to her home to teach. When old friends of her parents come

for a visit with their son, Stefan, Molly is attracted to the young man, but all he is interested in is talking about his position in the army. When he leaves to rejoin his regiment, Molly is both relieved and saddened. Can they overcome their differences and find love?"-- Provided by publisher.

  ISBN 978-1-62136-647-8 (paperback) -- ISBN 978-1-62136-648-5 (e-book)

1. Homecoming--Fiction. I. Title.
PS3618.O4655L67 2014
813'.6--dc23

2014024859

First edition

14 15 16 17 18 — 987654321
Printed in the United States of America

To Rex Rogers, my husband, who has stood beside me and encouraged me in all my writing. Thank you for fifty-five wonderful years.

ACKNOWLEDGMENTS

Thank you to:

- The St. Francisville Historical Society for their help in getting the information I needed for the town of St. Francisville and the surrounding area after the Civil War.

- My Whiteman cousins who continue to inspire me with plot ideas and for their support and encouragement throughout this series.

- My agent Tamela Hancock Murray and the Steve Laube Agency for always believing in me and looking out for my best interests.

- Lori and Deborah for always having the right suggestions and ideas for making my stories stronger and tighter. I'd be a mess without you.

- The team at Charisma Media. You have become like family to me and I love and appreciate each one of you on the team.

- My Lord and Savior who gives me the inspiration needed for each story and guides my path each day. To Him be all glory, honor and praise.

CHAPTER 1

MOLLY WAVED GOOD-BYE to her last student and plopped down at the top of the school steps. The last day always left her with mixed emotions. She loved the idea of three months without her students but she hated to see the semester end. Just when everyone had truly begun to understand and make so much progress, summer came along. How much would they forget over the summer?

Ellie Gordon, the upper grades teacher, joined her on the steps. "Well, another year gone by. I'm always amazed how much the boys in my classes grow in height during the year, and how quickly the girls grow into young ladies."

"I know what you mean. When I look at the first graders and then the fifth graders, I can't believe how much they change. You'll be getting a good group from those fifth graders next year." Molly stood and swiped at the dust on her skirt. "It's time for me to get my things and get home."

Old friends of her parents would arrive on the train tomorrow for a visit, and Molly had to help her mother get the house ready. Of course Mama had been working all week, but she wanted things to be perfect, so Molly had work to do.

She turned to hug Ellie, who now stood on the porch. "I'm so glad you're my teaching partner. If they hadn't decided that married ladies could teach as well as unmarried ones, no telling who I may have ended up with."

Ellie's laughter floated on the warm afternoon air. "Well, since I was the teacher before I married Levi, and our twin boys and Timothy are here in school, they figured I would be able to do as decent a job as any other. I'm happy you were here to take Miss Crabtree's place two years ago when she left. We were getting more students and she didn't want to handle that many."

"It's a good thing Levi and Micah and Mr. Hudson were concerned about our future and decided to enlarge the building and divide into two levels last summer." Molly turned to gaze at the expanded building that had opened in the fall. Two larger classrooms were joined by a coatroom. New maps, chalkboards, and pictures adorned the walls along with new desks, making for a good learning environment this past school year.

Ellie headed back to her classroom. "I'm going to gather my things and go down to Margaret's to collect my young'uns. They do love to play together, although, being cousins, they can create a lot of mischief, too."

Molly laughed and shook her head. How well she understood that since those same cousins occupied her classroom. After Ellie entered her side of the building, Molly stood on the porch a few minutes longer. How she loved this town where she'd lived since early childhood. It had grown and prospered in those years and now had two doctors to take care of the growing population. Her father had been delighted when one of Stoney Creek's own boys, Andrew Delmont, had returned as a doctor to partner in the practice.

One other thing that had changed happened to be the

female population. Many more girls had been born than boys, and now the female population of Stoney Creek had begun to overtake the males. And that now meant very few men single men her age were available. Besides that, younger families made up most of the new people coming into town. At least that trend bode well for the school.

Molly sighed, went back inside to collect her belongings, and gazed around her classroom once more before heading for the door. Silence surrounded her, and she ran her fingers along the desks as she walked up the center aisle. She'd miss the children this summer, and the months loomed ahead without much activity going on. At least July would be here before she knew it. She loved the celebration for the birthday of the United States of America.

Once outside, Molly realized she now had to rush to get home and help her mother with the final preparations for the Elliot family's arrival. The last time she'd seen them was back in Louisiana at her uncle's wedding, and that was over ten years ago. Stefan Elliot was only a few months older, and at the age of twelve, he and a few friends had teased and played jokes on Molly and Clarissa, Stefan's sister.

Clarissa would be with her parents, but Stefan had followed his father's footsteps and chosen the military as his career, so he most likely wouldn't be with his family. It would be interesting to have him around though since Andrew Delmont was too much like an older brother to be of interest other than as a friend.

Molly bounded up the steps to the clinic run by her father and Andrew. She darted through the waiting area and wiggled her fingers in her father's direction. The examination room's closed door meant Andrew was with a patient. She'd never be able to call him Dr. Delmont.

Mama's singing echoed from the kitchen where she made last-minute preparations for her guests. The doctor before them had a large family and had built a big house adjoining the area that served as an infirmary for the town, with room for six patients if they needed to stay overnight.

After depositing her box of things from school at the bottom of the stairs, Molly joined her mother in the kitchen. "Hi, Mama. I'm sorry I'm late, but it took me longer than I planned to close up for the summer."

Mama continued to roll out the pastry for a pie. "I understand. The last day of school is even more exciting than the first day of a new semester."

"Hmm, maybe, but I will miss the children." She swiped a few berries from the bowl on the counter then grabbed an apron. "What can I do to help?"

"What I need most right now is to see that Alice and Juliet have their things moved into Clara's room so we'll have their room for Mr. and Mrs. Elliot."

"It's nice to have five bedrooms for when we have company. I remember when Aunt Hannah lived with us, and how much fun it was. I'll go up now and check on Alice and Juliet." If Mama's other two babies had lived, the house would be much more crowded, but it suited a family with six children just fine. She and Clarissa would share a room, and what fun they would have catching up with each other.

At the top of the stairs the voices of her younger sisters reached the hallway. Their giggles meant they were either sharing a funny moment or up to a prank on Clara. Molly opened the door to find the two girls trying on some of Clara's clothes. "What's going on here?"

Their eyes widened and their cheeks burned red. Alice jumped up from the floor and nearly fell over trying to balance in Clara's best shoes. "Molly, we didn't know you were home."

Molly crossed her arms over her chest and tapped her foot on the hardwood floor. "Obviously. I don't think Clara would be happy with you or what you're doing with her things. Now get out of those clothes and put them back where they belong. You're lucky I found you and not Clara."

"Yes, ma'am, and please don't tell her." Alice pulled off the shoes and put them back in the wardrobe with the others.

Juliet slipped one of Clara's skirts down to her feet and stepped out of it. "Clara has pretty things, and we just wanted to see how they looked."

"I understand, but it's not nice to pry into someone else's belongings." Molly had to hide the smile that threatened to surface at the sight of the two younger girls scrambling to get things back in order. Alice had promoted to Ellie's class for next year, but Juliet would still be in Molly's. The two had been fairly well behaved in school, but Alice was one to be watched. Like most eleven year olds, she always had fun on her mind.

"Have you moved your clothes and things so Mr. and Mrs. Elliot will have plenty of room?"

Juliet bobbed her head. "Yes, we did. Clara was nice and made a space for us in the wardrobe and in the chest."

"And this is how you repay her kindness?" At the remorse in Juliet's big brown eyes, Molly's stern voice turned gentle. "I won't tell on you this time, but Mama and I both expect you two to be on your best behavior while the Elliot family is here."

At their firm nods, Molly wrapped her arms around them and kissed their heads. "I love you girls. Now play with your dolls or something else for a while."

Molly closed the door to their room and made her way to the one to be used by Mr. and Mrs. Elliot. Everything looked in order, including the empty drawers in the chest and the extra space in the wardrobe. Next she checked on her brothers' rooms. Now twelve and nineteen, they kept their room fairly neat, but Daniel's clothes discarded after school lay scattered on the floor.

Molly grinned and shook her head. Mama would have him clean it up later, or Tom would force him to. No telling where they were now, but they'd be back soon for supper. Tom should be off work by now and had probably taken Danny for a ride. Her youngest brother loved horses and wanted to work on his Uncle Micah's ranch someday.

By this time tomorrow the house would be full of people. She anticipated seeing Clarissa, but she wished Stefan could join them. He would certainly make for a more interesting visit. With everything in shape upstairs, she headed back to the kitchen.

Stefan rubbed his thumb along the handle of his cane. Two more weeks and he'd be rid of this thing and able to get back to his regiment. At least his injury had not been severe enough to prevent his return, but being off for these past weeks had been boring to say the least. He glanced through the train window as it clacked its way across East Texas and the piney woods. Not a whole lot different from the part of Louisiana they'd just come through. Still it was Texas and that made the difference.

Tomorrow morning they'd arrive in Stoney Creek to visit old friends of his family. His parents had talked of little else for weeks and then insisted that he join them. After much persuasion and pleading from Clarissa, he consented. Why, he wasn't sure, except that he did remember back ten years ago when Molly Whiteman visited for her uncle's wedding. If she was as pretty now as she was then, the visit just might prove to be worth the time and effort.

He fingered the brass buttons on his uniform. The army blue and gold had attracted more than one young lady, so it shouldn't be any different with Molly. She'd be impressed by the medals he earned for marksmanship as well as the one from the skirmish with outlaws that had caused his injury. Ever since childhood he'd planned to follow his father's footsteps and be a high-ranking officer in the United States Army. Now he was well on his way to that goal.

"Are you thinking about when you'll return to your regiment?" Clarissa leaned forward and pressed Stefan's arm.

He patted his sister's hand. "Yes and no. I'll be glad to get rid of this cane and get back to duty, but I was also thinking of our visit with the Whiteman family. Did I understand Mother to say they have six children?"

"Yes, they do. You remember Molly, don't you?"

Heat rose in his face. "Hmm, yes, and I...uh...I was wondering about her. If I remember correctly, she has red hair like her mother."

Clarissa sat back, a smirk filling her face. "You remember

correctly, and well you should with as much grief as you gave us when they were in Louisiana. I was ready to have Father string you up to dry."

"I must have lost that part of the memory." He frowned to hide the fact that he did indeed remember the teasing. He'd done it all to get Molly's attention and see if he could rouse the anger that was supposed to go along with having red hair. It had worked, and she had been even prettier with her anger riled up.

"I just bet you have." Clarissa's laughter burst forth and caused his parents to turn their heads toward him. A few of the other passengers also looked in their direction with curiosity written across their faces.

Stefan frowned at his sister. "Quiet down. You have everyone staring at us."

"And since when did *you* not want all the attention? I've seen you showing off your uniform and telling tall tales enough to know you enjoy it."

"This is different. Now sit back like a young lady and be quiet." What she said had an element of truth, but could he help it if he attracted young ladies with his uniform and stories, most of which were actually true?

Clarissa shook her head and clicked her tongue against her teeth. She gazed out the window a few minutes before turning back to face him. "I can't wait to see Molly again. It's been so long." A sly grin turned up the corners of her lips. "She's not the same little girl she was ten years ago."

"I should hope not. You aren't the same either." He grinned, but made no further comment. Under no circumstances would he admit his anticipation of seeing Molly again, but to express disinterest would be a lie. He may embellish the truth, but telling an outright lie was not his way. He'd have to be careful with his comments and reactions around Clarissa. The hours until their arrival in Stoney Creek couldn't pass quickly enough.

CHAPTER 2

STEFAN CHECKED HIS pocket watch for the time. They should be arriving in Stoney Creek within the next hour. The pine woods of East Texas had given way to green, rolling hills. He'd spotted farms as well as ranches dotting the countryside. What a versatile state this Texas had turned out to be. Although he'd traveled farther West with the army, he had not been through Texas before now.

The closer they came to the heart of the state, the more his desire to see Molly rose. If she had grown into a likeness of her mother she'd be most attractive, and that he could always enjoy. A smiled tilted his lips at the anticipation of her surprise at his arrival. As it had been a last-minute decision, there had been no time to inform Mrs. Whiteman that he was coming too.

Something tugged at his coat sleeve. Stefan glanced down into the eyes of a little boy. "Hey there, sonny, how are you?"

His round blue eyes opened wide. "Are you a soldier?"

"Yes, I am. I'm a lieutenant with the United States Cavalry, and normally I'm stationed at Fort Apache, Arizona." He turned so the boy could see the insignias on the dark blue jacket. "What's your name?"

"I'm Billy and I'm almost seven years old. Have you ever killed any injuns?" His little hand still gripped Stefan's sleeve.

What to say to this boy? Stefan didn't want to glorify

killing, but he also wanted to be truthful. A child this age shouldn't see killing as a good thing, even though Stefan himself had no problems with pulling the trigger against an enemy. He reached down and pulled the boy up onto his lap.

"Well, soldiers do kill others, but only when it's absolutely necessary to avoid being killed themselves, or to keep others from being killed."

A woman hurried their way. "I'm so sorry. Billy got away from me when I tended to his sister. He's been asking about you ever since we got on the train yesterday afternoon." She reached for the boy. "Billy, you know you shouldn't bother other people on the train. Let's go back to our seats and have a cookie." She held the boy close to her to still his squirming. "Again, I'm sorry he bothered you."

Stefan shook his head. "It's all right. He's just curious."

She nodded and turned to head back for her seat.

Clarissa leaned toward him. "That was a very good answer you gave that little boy."

"It's the truth, but boys that young don't need to be thinking about things like that yet." Wars and killing should never be taken lightly, but he understood the appeal of the military life since he'd fallen under the spell of it himself.

"That reminds me, did I tell you Molly is a schoolteacher now? She has the lower grades and another lady, who is married to one of Molly's uncles, teaches upper grades. I think that's exciting. If those children over there are going to Stoney Brook, Billy and his sister will most likely go to Molly's school. I wish I could learn some skills so I could work. Molly's aunt Hannah is a nurse even though she's married to a rancher, and she helps Dr. Whiteman when he needs her for surgeries and things like that. I want to be useful like that. Maybe I should go to college."

Stefan shook his head at his sister's ramblings. She could talk longer without saying much of anything than any woman he'd met so far. Her dissertation just now proved it. Who cared whose uncle or cousin or aunt or whatever taught school or ran a ranch? Clarissa and her ideas about wanting to work like Molly or Hannah would get nowhere with their father. He and Mother had brought up Clarissa to be a lady of the manor and expected her to marry well and carry out her role as hostess of a large home and family. No such plans filled his dreams of the future. He'd stay in the military and become a colonel or perhaps a general, and the woman he married must be content to live on army posts.

Next to him his sister sighed and picked up her book to continue reading, but the conductor came through to warn them that they'd be arriving in Stoney Creek in the next half hour. She laid her book aside and reached for the floral bag on the floor instead.

Stefan stood to stretch his muscles which had grown tight from prolonged sitting. He leaned on his cane with one hand and pulled out his brown leather satchel from under the seat. After setting it on an empty space across the aisle, he spotted Billy peering over the back of his seat. Stefan winked at the boy. Billy giggled and slid back down out of sight.

If their stop was also Stoney Creek, maybe he'd have the chance to see the boy in town. He enjoyed children, but he didn't let that be known among his mates in the regiment.

They might consider that trait to be too soft for a soldier trained to fight and kill when necessary.

However, he'd bet his last dime that if it came down to it, they'd all fight to the death for the safety of a child. As a matter of fact, wasn't that part of his duty? He'd been trained for battle, yes, but that training meant willingness to risk his life to ensure the safety of the citizens of the United States.

The cane now in his left hand proved that willingness, but he hoped such testing would not be necessary in the days ahead. A shudder passed through his body, and he shook his head. Time to get away from those thoughts and concentrate on enjoying the last weeks of his medical leave.

Molly rushed through morning chores and raced back to her room to get ready to meet the train. Less than half an hour remained until she'd see her friend once again. All the letters they'd exchanged in the past years had been fun, but seeing her in person and talking face-to-face would be so much better.

Molly's hair, once a much lighter red, now glowed a rich auburn with red-gold highlights. Thank goodness she no longer had orange-red hair like her brother. She tucked stray tendrils back and refastened the hair clip at the crown. Today she'd opted to let it hang loose from the clip. Besides, summer vacation had started, and she didn't need to keep her appearance so prim and proper.

With a last pinch to her cheeks, she nodded her head in satisfaction and picked up her handbag. With it hanging from her wrist, Molly hurried down the stairs to meet her sister and mother in the hallway.

Mama pulled on lace gloves and eyed Molly. "You certainly look eager and ready for that train. You and Clarissa have a lot of catching up to do." She turned to Clara now standing on the bottom stair. "Thank you for offering to stay with Alice and Juliet. We won't be gone long."

Clara looked toward the ceiling and sighed. "Of course we'll be fine. I'm seventeen now and old enough to have a child of my own."

Mama's eyebrows raised and she jerked her head back. "Don't even think a thing like that, Clara Louise Whiteman. You have plenty of time before marriage and children come into your life." She turned and headed out the door.

Molly exchanged a shrug of shoulders and raised eyebrows with Clara before following Mama outside to the carriage. Papa had gone ahead with the other buggy so there would be room for all to return to the house. She and Clarissa would share the buggy, and Mr. and Mrs. Elliot would ride in the carriage with Mama and Papa. That way she and Clarissa could begin sharing news right away.

The shrill train whistle signaled its arrival at the station at the same time Molly stepped down from the buggy and tethered her horse. Excitement flowed through her body in anticipation of seeing her childhood friend.

The train finally stopped and passengers began disembarking. A mother with three young children stepped down to the platform and was greeted by Mr. Olson, who had only recently moved to town and taken over the wheelwright shop.

Behind Mrs. Olson, Clarissa waved and called to Molly. "Here I am, Molly." Not a hair of her dark brown hair looked out of place, and the jaunty blue hat matched Clarissa's traveling dress. If she hadn't been stepping off the train, Molly would never have believed her friend had been traveling for two days.

As Clarissa descended to the platform, her parents followed her. Molly grabbed Clarissa and hugged her. "I'm so glad you've finally arrived. I brought the buggy so we could catch up on our lives on the way to our house."

"Well, we might have an extra rider with us if there's room." Clarissa's eyes danced with delight.

"An extra rider? Who came with you? One of your servant girls?" Molly furrowed her brow and tilted her head to the side.

"No, he's a surprise." Clarissa moved to the side and waved her arm toward a young man now descending the steps from the passenger car.

Molly gazed into the blue eyes of Stefan Elliot and her breath caught in her throat. He'd been handsome as a young boy even when he was teasing her, but now in his uniform, he was the most handsome man she'd ever seen, especially in Stoney Creek. "Mr. Elliot, this is a surprise."

He took her hand and raised it to his lips. "And you are a delightful surprise as well."

Heat flooded Molly's cheeks and she swallowed hard as his lips brushed her hand. "Thank you, Mr. Elliot. Or should I call you by your rank?" She looked doubtfully at the insignias on his uniform, not sure how to translate them.

His laughter rang in the air. "Now, Molly Whiteman,

don't you think we've known each other long enough for you to simply call me Stefan?"

Yes, they had been friends for many years, but calling him by his given name now—never mind that. She'd call him whatever he wanted while he was here.

Mama reached out and hugged Stefan. "It's wonderful that you could join your parents, but we're sorry about your injuries that have kept you from your duties."

For the first time, Molly became aware that Stefan leaned on a cane. Not wanting to be nosy, she blinked her eyes and glanced toward Clarissa. What had happened to cause such an injury? She didn't recall hearing Mama say anything about it before now.

"I'll be fine in another few weeks and will rejoin my regiment in Fort Apache at that time. It's been inconvenient, but I've enjoyed my furlough. Besides, it offered the opportunity to come here and visit."

Mama's hand went to her lips. "Oh, dear, you may have to bunk with our two boys. Your parents have the girls' room, and they've gone in with Clara."

Mrs. Elliot shook her head. "Oh, no, that won't be necessary. We'll make arrangements for Stefan to stay at the hotel."

Mama opened her mouth to most likely protest such a thing, but Mrs. Elliot shushed her before she could say a word. "No, don't say it'll be fine at the house. We knew it might crowd things a bit, so he'll register at the hotel and sleep there."

Clarissa pulled Molly to the side while their parents continued to talk. "Soon as we get our luggage loaded, let's ride out of here. Stefan may be a little lame still, but he's strong as an ox, which is why he's healed so quickly. He'll help get my things in the buggy."

Molly glanced over Clarissa's shoulder to discover that Stefan had already picked up one of Clarissa's bags and now walked toward them with his own and his sister's bags held with his free arm and hand. Indeed his strength became evident with his ease in handling the luggage. Molly's heart began a tap dance that sent a shiver through her veins.

Stefan stopped in front of Mama. "Where shall I stow these, Mrs. Whiteman?"

"Oh, over there in the buggy, I suppose. I'm sure you'd much rather ride with Clarissa and Molly than with us old folks."

A grin spread across Stefan's face as he fixed his gaze on Molly. "Yes, ma'am, I certainly would enjoy their company."

It meant that she and Clarissa wouldn't be able to share their thoughts, but they could do that later. Right now, riding with Stefan filled her heart with a new excitement.

Clarissa locked arms with Molly and the two set off for the buggy. "This is going to be the most fun two weeks. I heard your mama say they'd planned a party in our honor. That is the most wonderful thing I can imagine."

Molly laughed and shook her head. "She has arranged for one, but it won't be anything like the cotillions you have back in St. Francisville. Mama has told me of the grand parties they had at your father's place there and at your mother's home in Mississippi." Those stories of her mother's birthday and other grand occasions had thrilled Molly more than once, and sometimes she longed to attend such gatherings. Of course the parties and dances held here in Stoney Creek were fun in their own way, and now she could look forward to having Stefan at one.

"Maybe not, but I always like to try new things. It's exciting to just be here in Texas." She gazed up and down the street before allowing Stefan to assist her up onto the buggy seat. "I was really expecting to see a lot of cowboys here."

Molly laughed. "Oh, they'll be in later tonight. Saturday nights are sometimes a little wild, but they do have fun. Aunt Hannah has already invited us out to their ranch for Sunday dinner. We'll ride out there after church tomorrow. The Circle G is one of the biggest in these parts and you'll see lots of cowboys there."

Stefan helped Molly into the buggy then pulled himself up. "Do you mind if I drive?"

"Not at all. It's only about six or so blocks down that way to the infirmary. The stable is in the back, so you can pull around there. This way, I can point out things to you both without trying to keep my mind on the horse." Molly clasped her hands in her lap to stop their tremble at the nearness of Stefan.

Although the seat was big enough for three they barely fit, and if she relaxed one little bit she'd be almost leaning on Stefan. He glanced down at her with a grin that accented the dimple in his left cheek. That sent Molly's heart into a tailspin. How wonderful the days ahead would be with him here, especially since she wouldn't have to be busy teaching school.

Stefan flipped the reins and the buggy started forward with a lurch. Heat throbbed through the layers of her skirt as his thigh brushed against hers.

Papa followed close behind, and even from this distance,

Mama and Mrs. Elliot's voices carried to indicate they were already enjoying their time together. Molly stole a glance at Stefan, who happened to be gazing at her. A smile still curved the corner of his mouth, and heat once again flooded Molly's cheeks. Yes, this would be a most interesting two weeks with Stefan as their guest.

CHAPTER 3

THAT EVENING, ANDREW Delmont joined the family at dinner to welcome the Elliots to Stoney Creek. Molly bit her lip to hide her grin at Clarissa's reaction to the young doctor. Molly had known Andrew most of her life, or at least since they'd moved to Texas. He had become a handsome man, but even though he was one of the few men in town her age, Molly had no interest in him except as a good friend.

Clarissa smiled and batted her eyelashes as Andrew attended to her seating. Next to him of course. Mama must be in one of her matchmaking modes, which suited Molly just fine as she sat next to Stefan.

During a lull in the conversation, Danny rested his arms on the table and cocked his head toward Stefan. "I like your uniform. I might be a soldier one of these days." Then he leaned in closer. "How did you get hurt?"

Molly gulped and almost choked. War was not a topic she deemed appropriate for the dinner table, but no one voiced an objection. Heat flooded her cheeks, but she kept silent.

After a moment, Stefan laid down his napkin. "We ran into some renegade Indians who had been stealing horses. We got into a gunfight, and one of them shot my horse. When he went down, I landed under him and severely injured my leg. I was given a leave to recover, but I'll go back in a few weeks."

Danny's mouth turned down. "Oh. I thought maybe you got shot."

Molly's heart jumped to her throat, and the muscles across her shoulders tightened. The very idea sickened her.

Mama's fork clattered to her plate, and her face paled. "Daniel Whiteman, apologize to Lieutenant Elliot this minute. We would never want anyone shot for any reason."

Danny licked his lips before he said, "I'm sorry, Lieutenant. I didn't mean I wanted you to be shot."

"I understand, Danny, and I accept your apology." He pointed to the medal on his tunic. "I earned this medal with my men when we were able to successfully stop a stage coach robbery. Five outlaws tried to hold up a stage carrying a cash box with a lot of money in it. Even with two extra men on the stage as protection, the outlaws ambushed the stage. We had a small scouting patrol of five men not far away. When we heard the gunshots, we rode that way and prevented the men from getting away."

Danny gaped. "How did you stop them?"

Stefan glanced around the table, and seeming to notice Molly's discomfort, he sent a wink Danny's way then said, "Hearing about the cavalry is interesting, but I do think we can find a better topic of conversation for our meal." He turned to Molly. "Tell me about your classes. What do you teach and how many students do you have?"

Molly relaxed at the change in topic. Stefan had no way of knowing how much she hated talk of guns, shootings, and wars. Hearing about her father's war experiences from Grandma Whiteman had been more than enough battle stories for a lifetime.

"I have fifteen wonderful six- to ten-year-old children in my classes. They are still young and eager to learn. That doesn't mean the boys can't be mischievous and try a few tricks here and again. The secret is to let them know right away who is in charge."

Stefan grinned and nodded his head. "Yes, I can see you doing just that. I must say, though, that it's difficult to prevent boys from pulling pranks."

"Oh, and do you speak from experience?"

This time his laughter rang out so that others at the table turned in their direction. Molly's cheeks heated, but from the twinkle in Stefan's eyes, she must have been right on target. Then she remembered the things he'd done to her and Clarissa last time her family visited in Louisiana, like tweaking their braids and chasing them with a dead chicken.

"Yes, I'm afraid I was one of those mischievous boys, Molly Whiteman."

Embarrassed at his teasing, she lowered her gaze and concentrated on the food before her. Thankfully, her father rescued her with another question for Stefan.

The conversation around her buzzed, but she only half listened as Stefan talked with her father. Andrew and Clarissa were engrossed with each other, and Mama and Mrs. Elliot were deep into some topic most likely to do with plans for tomorrow. For once her siblings sat in their places and ate in silence.

She glanced up to find her mother frowning. Molly smiled, but her mother only slightly nodded which meant she wanted Molly to pay more attention to their guests. With everyone's but Clara's attention drawn elsewhere, she'd talk with her sister who sat on her left. Come to think of it, Clara did appear to be somewhat bored with the whole thing.

Molly leaned over. "Looks like everyone has som
to say but us. Wonder what would happen if one ᴄ
swooned right here and landed our face in the middle
our plate?"

Clara almost choked on a bite of potato. She swallowed
hard then giggled. "You wouldn't dare."

Another stern glance from Mama quieted Clara, but her
lips still curved in a smile. Molly lowered her voice. "No, I
wouldn't, but it'd be interesting." Indeed it would, but not
worth the embarrassment in front of Stefan. She sighed
and picked up her knife to butter a piece of bread.

Clara's giggle drew Stefan's attention to Molly. She and her
sister shared some private amusement, and Molly's smile
lightened his heart. All during the story he'd told Danny,
her displeasure filled her face at the mention of the gun
fight and being shot. He'd heard that Molly's father had
terrible experiences in a Yankee prison. That would be
enough to make any young woman reluctant to hear war
stories, but the military was a part of his life.

He leaned toward Molly. "It's good to see you smile.
You didn't look too pleased earlier when I was telling army
stories." Unlike other young women he'd known, she had
seemed more repelled than impressed at this tales.

A pink blush filled her cheeks. "I'm sorry you noticed
that. I didn't like hearing about your getting hurt. It could
have been a lot worse, and I don't like hearing about guns
and killings at all."

"Then we'll talk about them no more." He leaned forward and addressed Clara. "And what interests you, Clara?"

Clara flushed pink, but delight filled her eyes. "I love the horses at Uncle Micah's ranch and want to help train them, but Papa says I have to finish my schooling first. I enjoy riding, and when I'm through with school, Uncle Micah promised me a horse of my own. Then I can go riding whenever I want."

She stopped suddenly and blinked her eyes. "I'm terribly sorry, but I do tend to get carried away when I talk about riding and such."

"That's quite all right. I tend to have a special place in my heart for horses. I hope to pick out a new one while we're here. Your father tells me the Gordon ranch has some of the finest horses to be found in these parts."

Molly clasped her hands in her lap and beamed at Stefan. "Yes, they do. We're going out there tomorrow after church, so you'll get to see firsthand how beautiful they are."

"I look forward to the trip." Indeed he did. Finding a new horse to replace Black Knight would be a bonus to what already promised to be a most pleasant visit.

Andrew had listened with some interest to Stefan's story, but with him now engaged in talk with Dr. Whiteman, Andrew would much rather pay attention to the delightful young woman seated beside him. Molly had gone on about her friend for weeks, but had he known how beautiful she'd be, he'd have listened more carefully. Clarissa smiled at him now, and eyes that defied description sparkled in the light from the gas-lit chandelier.

"Dr. Delmont, Mrs. Whiteman tells me that you are a partner with Dr. Whiteman. I'm not sure I could be around sick and injured people that much without getting depressed."

"If I'm able to ease the pain and misery of my patients who come in with severe illness or injury, then I'm anything but depressed. I watched Dr. Whiteman while I was growing up and admired all he did for our community. That's why I decided to take up medicine myself."

"I guess it would be very rewarding to see a patient cured or healed, but some die, too, don't they?"

"Yes, they do, and it can be heartbreaking, but thankfully, we cure and heal more than we lose. We have all kinds of new equipment and treatments for injuries and illnesses now." He fingered the napkin in his lap. Being this near to a beautiful young woman sent the blood racing through his veins.

Once again she smiled at him then picked up her water glass and sipped the contents, her enticing eyes peering at him over the rim of the glass.

All his years of learning proper etiquette left him as swiftly as the fluff of dandelions floats away with the breeze. He searched for a topic of interest for Clarissa. Her life? Of course, most people liked to talk about themselves. "Tell me about your home in St. Francisville."

She set her glass back down. "It's a quiet town just up the hill from the Mississippi River. We live in the house where my father grew up, but it seems awfully big with only three of us there now. The thing I love most about it is the garden and all the beautiful flowers Mother tends."

Her voice held such a musical quality to it that Andrew could listen to it all evening. "Sounds like a beautiful place to live. Tell me more."

"It isn't as large as it used to be. Since Father left the

military and took over for Grandfather Elliot, he's had to sell some of the land because he didn't have as many workers, but he still has a good sugarcane crop."

The question of whether or not they employed their former slaves crossed his mind, but then that may be a bit too controversial and private to ask at a dinner table. Instead he asked, "Do you see much of the Mississippi River?"

"Oh, yes. I sometimes go down with Father when they load our sugarcane at the docks. Dr. Whiteman's brothers run the shipping company there. Occasionally Father even takes Mother and me down to New Orleans on the river boats."

As she went on to describe the wonders of New Orleans, he found himself wondering how a small-town doctor could ever compete with riverboat rides to New Orleans and living on a plantation. What a country bumpkin he must appear to someone with her background! He sighed inwardly, resolving to enjoy Clarissa's presence while she was here, with no expectations for the future.

CHAPTER 4

MOLLY DRESSED WITH extra care the next morning. Her clothes were nothing like Clarissa's latest fashions, but then no one in town but the banker's daughter Camilla Hightower wore such high-fashion clothes. Still Molly wanted to look her best. While Clarissa finished pinning the curls in her hair, Molly selected her emerald green dress because it set off her hair and eyes and had brought many compliments before.

"Oh, Molly, that dress is perfect for you." Clarissa turned from the dressing table and fingered the lawn fabric.

"Thank you. It's one of my favorites. Mrs. Culpepper here in town made it for me. Mama never learned to sew, so we have them made."

"I understand that. Mrs. Tenney and her daughter Miriam still make ours in St. Francisville. Of course we now have catalogs and can order them ready-made or go down to New Orleans and purchase beautiful dresses and hats there."

Molly sighed and turned to let Clarissa finish closing the last few buttons. "I'd love to go to New Orleans sometime. Grandma Dyer speaks of it often when we visit. She even talked to Papa about Daniel and Tom going to Louisiana for college at either Tulane or Louisiana State University, but he says if they go to Louisiana for college, they'll go to Centenary like he did. Then Tom decided Texas schools are good enough for him."

"That's good because I don't think Centenary has the

standing it once did." Clarissa fluffed the lace around Molly's neck. "But why are we talking about school of all things? That's boring. Tell me more about the young men here in town."

Molly laughed and picked up her brush to smooth the tangles of her curls. "You met Papa's partner, Dr. Delmont. He'll be at church this morning, but he won't go to the ranch with us because he needs to stay here and take care of any emergencies that might arise."

"Oh, I was looking forward to seeing him again as well as any others who may be around. After all, we're not getting any younger, and men are scarce as gold nuggets back home."

How well Molly remembered her last visit and the party Mr. and Mrs. Elliot had for her parents. Six girls the ages of Molly and Clarissa were there for Molly, but only two young men besides Stefan. Of course the young men loved it, but the girls had been dismayed.

"That's somewhat of a problem around here, too. Andrew is more like a big brother to me than a man I might consider for courting, and most of the cowboys are rough. Besides, my being a schoolteacher turns a lot of them away. I wonder if there's such a thing as a mail-order husband. If it works for the men, why couldn't it work for women?"

Clarissa laughed and shook her head. "Now that's an idea I never considered. Might be interesting, but I think I'd rather know who I was getting right up front."

A knock on the door stilled their conversation. Molly giggled and called out, "Come in."

Mama opened the door and thrust her head through the opening. "We're all ready to go, so you two had better hurry or you'll be walking to church."

"Yes, ma'am. We'll be right down." Molly covered her grin with her fingers and glanced at Clarissa.

"Whatever has you so amused can be continued later. Let's don't keep your father waiting." Mama pulled the door closed and her footsteps echoed on the stairs.

"Guess that means we're ready whether we like it or not." Molly picked up her straw hat decorated with white daisies and a green ribbon. She secured it to her hair with pearl hatpins.

A few moments later Molly followed Clarissa to the buggy where Stefan now stood holding the reins of the horse. Her heart did a double flip at the sight of him in uniform. His dark blue jacket had gold stripes on the sleeves, and his white gloved hands held a hat with crossed sabers and gold cord decorating the crown.

"I must say, you two ladies look lovely this morning. It'll be a pleasure to escort you both." He grinned, showing off that dimple again, and helped them up to the seat.

After listening to his stories last night, Molly admired him even though she didn't really approve of wars and the military. One thing for certain, she'd be the envy of every young woman under age twenty-five at church and maybe even a few older ones as well. With that satisfaction filling her heart, Molly sat back to enjoy the ride to church.

Sallie Whiteman and Jenny Elliot sat in the back seat of the carriage. They'd been best friends since childhood and had endured terrible things during the war that spring of 1865 before the Armistice.

In the bright sunshine of the June morning, Jenny's face

glowed with happiness that mirrored Sallie's own. "Could you imagine back during those days when you waited for Manfred to come home and I recuperated at your home that we'd be where we are today?"

"No, and although I would follow Manfred to the ends of the earth if he asked, I do miss St. Francisville, Woodville, and the times we had together. When my father decided to move his business to St. Francisville to be closer to Grandma and Grandpa, I was delighted to have them in the same place Manfred and I lived. Those were wonderful days, but so have these days in Texas been wonderful."

Jenny reached over and squeezed Sallie's hands. "I'm so glad you've been happy. We shared so much heartache as young women."

Sallie let her thoughts wander back to that day in St. Francisville when Papa had brought Jenny home after her harrowing experience with the Union Army. The young officer who had helped Jenny and her brother get home safely had another reason to accompany them. He came to claim the body of his younger brother, the young soldier Sallie had killed in a terrible skirmish in her parents' home. Sallie blinked her eyes and willed the horrible memory back to the recesses of her mind. She had no time for such dark memories on a beautiful summer day as this one.

She turned her brightest smile to Jenny. "Look how gracious the Lord has been to us. We have beautiful children, wonderful husbands, and lovely homes."

"Oh, indeed. Without our faith during those years, we would never have made it this far." Jenny's face clouded for a moment as sadness passed through her gaze. "My only regret is not having more children. You can understand since you had two of your own who did not live."

Sallie nodded. "I do understand, but I must say the house does get crowded with six children to feed and keep out of mischief. It's much better now that Molly and Clara and are older and Tom is off for school again next fall. He has a head for numbers like his uncle, and he loves to write. His job at the newspaper this summer will be good for him."

The two ladies fell silent for a moment until Jenny leaned toward Sallie and whispered, "Look at our older children. They act as though they've been together all these years instead of across the state line." A grin played about her lips. "Wouldn't it be nice if Molly and Stefan became close? That's one reason I was delighted he decided to come with us."

Sallie pondered the idea. They did make a striking couple. "Let's see how they get on these two weeks. They may not be compatible at all." She did not think it likely that Molly would want to marry a military man, but she could be wrong.

Stefan listened with a smile as his sister and Molly chatted about the people they'd meet today. A few had come by the doctor's house last evening to pay their respects, and many more would greet them at church. His gaze landed on the steeple of the church and moved down to the building itself. This was no ordinary country building. The original wood frame structure sat off to the side with a smaller steeple and single front door. The new one stood tall and stately with white columns, double doors, and colorful stained glass windows. It reminded him of some of the churches he'd seen in Maryland when he attended West Point.

God had been good to him, and Stefan had made sure he'd attended church no matter where he might be. Even at the fort, the chaplain held services each week. He looked forward to church today, especially in the company of a pretty young woman like Molly.

He stopped the buggy and climbed down to tether the horse then limped over to help his sister and Molly step down. He released his sister's hand quickly to grasp Molly's. "Watch your step, Miss Whiteman."

She grinned. "Now, Stefan, we settled that yesterday. If I'm to call you Stefan, you are to call me Molly. Remember?"

"Yes, I know, but—never mind. Molly it is."

The two young women, one with dark hair, the other with sun-kissed red-gold, leaned on each other with their arms interlocked as they climbed the few steps to the church doorway. They made a pretty sight, and one he wouldn't tire of seeing the next few weeks.

A voice at his side made him turn, and he spotted the young doctor he had met last night. "Oh, good morning, Dr. Delmont. I'm sorry, what was that you said?"

Red tinged the doctor's cheeks. "I was commenting on how pretty your sister is. Her eyes are a most unusual color."

Stefan tilted his head. "Do I detect a spark of interest in my sister?"

Andrew Delmont's cheeks burned brighter. "After our visit last evening, yes, I would like to become better acquainted."

"Then I'll see what I can do to make that happen." As

long as the young doctor's interests didn't lie in Molly, he'd help the attraction along with pleasure.

"Thank you, Stefan. I do appreciate that."

"Then let's go inside and see if we can find seats with them." Stefan grinned and climbed the steps with Andrew close behind. Having another young man near his own age, and who was not interested in Molly, would make for an even better visit. However, he'd have to find out more about Andrew Delmont before actually helping him in his pursuit of Clarissa. After all, she was his only sister, and nothing but the best would be good enough for her. Two weeks with the attention of the doctor would make her time more enjoyable, too, as long as it didn't go beyond that.

Inside the church Stefan spotted Molly's green beribboned hat and noted the space beside her. He winked at Andrew then nodded toward the two young women. "Looks like we're in luck."

He headed down the aisle to the pew where Molly and Clarissa sat. "Are these places taken?"

Molly's smile sent his heart reeling. She glanced at the empty space beside her then back at him. "Well we were saving them for someone special, but I suppose you two will do."

Stefan laughed and stepped over to claim a seat next to Molly while Andrew sat beside Clarissa. That had worked perfectly. Now if the rest of the day went as well, he'd consider it to be a very good day indeed.

CHAPTER 5

AFTER CHURCH TOM drove the team leading the two-seated surrey out to the Gordon ranch. Molly sat beside Stefan and searched for a topic of conversation that would not bore him to pieces. They'd talked about his medal and injury last night, and the idea he'd been in a fight with Indians didn't sit well with her anyway.

Stories about the war from her pa and his brothers always left a bitter taste in her mouth. Stefan may be a handsome hero, but she couldn't bring herself to admire his killing anyone, Indians or robbers. While Pa and Mr. Elliot went on about what the army was doing to keep peace in the land, Molly could think only of the deaths of young men in the last war.

"What, may I ask, is going on in that pretty head of yours, Molly Whiteman?" Stefan grinned, and the dimple in his left cheek winked at her.

Oh, he was handsome all right, and her heart jumped when he smiled at her like that. She swallowed hard to compose her mind before speaking. She didn't dare tell him she'd been thinking of war and death. "Nothing really. It's such a glorious day for June. We're still getting a few cooling breezes to keep our temperatures from being unbearable."

Gracious, talking about the weather. Now nothing could be more boring than that. "I hope you aren't overwhelmed by all the family you're about to meet. We only had time for a scant few introductions at the church, but you'll see the whole lot today. Mrs. Gordon, Uncle Micah's ma, does the cooking for them all still, and she's one of the best around. I love to come out here on Sundays when it's her turn for the family. I hope she has a couple of her apple pies for dessert." She stopped short. First the weather and then rambling on like Stoney Creek after a good rain. Stefan must think her to be a complete ninny with no conversation ability at all.

"How did you like church this morning?" Maybe that would be a safer topic.

"It was very nice. Your pastor is quite capable and seems to know his Bible well. He preached a timely topic of caring for your Christian brothers and sisters in time of need."

That hadn't been exactly what Reverend Weatherby had said. He'd indicated caring about all mankind, not just our Christian brothers and sisters, but no sense in getting into an argument with Stefan over semantics. "Yes, he was very good. He's been here ever since we came. A new doctor and a new reverend at the same time created quite a stir."

Tom turned his head toward Stefan. "And that's what allows our father to enjoy a day like today. With Andrew in town to take care of emergencies, Pa can come with us. Before, he stayed in town so people wouldn't have to hunt him down if needed."

Molly noted the slight blush on Clarissa's cheeks. She and Andrew had met last evening and a spark of interest developed right away. Now that would be a fun match, especially if it meant Clarissa living in Stoney Creek. Mercy sakes, here she was having them married and they'd barely even met. She'd best gain control of her thoughts or no telling what might pop out of her mouth.

To Molly's relief, Tom continued his dialogue. "Aunt Hannah's cooking has improved a lot, but Uncle Micah's ma still does most of the cooking. Pa even looks forward to these dinners and Aunt Hannah's desserts. I remember her first attempts. She's a much better nurse than cook."

That may have been true ten years ago, but not now. Despite her handicap of one leg shorter than the other, Aunt Hannah had done a remarkable job as a wife of a rancher and a mother of two children.

Stefan touched her arm. "I do believe you left us there for a minute, Molly."

Heat filled her cheeks. "I'm sorry, I was thinking about Aunt Hannah and how much she has accomplished in her life."

"I don't remember her that well since she's older, but every time she visited Mother before moving here, she was very nice. It was good to see her again at church."

Tom pulled the wagon into the Gordon yard, and Molly leaned toward Stefan. "Get ready for the onslaught of Gordon relatives. There's a bunch of them."

Stefan laughed. "I'm looking forward to it. I enjoy big families. Besides, I will have you with me to help with names through the afternoon."

When Tom pulled to a stop, Stefan stepped down then offered his hand to Molly. When he grasped hers, the warmth of his palm spread through her like butter melting on a biscuit. "Yes, I will keep everyone sorted out for you. I look forward to our afternoon."

Aunt Hannah stood on the porch with Uncle Micah.

Grace and Joel, her cousins, ran out to grab Molly around the waist. Molly laughed and disentangled herself. "Whoa, that's quite a greeting. I just saw you at church."

Grace stepped back and planted her hands at her hips. "Yes, but it's been a while since you came out to the ranch. I want to show you my new horse. She's still too young to ride, but Pa says she's mine to train. He brought her home a few weeks ago."

From the corner of her eye, Molly watched Joel stare in awe at Stefan's uniform. Stefan shook hands with the boy, and from the look on his face, Stefan had a friend for life in her seven-year-old cousin. She turned her attention to Grace.

"I'm looking forward to meeting your horse, but first I'm looking forward to your grandma and ma's dinner." She locked arms with Grace and headed to the house. Mama and Papa had already gone in with Mr. and Mrs. Elliot. Joel and Stefan trailed behind with Joel bombarding Stefan with questions about the army.

Stefan smiled down at the young boy at his side. "Being in the cavalry isn't always exciting. We have lots of things we have to do to make sure we're ready when duty calls."

Joel scrunched his eyebrows together. "You mean you're not out fighting injuns and bad men all the time?"

"No, son. We have to take care of our horses and our equipment as well as keep things in order around the fort. We have reveille in the mornings and then we have drills until noon."

"But you do chase bad people and shoot at 'em, don't you?"

"Yes, but only when it's necessary to protect a town, a shipment, or the fort."

Joel seemed to ponder that a moment before his eyes lit up again. "I bets you know how to shoot better than anyone else, even my uncle Levi, and he's the best shooter in these parts, exceptin' for my pa."

Micah Gordon stepped forward and extended his hand in greeting. "Welcome to the ranch, Stefan. I hope our little chatterbox here hasn't bored you."

"No, he hasn't. He's quite the talker for his age."

Micah patted Joel's shoulder. "Go on into the house and find your cousins." When the boy disappeared inside, Micah grinned. "Yes, he is quite the talker. Just ask Molly about what he does at school. She says he asks more questions than any other student."

"An inquisitive mind is a good thing to have. As he gets older, he should do well in school."

"That's our hope. Now, let's go inside where you can meet the rest of the family."

Stefan followed Micah into the house and marveled at the amount of room inside. A large parlor with a fireplace opened out from the doorway, and a stairway ascended to the second floor. It separated the parlor from a large dining area. He noted two tables were set with dishes and linens. Not the fancy crystal and china his family used at home, but perfect in this setting.

A young couple joined them. The woman held a little girl on her hip, and the man held the hand of a young boy. Stefan recognized the man as James Hempstead, whom he had met at the general store yesterday in town.

The man extended his hand. "Good to see you again, Stefan. Sorry the store was so busy that we didn't have time to talk yesterday." He wrapped his free arm around the woman's shoulder. "This is my wife, Margaret. She's Micah Gordon's sister, and these are our children, Elizabeth and Davy. Our oldest, Jimmy, is with his cousins."

"I'm pleased to meet you, Mrs. Hempstead. You have a fine-looking family." He bent down to shake Davy's hand. "And it's a pleasure to meet such a handsome young man here."

The boy stood taller and grinned, exposing the absence of two teeth, one on top and one on bottom. "I'm seven, and Miss Whiteman is my teacher." His brown eyes sparkled. "And you're a soldier. Do you fight the bad men?"

"Yes, I do, sometimes when I need to defend myself." It seemed as though all the boys Jimmy's age were interested in fighting. He turned his attention back to James, not to ignore the young boy's interest, but to take the child's mind elsewhere. "You have a fine store. I didn't expect to see one so large out here."

"Thank you. We expanded a year or so ago and carry just about anything you want, and if we don't have it, we can order it from our catalogs."

"Now don't go hogging all the attention, Margaret." Another man dressed in denim pants and a plaid shirt extended his hand toward Stefan. "I'm Levi Gordon, part owner of the Circle G. We're glad to have you out visiting today. Give you a real taste of Texas living."

He turned to the woman with him. "This is my wife, Ellie. She teaches at the school with Molly. The twin boys who just scooted through here are ours, Josiah and Jeremy, and we have another son, Timothy, as well as little Sarah here."

Stefan absorbed the names and faces as best he could with so many running about. Levi and Micah were brothers and married to Hannah and Ellie. Margaret was their sister married to James, the storekeeper. At least he had the adults right, but he'd have to take it slower with the children with so many of them. "It's a pleasure to meet all of you. I'm looking forward to seeing your ranch. Molly tells me it's quite a spread."

"Since we added horses to our livestock, it's grown to be the second largest next to Mr. Hudson's spread to the west. Micah and I will be happy to take you out to see our land. We'll fix you up with a horse and saddle after dinner."

Ellie Gordon tugged at Levi's sleeve. "Speaking of dinner, I believe your ma has the table ready. You and James need to round up the children and get them cleaned up to eat." She shifted the sleeping child in her arms. "Molly has looked forward to your visit for weeks. We're glad you're here, and welcome to Texas. I hope you enjoy your visit. Now if you'll excuse me, I'm going to put this one down for her nap."

As she turned to leave, Molly grasped his arm. "Looks like you've met them all but Rose. She's been in the kitchen helping her ma with the meal. Rose is the youngest of the Gordon clan and has just made plans to marry one of the cowboys over at the Hudson place."

"I think I can keep everyone straight." He gazed into Molly's green eyes and hoped they'd have some time together this afternoon. "I'm looking forward to getting to know them better." He placed his hand over

Molly's resting on his arm. "And especially one doctor's daughter."

The pink that flooded her face brought a smile to his heart. He led her to the dining area where the older children seated themselves around one table and the adults with the youngest settled at the larger dining table.

Accustomed to only four at the family table for meals, Stefan shook his head in wonder at the happy chatter and bustling about of fifteen adults and who knew how many children finding places to sit. In only a few minutes, quiet fell over the group, and Micah Gordon stood at the head of the table.

"Welcome to our home and to the bountiful blessings of our meal. Let's join hands and thank our Lord for what He has provided."

All around hands clasped and heads bowed. Micah's strong voice called upon the Lord. "Lord, for these and all thy bountiful blessings, we give You thanks this day. Thank You for the safe journey for Mr. and Mrs. Elliot and their son and daughter. Thank You for the message this morning that nourished our souls in Your house. Now bless the hands that prepared this food today and bless it to the nourishment of our bodies. Amen."

As Micah finished the prayer, chatter again erupted and hands reached out to pass around the platters of meat, vegetables, and hot, fresh bread. The delightful aroma sent a rumble through Stefan's belly. It'd been hours since breakfast and he eagerly anticipated the meal.

He glanced down the table toward his sister, who leaned toward a young woman in deep conversation. That must be Rose, the youngest Gordon girl. She and Clarissa had evidently found an interest they shared.

Molly handed him the basket of bread. As their hands touched, a most pleasant, but unusual feeling shot up his arm. Once again he gazed at Molly. The beauty of her smile caused a lump to form in his throat. If he didn't have to report back to his regiment in two weeks, he'd be sorely tempted to ask his parents to plan for an extended stay. As it stood, he'd have to seize every moment of opportunity he could get to be alone with Molly. How could he have known about her for so many years, but not truly known her? He planned to remedy that as soon as possible.

CHAPTER 6

MOLLY FIDGETED WITH the lace about the collar of her white shirtwaist and strolled again to the window. The men had been gone a long time. Plenty of time to see the ranch and livestock, but no dust cloud announced their return. A sigh escaped her lips. Her plans for time alone with Stefan receded to the background as quickly as the fresh bread had disappeared at dinner.

Clarissa stepped up behind Molly. "Watching for them isn't going to bring them back any sooner."

"Oh, dear, am I that obvious?" Molly bit her lip, but couldn't resist another glance out the window.

"Yes, you are. Now come on and join Rose and me. She was telling me about her wedding plans." Clarissa tugged Molly's arm back toward the parlor. "All the other women are in the kitchen or taking care of the youngest ones just waking from their naps. I must say I really enjoy all the hustle and bustle of such a large family. We have only the three of us now with occasional visits from Papa's brother and his family. They live in New Orleans and don't come up to St. Francisville very often."

Sometimes having such a large family wasn't as much fun as others may think. Once in a while Molly wouldn't mind having a quiet Sunday afternoon at home without so many cousins around, but then again she never had to complain about being lonely. Having no family around at all would not be fun.

Rose glanced up when Molly and Clarissa returned to the sofa. "You're going to wear the carpet out between here and that window. They'll be back shortly because those boys will want more of that pie Ma made today." She patted the sofa beside her. "I was telling Clarissa about my wedding plans for August."

Right now the last thing Molly wanted to talk about would be weddings—or at least somebody else's wedding. She shouldn't have been so obvious in her desire to have the men return. With all that Mama had planned for the next two weeks, she and Stefan would be hard put to find time to be alone and get to know each other as adults rather than children.

The other women filed into the parlor and seated themselves. Molly gazed at the women as they filled the room. Three different generations represented, yet they spoke and laughed as though all the same age. Mrs. Gordon's hair had only a few streaks of black still running through the silver, and now she sat beaming at her daughters and the two women her sons had married.

In the years since Hannah had married Micah, Ruth Gordon had become like the Louisiana grandmother Molly sorely missed since Papa's practice didn't leave much time for trips back to St. Francisville. Someone spoke her name. "I'm sorry, what did you say?"

Ruth Gordon laughed. "I was commenting on the fact that you and Clara are the last two girls of marrying age in the family, but I do believe a certain young man has already caught your fancy."

Heat rushed to Molly's cheeks as she stole a peek at her mother and Mrs. Elliot. Both women wore smiles that stretched clean across their faces. What must they be thinking about her behavior this afternoon?

Clarissa joined in the teasing. "I must say my brother does present a handsome figure in his uniform." Then she leaned forward with a grin. "I do believe he has a mutual interest in you, Molly."

"But we've only seen each other this once for all these years. Why, I hardly know him."

Clarissa wrapped her arm around Molly's shoulder. "Oh, but you have two whole weeks to get to know him." She winked at her mother. "I think we can arrange for that, can't we, Mama."

Molly sought to change the subject. "I say, it's quiet in here. Where are all the children?"

"The older boys are with their fathers riding around the ranch. The girls are upstairs playing with their dolls, and the babies are here. All are accounted for." Ellie bounced her little girl on her knee. "This one is rested, fed, and ready for some attention."

"Oh, let me hold her." Molly stood and reached out for the baby. At eighteen months of age, Elizabeth had recently learned to walk and squirmed on her mother's lap.

"Looks like you want to go for a walk, young lady." Molly grasped the child about the waist then set her feet on the floor. "We'll just take a stroll around the room."

Ellie's voice followed her. "She likes to look out the window, too."

Heat again rose in Molly's cheeks as the women behind her laughed then resumed their conversation. Never mind them, she did want Stefan to return.

"Molly, Molly, it's time to go see my horse." Grace raced up from behind and wrapped her arms about Molly's waist.

"So it is." She picked up Elizabeth. "Do you think it'd be okay for our little cousin to join us?" She looked to Ellie for approval. At her nod, Molly then looked to Grace.

The young girl bit her lip. "I s'pose it's okay. Pa put me up on my first horse when I was just a little older than she is."

"Well, I don't intend to put her on any horse today, but we'd like to get acquainted with yours. Wouldn't we, Elizabeth?"

"Horsie. Horsie." Elizabeth grinned and clapped her hands.

"All right, let's go." She turned to the women and headed to the door. "We won't be gone long."

Clarissa rose from her chair and hurried to join Molly and the children. "I'd love to meet your horse, too, Miss Grace."

The ten-year-old girl beamed her approval and raced ahead outside to open the stable doors. "Come on. Starlight is waiting."

They entered the building and Clarissa grabbed Molly's arm and gazed about in wide-eyed awe at the size of the stables. Molly's heart filled with pride at what Micah and Levi had accomplished. Stalls lined the walls for all the family horses as well as all the horses used by the ranch hands in their daily work. A door opened into a storage room, and saddles of every color and description strad-dled lengths of wood near the stalls.

She breathed deeply and savored the smell of horse flesh, but then she laughed as Clarissa wrinkled her nose and pinched it.

"Ew, it stinks, but I've never seen a barn so big. How many horses do they have?"

Before Molly could speak, Grace poured a few oats into a bucket and answered. "About twenty, maybe thirty, I think. All the cowboys have one, plus Pa, Ma, and Joel each have one, and then there's my new horse, and a few extra they take on round-ups. That's what they call a remuda."

"My, my, you certainly know a lot about horses." Clarissa let go of her nose to pick up her skirts to keep them off the ground.

"Sure I do. I'm gonna ride Starlight to school once she's saddle broke. Pa says he'll do that soon as she's old enough. He even got me my very own saddle." She chattered as she led them to a stall where an inky black filly stood. When Grace drew near, Starlight nuzzled Grace's neck. "Hey, Starlight. I brought some visitors to meet you."

"Oh, my, she's a gorgeous horse." Molly shifted Elizabeth to her left side and reached up to caress the white dots on Starlight's forehead. "This must be why you named her Starlight. All these small circles look like stars in the sky at night." She held Elizabeth's hand toward the horse. "See, pretty horsie."

A giggle bubbled from the baby's throat as she leaned forward and said, "Horsie."

Grace held out a handful of oats, and Starlight ate from her hand. "Good girl, Elizabeth. She likes you. You're right about the name, Molly. Pa and Joel thought it silly, but Ma and Grandma like it."

Clarissa stepped closer, but didn't reach out toward the horse. "These horses are much bigger than the ones we have at home. Father and Stefan ride, but Mother and I prefer the buggy or carriage. You say you've been riding since you were Elizabeth's age."

"Sure have. Pa put me in front of him on the saddle before I was two years old. I rode by myself the first time when I was four. I had another horse, but he was old, so last year Pa promised me a new one."

A male voice interrupted. "Well, I figured I'd find you in here showing off Starlight."

Grace squealed, dropped her bucket, and ran to Micah. "Pa." She threw her arms around his waist.

Levi followed his brother and reached toward Elizabeth, who held her arms out to him and grinned, exposing the two rows of baby teeth in her cherub mouth.

Molly let her go, but her eyes searched behind her uncle. Stefan stood a few feet away, and her heart did a jump skip when she locked gazes with him. "How...how was the ride?"

His dimple flashed again. "Hot, but enlightening."

Everyone made their way from the stables, and Stefan stepped closer to her. "Your mother said we'd be leaving for town in an hour. May I ask for that time with you? I've hardly had a chance to speak with you since our carriage ride out here."

Heat crept into Molly's cheeks, but she accepted his extended arm and hooked her hand to his elbow. "Why don't we get something cool to drink, and then we can take a walk or sit on the porch."

A few minutes later they sat with glasses of cold lemonade on the porch of the Gordon home. Stefan wished to discard the sweltering uniform jacket, but it wouldn't be protocol for him to do so with Molly seated next to him. The air hung thick and hot as the afternoon sun moved to the west. He'd enjoyed the trip around the ranch, and especially the interest Micah and Levi Gordon had shown in his military action. With the younger boys scampering ahead and playing with their mounts, Stefan had spoken freely on his military service, a subject dear to his heart.

Molly sipped her lemonade and her eyes danced with amusement. "You're here on the porch with me, but for a moment there, I truly thought you were somewhere else."

What was he thinking? This time with Molly was what he'd anticipated all afternoon, and here he was letting his mind wander. "I apologize. I've looked forward to having some time with you this afternoon. I do hope you'll forgive me."

"Forgiven. But tell me, what do you think of the ranch?"

"I'd say it's quite remarkable. In Louisiana we have fields and fields of cotton plants and sugarcane, but here I saw nothing but acres of cattle and horses. The land around here is so wild and untamed. I'm accustomed to the moss-covered trees and easygoing life of the South."

Molly laughed and set her glass on the table. "It's pretty hectic around here most times, I must admit, but you'll get used to it. I remember those lazy afternoons at Grandmother Woodruff's home. Sunday afternoons were for resting and quiet time, but not around the Gordon and Whiteman families. We're all about family and having fun together."

"Yes, I've seen that, and I do envy it some. We hardly ever see any of ours."

"That's what Clarissa told me." She leaned forward. "Enough talk about the Gordon family and the ranch. It's been a long time since we last saw each other. Tell me what you've done in those years. I know you went to West Point and now you're an officer like your father, but what do you do all the time?"

Stefan gazed about the well-kept yard of the ranch house and out toward the stables and corral. What could he tell her? Most of his military life, though busy, consisted mostly of drills, routine maintenance of equipment, and occasional patrols.

"Since the Indian raids have died down, we spend most of our time at the fort. On occasion we're called on to escort a shipment of gold somewhere or payroll from the depot to the fort. Sometimes we get so bored we almost wish for a battle like our fathers experienced."

Molly's eyes opened wide. "Oh no, that was horrible. I've heard a few stories about those days, and I'm glad we have nothing like that today. The thought of fighting and killing other men gives me the chills."

She wrapped her arms around her waist as though to actually ward off the cold. Stefan bit his lip. How would she feel if she knew his drills and training were all about just that? His father's war had been terrible, but Indians had made life miserable for settlers, and outlaws still roamed the land looking to steal and rob. That meant someone had to defend the innocent, and he'd just as soon be a part of that as not.

"I'm sorry, Molly. War is a tough subject." He had to change the direction of this conversation. He remembered Mrs. Whiteman speaking of a party in honor of his parents. "I say, I'm looking forward to the party your mother is planning for us next week. I'm sure it will be quite different from those we have at home."

Relief flooded Molly's face as she sat back in her chair.

"Oh, it will be, but it may well be the most fun you've ever had at a party."

"Is that so? Pray tell how that may be?" He could imagine the music and the dances. They would probably be much like the ones at the fort, but he'd still rather hear Molly's description of the event.

As she told him of the fiddle music and the reel dances they'd be doing, he listened, but at the same time enjoyed the beauty of the young woman before him. Her gold-flecked green eyes sparkled with excitement, and her hands danced with enthusiasm as she described what would take place a week from Friday at the town hall. He reached over and grasped her hands to still them.

"May I be so bold as to ask that I be your escort for that evening, Miss Whiteman?"

A shade of pink he couldn't quite describe flushed her cheeks. She gazed at him a moment before answering. "There you go with that 'Miss' business again, but I would be honored to attend the dance with you."

"Thank you. I'm glad that's settled." And he'd be sure he didn't discuss or mention anything having to do with war or the military. Clearly that was one subject to avoid with Molly. As pretty and smart as she was, she simply didn't understand the necessities that came along with protecting one's country and freedoms. Killing may not be the best choice, but sometimes there was no alternative.

CHAPTER 7

ANDREW WASHED AND dried his hands then went to the desk to fill out the information for his report. Only two patients had come in this afternoon, but it was enough to make him glad he'd insisted on staying in town so Dr. Whiteman could enjoy the time with his family.

One patient had fallen from his horse and required stitches in a cut on his forehead, and the other was a fainting spell by one of their elderly patients. He'd rushed to her home and taken care of her there. Now he sat at his desk in the quiet infirmary. After the last of the notes had been entered on patient charts, he sat back and swiveled around in his chair to gaze out the window toward Main Street.

He didn't see what was there because a pretty, dark-haired young woman filled his mind and thoughts. Clarissa Elliot not only possessed good looks, but also had a wit about her that charmed him right out of his shoes. He hadn't paid much attention to women in the past few years because of his focus on his medical career. However, only a blind man could miss the attractiveness of Miss Elliot.

They'd be here for two weeks, but that was little time in the grand scheme of things to even get to know a person, much less entertain any romantic thoughts. Besides, at the end of the two weeks she'd return to Louisiana with her family and forget all about him. Still, it would be nice to enjoy her company while she was here. He shook his head to clear it. Best get his mind off that subject and check the supplies for the coming week.

With the sun making its way to the horizon, Andrew turned on the gas lights on the wall behind his desk then proceeded to light several other lamps to give him light enough to carry out his duties.

He'd begun to check the rolls of bandages and the supplies for stitching up gashes when the rattle of carriage wheels filtered in through the open window. Must be the Whiteman family and their guests returning. Dr. Whiteman had said they'd be home before sunset.

After a cursory glance through the supplies, he closed the cabinet and headed for the hallway where voices now chased away the silence of the evening. Before stepping through the doorway leading to the Whiteman home, Andrew adjusted his jacket and straightened his tie. Maybe Miss Elliot would still be downstairs.

Molly turned and her face lit up with a smile. "Andrew, did you have a quiet afternoon, or were you overrun with patients eager for your services?"

Miss Elliot stood behind Molly and she too turned to peer at Andrew. His gaze caught hers as he answered Molly. "Bill Crachitt had to have stitches on his forehead after a fall from his horse, and elderly Mrs. Dennis had a fainting spell that worried her daughter, but she'll be fine. How was your afternoon?"

"Very nice, but next time you'll have to come with us. Mrs. Gordon is a wonderful cook, and we had a chance to see Grace's new horse." Molly pulled off her gloves then unpinned her hat.

"And you enjoyed the afternoon, too, Miss Elliot?"

Clarissa's eyes, more violet than blue, shone in the light from the lamps and stabbed his heart with delight.

"Yes. I've never been on a real ranch before, and I've never seen so many horses in one place. We have stables at home but only horses for the carriage are housed there. Stefan rode one of the Gordon horses to view the ranch with the other men."

"I've been on that ride. They own a lot of land and a great herd of cattle so horses are a necessary part of their livelihood."

"Andrew, I'm preparing a light supper for everyone. Would you like to stay and join us?" Mrs. Whiteman nodded toward him as she removed her hat.

He hesitated only a moment. An opportunity to have more time around Miss Elliot was too good to pass up. His mother would understand as he often didn't come home until late on Sunday evenings when he manned the clinic.

"I'd be delighted to join you, and thank you for the invitation. I look forward to hearing more about your afternoon." As well as perhaps having a few moments to speak with Miss Elliot.

"The colonel and Mrs. Elliot have retired to their room and the others were sent to clean up a little. Molly, you come and help me. Andrew, you take the time to entertain Clarissa and Stefan." She grasped Molly's arm and headed to the kitchen, ignoring Molly's sputtering objections.

Stefan raised an eyebrow, a hint of amusement crossing his lips. "I think I'd like to get some of this dust off before dining again. I'm sure you two can find plenty to talk about." He winked at his sister then turned to head upstairs.

A deep pink rose in Clarissa's cheeks. "I'm sorry, but it looks you've been stranded with me for a while."

Nothing could please him more. "Are you sure you don't want to rest before supper?"

"Oh, no, I'm much too excited to rest even a teensy bit. Being in Texas is the most exciting thing we've done in a long while. Of course we do go to New Orleans often to see my aunt and uncle and cousins, but never have we traveled this far. The wide open spaces are amazing, and the people are so friendly. I don't know what I expected, but it's been wonderful so far." She stopped and her fingers went to her lips. The pink blush returned to her cheeks.

"I'm sorry. I don't mean to ramble on so. I guess it's just the excitement of being here with Molly finally. I'm sure you're not interested in all that."

Andrew didn't care what she said or the topic. He simply appreciated this amount of time to be alone no matter how long or short that time may be.

"Shall we go into the parlor where we can be more comfortable? I'd be happy to listen to tales of your journey and all the plans for your stay with the Whiteman family." He offered his arm to her, and she placed her hand under his elbow.

❦

Molly met Andrew and Clarissa in the entrance to the parlor. From the pink in Clarissa's cheeks and the smile on Andrew's face, something had been interrupted. Andrew couldn't help but be attracted to a girl as pretty as Clarissa. There may be a difference of several years in their age, but that didn't matter in places like Stoney Creek.

"Oh, I was coming to find you two. Supper will be ready in about half an hour. Go on into the parlor and I'll find Stefan and the others."

"You needn't look far for me."

Stefan's voice sounded so close behind her that Molly jumped and stumbled backward. "Where did you come from?"

He laughed and reached out to steady her. "I'm sorry. I didn't mean to startle you."

Andrew glanced down at Clarissa. "If you two don't mind, we'll be in the parlor. Let us know when it's time to eat."

Molly gazed down at Stefan's hand on her arm. Heat filled the spot and she'd just as soon he left it there as not. "Thank you for keeping me upright. I wasn't expecting you to be behind me is all."

"I gathered that you were somewhat surprised." Amusement filled his blue eyes.

Molly's tongue decided to attach itself to the roof of her mouth. Even if she wanted to speak, she couldn't. Whatever cords Stefan had wound around her heart earlier in the day tightened themselves now. She must remember he would be here only a short time.

As if reading her mind Stefan said, "With only two weeks to explore this wonderful land of yours, would you consider riding with me tomorrow and pointing out places of interest?"

Would she consider such a thing? Of course she would. "It'd be my pleasure to show you around." Then she remembered Clarissa. "We must include Clarissa. I'd hate for her to be left out of anything."

"Oh, I don't think you have to worry about that. If my

eyes don't deceive me, I do believe the good doctor has taken an interest in my sister."

"You really think so? With more women than eligible men in town the past few years, he could have his pick of ladies to escort around. Of course Clarissa is so pretty that she'd turn any man's head without lifting a finger." Molly envied her friend's flawless cream complexion and dark hair as well as her gorgeous eyes. "She's really beautiful, you know."

Stefan laughed. "Yes, I do. Papa says he's not going to let any man get close to her for many years yet. I think he has a harder job than he imagines." He tilted his head and lifted an eyebrow. "How about yourself? You could have your pick of young men as well."

"Hah! If there were any around to pick. I'm of a mind to start a mail-order groom service like they do for brides. I'm sure I can find enough single women who would be interested."

"Yes, you probably would. With your energy and enthusiasm, you could do just about anything you put your mind to."

Molly bunched her eyebrows. What did he mean by that? But before she had time to figure it out, Stefan smiled and took her hand. "I meant that as a most sincere compliment."

"Thank you, I guess. If all the cowboys around came into town and sought us out instead of drinking and gambling down at the saloon, we would have plenty, but that's not going to happen unless...well, never mind."

What in the world was she doing talking about getting the attention of other men? Here she had a wonderful man like Stefan and she couldn't find a better topic of conversation than the lack of males in town. How inconsiderate was that?

Juliet bounced in dancing on her tiptoes. "Mama says supper is ready, and I'm to fetch you and Clarissa." She glanced around. "Where are Clarissa and Andrew?"

"In the parlor."

Juliet swished her skirts and went seeking the other couple. Molly cringed. She'd certainly botched that little time with Stefan. Maybe they could still manage some time before the evening ended, but that most likely wouldn't happen with all the family around.

Stefan patted the hand still on his arm. "Shall we go in and join the others? Maybe we can have a few minutes after supper to continue our conversation."

Molly gulped and her heart thudded. He did want to spend more time with her. Of course he did or he wouldn't have asked to see her tomorrow.

All through the laughter and conversation around the table, Molly found Stefan gazing at her several times when she sneaked a peek in his direction. Heat flooded her face each time, and trying to concentrate on her food became even more difficult.

Andrew leaned forward to address Molly. "Since I have tomorrow free, Clarissa has accepted my invitation to go on a ride. Do you and Stefan wish to join us?"

From the look in his eyes, he desired a negative answer. "No, I'm sure Clarissa will enjoy things that Stefan won't. We plan a little excursion ourselves, but we will probably find different places to visit than you two will." Not that there were any she could think of for the moment, but at least that did give her some excuse for not tagging along with them.

Evidently Andrew preferred to be alone with Clarissa, but Molly desired the same thing with Stefan. Whenever Andrew filled in for Manfred on Saturday and Sunday, her father gave Andrew the next two days off for his own pursuits. Looked like one of them this week would be spent with Clarissa. And to that Molly had no objections.

CHAPTER 8

A FTER BREAKFAST MONDAY morning Molly sat on her bed and made plans with Clarissa for their respective tours of the area. Although Andrew had grown up in Stoney Creek, Molly wanted to make sure Clarissa would learn everything about the town in her ride. She already had a list of places she'd go with Stefan.

Clarissa lay on her stomach with her chin propped in her hands. "If we plan this right, we could all meet up for lunch at the hotel." She rolled over to her back. "That is unless your mother has something planned for us here."

"No, I don't think she does. She and your mother want to do a bit of shopping at that new dress shop. I think she also wants to pay a visit to Mrs. Olson and welcome her to Stoney Creek. She didn't have time to do that properly at church on Sunday."

"Good. The hotel would be perfect for lunch with two of the most handsome men in town. Not that I'm prejudiced for my brother, but he is dashing in his uniform."

"Yes, he is, and Andrew is quite attractive himself." If only Stefan's uniform didn't remind her every second of what he did, she'd be much happier to be seen with him in it. "Does he wear that uniform all the time?"

"Well, when we're at home he wears any old thing, but when we're out in public, he really likes to wear it as a reminder that we have men protecting our country for us." She sat up and tucked her legs beneath her. "Please tell me more about Andrew."

Laughter spilled from Molly's lips. She'd already told everything she could rightly remember. He'd been ahead of her in school, so she hadn't paid that much attention to him. Well, she had, but he'd been too busy making good grades to be bothered with any girls, much less one two years behind him.

"I think I've told you about everything there is. We've known each other practically all our lives. I think I did like him from afar when were in school but he never paid me any mind. I do remember he was a good athlete. He could run fast and throw a ball hard."

Clarissa's eyes clouded over as though she had gone into deep thinking. Molly let her be and stood to smooth out her skirt. Stefan would arrive from the hotel shortly, and she wanted to be ready.

Molly glanced back at the bed and Clarissa. "Won't Andrew be here about the same time as Stefan?"

With a shake of her head, Clarissa puffed out a breath. "Yes, and I must be getting ready for him." She stood and pirouetted with her hands crossed over her chest. "Oh, Molly, do you think Dr. Delmont will find me as attractive as I find him? He's so tall and strong. And he must be smart to be a doctor with your papa."

Molly pinned her hat in place over her curls. "Clarissa Elliot, are you smitten with our good doctor?" She grinned over her shoulder at her friend. One thing for certain, Andrew and Clarissa would make a fine-looking couple. With two whole weeks ahead, no telling what could happen.

A blush colored Clarissa's cheeks. "I think he's a very handsome and nice young man, and I'm glad he's taking me around town this morning so I can get to know him better." She grabbed Molly's hand. "Please say you'll ask Stefan to take you to the hotel and meet us there."

"I will do that. The hotel has good food, and a very pleasant atmosphere." Molly had only dined there once, but the food had been delicious and the dining room was beautiful. Still, she couldn't help but tease a bit. "I thought you'd rather spend all your time with Andrew. Why share the time with us?"

Clarissa closed her eyes and sighed as though going into a swoon. "I thought it would be nice for Stefan to get to know Dr. Elliot, too. He's always so critical of any man interested in me." Her eyes opened wide. "Has he said anything to you about me?"

"No, he hasn't." The last thing on her mind to discuss with Stefan would be his sister and her love life. "Come, it's time for them to be here. We can save time by being downstairs waiting for them."

"But...but I thought it was better to keep men waiting in anticipation for our appearance."

"Oh, posh, that may be fine in your social circles, but out here in Texas, we don't waste a minute that could be spent with someone we like." Molly checked her hat one more time before heading out the door. If Clarissa wanted to dillydally, then she could, but she would not make Stefan wait one second longer than absolutely necessary.

Stefan and Andrew entered the hallway as Molly reached the last step. "It's nice to see you both being so punctual. I'm all ready to go." Stefan wasn't wearing his uniform today, but his western-style shirt and dark pants did nothing to detract from his good looks.

The two young men smiled at her, but Andrew's gaze

trailed up the stairway behind her. Good, Clarissa must have decided to come too.

Stefan reached for Molly's hand. "You look lovely this morning. Like a ray of sunshine in your yellow dress."

"Thank you, and I see you've paid a visit to the Hempstead store. You might even pass for a Texan." Even through her lace gloves, the heat from his hand sent shivers of delight through her arm and to her heart. Would three hours alone be enough to get to know more about this man?

Andrew tucked Clarissa's hand under his arm. "And you are lovely as well, Miss Elliot."

Anticipation for the day ahead shone in Clarissa's eyes as she glanced at Molly. "Thank you, Dr. Delmont. Molly and I decided that lunch together at the hotel would be a nice way to end our morning."

Stefan chuckled. "Oh, you did, did you? Nice that you're willing to spend some time with your big brother." He saluted her with two fingers. "We'll see you there."

"Now it's time for a tour of Stoney Creek, Texas, and all her glories." He guided Molly to the door and turned to glance back at his sister and winked. "Don't get lost, you two. See you at the hotel at noon."

"Now y'all weren't going to leave here without saying hello, were you?" Mama made her way from the kitchen with Mrs. Elliot right behind. "We were on our way out, too. All my family is accounted for now."

Clarissa kissed her mother's cheek then asked, "What will Father do today?"

"He's taking Tom and Danny out to the Gordon spread to look into purchasing a couple of horses for our place back home."

"And Clara is entertaining Alice and Juliet, so it's time

to be about our business. Come, Jenny. Let's leave these young people to their fun." Mama reached for her parasol in the hall stand. "Don't forget yours, Molly. You know what the sun does to your complexion." She headed for the door. "We'll see you back here sometime this afternoon."

Mama would have to remind her about the freckles that popped out with too much sun. She grabbed up her parasol as Andrew escorted Clarissa out to the buggy he'd rented at the livery.

Stefan placed her hand on his forearm. "I'm sure our mothers will have themselves quite the time this morning. Mine loves to check out all the stores in every town she visits." He assisted her up to the seat in Papa's buggy then climbed up beside her. "Where to, m'lady?"

She pointed down Main Street. "Let's start at the end by the courthouse." Of course it wouldn't take any time to make the eight blocks and the town square, but then they could drive down by the creek that gave the town its name. Her mind went blank. What in the world would they talk about for three hours?

&

Stefan clicked the reins and guided the horse toward town. He didn't really care about the courthouse or any other building, but as long as he could spend time with Molly, where they went or what they said didn't matter one whit.

She loved her town, and her enthusiasm made her even more charming. How lucky her students were to have such a beautiful teacher. As he listened to her expound on the background of the courthouse, the musical lilt to her voice made whatever she said a delight to hear.

If he ever decided to settle down with a girl, it'd be someone like Molly, but with his military career, he hesitated to even think of a future with a girl like her. Life on an army post wasn't easy for wives and families. Safer than in the past, yes, but not as comfortable as living in an established town.

They passed a building nearing completion, and Molly's face lit up with a warm glow. She grasped his arm.

"Oh, Stefan, stop for a moment. This is our new theater. It opens Friday evening, and I believe Papa has purchased tickets for us all to attend the first concert."

The red-brick two-story building stood out in its glory among the other less elaborate businesses. Workmen scurried about their duties taking boxes and trunks of items through the leaded glass doors. Arched stone edifices sat atop each window on the second floor and allowed the noise of construction to reach the outdoors. A large poster advertised the first performance at Stoney Creek Auditorium on Friday, June 8.

"Theater is becoming more popular than ever these days. My parents have taken Clarissa and me to several shows on the showboats that come along the Mississippi to New Orleans. It's no wonder Stoney Creek wanted to have a theater of its own."

"I've read about some of those shows as well as the ones where all the actors put black on their faces and perform songs and dances. I've never actually been to a professional play or concert, and I'm so looking forward to it. The first performer to come our way is Caroline Cushing. She's supposed to be a wonderful singer."

"Yes, I've heard she is. I'm sure we'll have a pleasant evening." Once more he flicked the reins across the horse's back and proceeded toward the other end of town. Along the way, Molly pointed out the bakery, a new dress shop, the wheelwright business, and several others, but Stefan barely listened to the words, simply enjoying the sound of her voice and the animation in her gestures as she described the various points of interest.

Molly stopped talking and turned to grasp his arm again. "I'm so sorry, Stefan. This must all be so boring to you what with seeing the likes of New Orleans and other places much larger than Stoney Creek."

"Nothing is boring as long as I'm beside you." That was the truth, and he wanted her to know she was more important than seeing the sights. He hid a smile as red stained her cheeks. "I didn't mean to embarrass you. I do enjoy your company, so anywhere we go is fine with me."

She bit her lip, and a smile lifted one corner of her mouth. "Then let's go out to my favorite spot along the creek. The bluebonnets and Indian paintbrushes are long gone, but it's still pretty there."

"Lead the way, as your plans are my plans." He drove to the end of Main Street and turned down a road leading out of town. They left behind the smells of animals and people and the hustle-and-bustle sounds of a town at work. In a few minutes the houses thinned out until they were in open country where the fresh air soothed his lungs.

He breathed deeply and smiled. "Now this is more like it. Nothing like nature to fill your senses."

"Yes, it is much more pleasant out here, but I do love the activity of town. I only come out here when I want to have quiet time." She pointed to the west. "The creek is over thataways. It's not far."

In a few minutes they were at the creek trickling its

way between two rocky banks. Stefan hopped down then assisted Molly. With his hands on her waist, he set her on the ground, but didn't move his hands. He stared into her eyes that were only slightly below his and noted how the yellow dress she wore today brought out the green in her eyes. Any other woman and he'd lean down for a kiss, but not with Molly, not yet.

She cleared her throat and he dropped his hands to his side. Her gaze pierced his with an intensity that set every nerve in his body on edge. How could she have such an effect on him in a only a few days?

Molly reached up and unpinned her hat then set it on the seat of the buggy. The sun picked up the red-gold highlights in her hair and stole Stefan's breath. She reached for his hand then led him to the creek bank. Right here and now, he'd follow her wherever she led him, even into the rippling waters of the creek.

"This is my favorite spot. The trees give plenty of shade from the heat of the sun, the creek babbles along its way, and little creatures dart here and about if you're really quiet."

She stopped at a large rock and climbed a few steps to sit perched on top. She patted the space beside her. "There's plenty of room for both of us."

Yes, there would be if they sat very close to each other, and he didn't mind that a bit. He grabbed hold of the edge and pulled himself up to the spot next to her. She gazed out across the creek, but his eyes stayed glued to her face.

"Tell me, Miss Molly, how do you like teaching?"

The green in her eyes sparkled with enthusiasm. "I love the children and all the things we get to do. We have two rooms, one for the lower grades and one for the upper ones. You met the other teacher, Levi's wife, Ellie. I think she has the harder job."

"And how many of the children are related to you in one way or the other?" He'd met enough children at the Gordon ranch for a small town school.

"Only seven of the twenty in lower school are related, but it sometimes seems to be a lot more than that. One of my favorites is Grace, Aunt Hannah's girl. She loves horses and riding to the point that's all she talks about most of the time. She can play the piano, too. Gets that from her mama. Aunt Hannah is a talented pianist as well as a nurse."

With her legs pulled up to her chest, she rested her chin on her knees and clasped her hands about her skirt. "You know, we left St. Francisville when I was a little girl, so I don't remember a lot about it. What I do remember is seeing the mighty river down the road at Bayou Sara. Papa's brothers worked that river and it always impressed me. One time I thought how much fun it would be to get on a boat and go down to New Orleans and see the great ocean at the end of the river."

Stefan balanced himself so as not to crowd Molly. He could sit and listen to her talk all day. The more she talked, the less he'd have to reveal about himself. She'd already expressed her distaste for his being in the military, so he had no desire to say anything more about it.

Molly raised her hand to point to an area across the river. "Years ago, before we ever came here, there was a great Indian battle right over there. Some of the Indians escaped and went around another way to the town and started burning buildings. A lot of people died that day, but the men of Stoney Creek held their ground and finally forced the Indians to retreat. People still talk about it, but not near as much as they did when we first came here."

Stefan didn't comment for fear he'd say something to spoil the mood. Couldn't she see from that skirmish how sometimes killing was necessary to protect property and those you loved? He'd killed a few men himself, and it never felt good, even when the men were outlaws or murderers. Killing unnecessarily went against God's laws, but the apostle Paul himself said that authorities had both the reason and the right to punish the wrongdoer with the sword.

"Stefan, when I think about fighting and battles it makes me sad. Mama told me about a time she had to kill a Yankee soldier, and she hoped I'd never be in a spot where I'd have to do something like that."

He'd heard the story from his mother, and it helped him understand even more Molly's distaste for killing. "Your mother and mine endured some hard times when they were young, and your father and mine both fought in a terrible war. I'm thankful those days are behind us."

She reached over and placed a hand on his arm. "Nothing against you or our fathers, Stefan, but I hated to hear those stories of soldiers and battles. I'm sure what you do is necessary but I don't think I could stand being around soldiers all the time knowing that they are being trained to kill." She put her hand to her mouth and shot him a glance, indicating that her true opinion had just spilled out, and she feared how he would respond.

Not wanting to go deeper into the subject, Stefan chose to make light of it. "Oh, you get used to it after a while."

She smiled slightly, then changing the subject, began to talk about the local ranches. But her words stayed with

Stefan. And that was precisely why, no matter how much he might be attracted to her, he could never consider taking someone like Molly for his wife. But how could he convince his heart of that?

CHAPTER 9

A FTER THE WONDERFUL lunch at the hotel Molly didn't see how she could sit through a large evening meal. At least there had been no more talk about wars or battles, but then that might indicate she'd offended Stefan in some way with her outspoken opinion. She'd have to be more careful with her words in the future.

Clarissa and Andrew had certainly appeared to enjoy their time together, and Clarissa positively glowed all afternoon. Mama must have noticed as well since she included Andrew again for the evening meal. At least Mama hadn't prepared a heavy dinner. The cold ham was just enough.

After they finished supper, Molly moved to the parlor with Clarissa while the men headed for Pa's study. Soon after they had settled themselves for a chat, Mama strode through the doorway with Mrs. Elliot, Clara, and Alice behind her. "The kitchen is finally clean." She waved her hand toward Molly. "It's now time for some entertainment. Molly, will you play for us first?"

"Yes, but only if Clarissa agrees to sing after that. She has a beautiful voice."

The men ambled in and joined the ladies. Stefan nodded to his sister. "Even if I may be somewhat prejudiced, she does know how to sing." He glanced over at Molly and winked. "But I haven't heard you play the piano since you were in St. Francisville for your uncle's wedding. I don't imagine you've lost your touch."

Heat bloomed in Molly's cheeks at the memory of that

evening at the Elliot home when Papa had insisted she play for them. She'd been smitten with Stefan even as a twelve-year-old, and to think he'd remembered all these years sent her heart to fluttering.

"Thank you. I'll play Papa's favorite first, a polonaise. He loves Chopin." As her fingers touched the keys her heart and soul went into her music. As usual everything else in the room dissolved, and she became part of the notes she played. She'd disliked practicing when she was a child, but now as she became one with the music her heart swelled with joy and gratitude for those hard lessons.

As the last notes faded, silence greeted her, but the ensuing praise that came as everyone clapped brought heat to her face. Papa stood behind her, hands on her shoulder.

"Well done, my sweet girl. It's been a while since I heard you play like that." He bent and kissed the top of her head and whispered, "I'm so proud of you."

Clarissa moaned. "How will I ever sing after something that beautiful?"

Mrs. Elliot reached across for Clarissa's hand. "Yes, it was beautiful, but you have a wonderful voice. We'll be delighted to hear from you."

"Oh, yes, Clarissa. Tell me what you want to sing, and if I can't play it, Mama can." Molly started shifting sheets of music around. There should be something she could play for Clarissa to sing.

As Clarissa's pure soprano voice filled the room with Foster's "Beautiful Dreamer," Molly stole a glance at Andrew and stifled a grin. The enraptured expression on his face left no doubt he was smitten hard with the beautiful singer. What a wonderful match, a small-town doctor and a plantation girl. The more Molly considered it, the more delight filled her, and she let her smile become full blown.

As before, a moment of silence preceded the clapping and compliments. Molly stood and wrapped her arm around Clarissa's waist. "I think we make quite a pair." She giggled and nudged Clarissa. "Let's run off and join the theater and travel all over the country singing."

After laughter and more remarks about her voice, Clarissa raised her hand in the air. "Now let's sing something fun for all of us. Molly, strike up 'Oh, Susannah.'"

As everyone sang, Juliet and Alice linked arms and danced in a circle. The boys clapped and sang along then Tom grabbed Clara and whirled her around the room. When they finished, Mama fanned her face.

"Y'all did all the work but I feel like I've been to a barn dance. What fun, but I see two little girls who need to go to bed." She reached for Alice's and Juliet's hands. "C'mon girls, it's time to leave this party."

Juliet protested with a frown. "But, Mama..." A yawn stopped her words. Papa picked her up and headed to the stairs. "We'll be back in a few minutes. Entertain yourselves while we're gone."

Stefan called after Papa, "Dr. Whiteman, may I take Molly for a walk?"

Papa grinned and waved his free hand. "Yes, go enjoy yourselves."

Andrew turned to Mr. Elliot. "And may I do the same with Miss Elliot?"

At his nod, Andrew grasped Clarissa's elbow. "I don't think you'll need a hat or parasol this late in the evening."

Pink bloomed in Clarissa's cheeks as he tucked her

hand under his arm. They walked to the door and Stefan grasped Molly's hand. "Are you ready for a stroll?"

"Yes, but sitting on the porch would be much nicer, don't you think? Andrew and Clarissa can stroll about all they want, but I'd prefer to sit." She wasn't sure how much weight Stefan was allowed to put on his leg, but she wanted to make sure he wouldn't be tired. He did have to walk back to the hotel later.

"Whatever you wish, my dear Molly." He placed one hand at her back and pushed the door open with the other.

A gentle breeze wafted across the porch, ruffling the leaves of the ivy plants along the porch rail. A white wicker table and several chairs sat to the left of the door. After they sat down, the murmur of voices drifted out from the parlor to break the silence of the evening.

"This is nice. I'm glad you suggested it. It's good to have a large front porch like this. Someday I plan to have a house with a porch and railings that go all the way around."

Molly settled in the chair and smoothed her skirt. "Oh, do you not plan to stay in the military?" That possibility had never occurred to her. If he was willing to leave the military, she'd be more willing to have a relationship with him.

He laughed. "Being in the military doesn't preclude having a life of my own. A home and family are within my goals as well."

"I see." She bit her lip. Could she handle being married to someone on active duty? Curiosity ate at her.

"Do they have many wives and families at the fort where you are?"

"We have a number of the officers and enlisted men whose wives have joined them. They have special living quarters that are nicer than the bachelor officer barracks. They bring a social atmosphere that is actually quite pleasant, and most of them are very good cooks. The commanding colonel's wife bakes wonderful cakes and cookies to have on hand to greet us when we return from patrol."

"It seems like it would be awfully dangerous to live out in the wilderness. Who protects them when you're out fighting or on patrol or whatever it is you do?" How could they endure being so far away from civilization? She shuddered to think of the distance from her own home and family.

"We don't all go out at once unless it's a big Indian attack, and we haven't had one of those since Geronimo was captured a few years ago. Most of the Indians are now on reservations, and we have a large one near the fort. However, many were relocated to New Mexico and Colorado. That was before my time, but I've heard many stories."

"Well then, exactly what is it that you do with your time?"

Stefan swallowed hard. How could he answer her and not make her angry? Why were they even discussing this anyway? He should have asked her about herself first rather than bring up his hopes for the future.

"Mostly drills and other boring stuff like cleaning and taking care of our equipment and horses. We go out on patrols to check the area around the fort, and that sometimes may take a week depending on how much territory we need to cover." Maybe that would satisfy her questions for now.

"So the women are left on the fort alone?"

"No, of course not. We don't all go on patrol at one time. We always leave a group behind to man the fort." He grinned and reached for her hand. "Now that's plenty about me. I want to know more about you. You told me about your students and school, but do you plan to teach the rest of your life?"

Her smile warmed his heart even as she withdrew her hand from his. Her cheeks once more turned a delightful shade of pink. She embarrassed easily, but that only endeared her to him more than ever. He sat back in his chair, trying to remind himself that under the present circumstances they most likely would never be more than friends.

She tilted her head, but the grin had disappeared and she pursed her lips. After a moment she said, "No, I don't intend to teach all my life. I want to find someone like Aunt Hannah and Ellie did and settle down here in Stoney Creek with a home and family."

Exactly what he'd figured she'd say and more reason than ever to keep their relationship strictly on the friendship level. "They both married ranchers. Is that what you want to do?"

"Not really. I love the ranch and going out there to visit, but I'd much rather live here in town and be where there are more people and activities. What about you? You said you want a large home with a porch like this one. Would that be in town or out in the country?"

"You know our plantation is outside of town, but close enough that Clarissa and my mother can go into St. Francisville frequently for social visits with friends and to shop. I rather like the plantation myself. It's quiet and secluded. That's why I'm considering raising horses after the military." Nothing like the hustle and bustle of the fort where he could hardly have a moment of privacy.

"So the home and family you want won't be at the fort?"

"Only at first. I'd like to stay long enough to reach the rank of major."

"How long does that take?"

"Several years at least since I'm now a first lieutenant. It depends on the opportunities that come my way."

A cloud passed over her face and dimmed her eyes for a moment. Then her old sparkle returned. "With your skills and bravery, I'm sure you will be promoted quickly."

"Why, thank you. I'm not sure you've seen either of those traits exhibited, but I'm gratified that you think so highly of me." He changed the subject. "I'm curious. With all the ranches hereabouts, what do you think of life on a ranch?"

"Ellie and Hannah don't seem to mind, but I think it'd be rather lonely. When the men are out on the range they are sometimes gone for days. If Ellie didn't come into town to teach, she'd have only her children to keep her company all day."

Stefan had to chuckle at that. After meeting the Gordon twins he doubted Ellie had much time to be lonely. Caring for four children would be a full-time job for any woman. "So, couldn't you do the same as Ellie and come into town and teach if you married a rancher?"

"Perhaps, but right now there's not an eligible rancher near my age so I don't have to worry about that."

If town living was her preference, he had one more hurdle added to the list of reasons he shouldn't think of Molly in his future. "So what do you do with your time in town?"

"I do volunteer work with our church ladies' group, visit

our new library, and of course I help Mama around our house. She and I visit different friends for tea, and then there's the new theater."

The enthusiasm in her voice and the gleam in her eyes told the truth of her love for living in town. She had to love people or she wouldn't be a very good teacher and the students wouldn't like her either. His gaze came to rest on her lips. The urge to lean over and kiss them flooded through him.

Molly stopped talking and knit her brows together, and her fingers went to her cheek. "What is it? You're looking at me strangely. Do I have something on my face?"

Stefan blinked his eyes and shook his head. "No, nothing like that." He had to think fast to get his mind away from where it was headed. "I was enjoying listening to you talk. You're really passionate about so many things."

"Oh, I guess I am." She leaned back with her hands on her cheeks. "Dear me, I'm not boring you then?"

"No, you're doing anything but. If you care about people with as much passion as you put into your music earlier, then you're a young woman after God's own heart."

Again her cheeks turned pink. "That's beautiful. No one ever said anything like that to me before. I do love people and I love my Lord even more."

Under any other circumstances, this beautiful young woman before him would be the perfect one for his wife, but with her negative feelings about the military and ranch living, such a relationship could never be. The one thing they did have in common and one that would bind their friendship was their love for the Lord. God had protected him so many times in the past that he couldn't imagine not trusting God and relying on Him for strength.

He reached over and grasped her hands again. "Molly, you are truly a remarkable young woman. May you never lose your love for God and people. Without Him and without love, we are nothing but sounding brass or a tinkling cymbal."

"That's from Paul's letter to the Corinthians, isn't it? I've learned that God's love never fails us no matter how many times we fail Him. I don't know about you, but it gives me great hope for the future. With God as our guide, we can't go wrong."

He smiled and nodded. God was in control, but he was afraid that if he didn't forget about loving Molly everything could go wrong.

CHAPTER 10

On Friday afternoon Sallie sat with Jenny in the kitchen. She had observed her daughter and Stefan during the week, and as delighted as she was to see Stefan's interest in Molly, knowing he would soon return to his regiment disturbed her.

After discussing the dresses they'd be wearing to the theater that evening and the party coming up next Friday, Sallie switched the topic to their children. "So, is Stefan set on a military career?"

"Yes, I'm afraid so. I really didn't want him to enlist at all, but Ben loved the military and taught Stefan to do the same. From the time he was a little boy and learned to ride, all he talked about was riding in the cavalry. I had hoped this injury would make him think twice about going back, but he seems more determined than ever to prove he's as brave as his father."

"What about your plantation?"

Jenny toyed with the handle of her cup. "Things aren't what they used to be. The plantation flourished when Ben's father had a full crew of slaves to take care of it, but now that's not the case. Only a few of them stayed behind after being given their freedom. We can't raise as large a crop as the land once produced. In fact, Ben's father sold some of it after the war in order to keep the place going." She raised somber eyes to Sallie.

"Stefan has never really liked working on the plantation. It grieved Ben at first, but then he realized if he forced

Stefan to farm, he might lose him altogether. So, it's the military for our son right now."

"I know how worried you must be about him." Sallie refilled her cup and Jenny's with minted tea.

After the months she'd spent waiting on Manfred to return home from the war, Sallie had no desire for Molly to experience the same. Sallie hated war as much as Molly, and she had to admit to herself that it had been a bit disturbing to have a soldier like Stefan around, stirring up old memories.

Jenny added a bit of honey to her tea. "I'm not worried so much now that the Indians have quit attacking. They mostly go out on patrols and ride along as protection for certain army or other government shipments. Once in a while they'll assist the local law in apprehending those who break the law. I'm thankful there is no war. No one should have to experience what we did."

Sallie couldn't agree more. The memory of the day her father brought Jenny to Grandma Woodruff's home in St. Francisville still produced a chill in Sallie's bones, and the memory of shooting that young soldier in her mama's kitchen would never be erased. Fighting and killing did strange things to people, and she didn't want Molly to experience any of it.

"Perhaps it's best that you won't be here for a long period of time. Stefan and Molly are growing close, but there's no time for it to develop. If she falls in love with him, she'll end up worrying and waiting just like I did for Manfred."

Jenny reached over and grasped Sallie's hand. "But look how wonderful that turned out."

"I know, but I wish she could find someone here. Andrew is only a few years older than she, but he's been like a brother to her since he went away to school." Short of the cowboys out at the ranches, few eligible young men lived in the area. She'd hoped for an attraction between Andrew and Molly, but that hadn't happened, and from the look on his face when he was around Clarissa, it wouldn't.

Jenny said, "Speaking of Andrew, I've noticed how much attention he's paying to Clarissa, and she seems to be enjoying the attention. He's a fine young man, but I don't imagine there's any hope of his coming to Louisiana to practice medicine."

Sallie laughed and shook her head. "I think Manfred would hog-tie the boy to the fence out back before he'd let him run off somewhere else. He really does relieve the load for Manfred." With Manfred's kind heart, he'd probably support Andrew wherever he wanted to go, but no need to tell Jenny that fact.

She sat back to enjoy the last few minutes with Jenny before they needed to get ready for their evening at the theater. She'd planned to speak with Molly about her feelings for Stefan, but that would have to wait another day. Tonight she'd keep a close eye on them to see if her suspicions were justified.

***

Stefan strolled down Main Street in the direction of the Whiteman home. The theater sat in its regal splendor all prepared for the opening performance that evening. Molly would be resting with Clarissa in preparation for the full evening of entertainment ahead, but perhaps he could catch Andrew in a lull and talk with him. If what he'd seen meant anything, romance was brewing between the doctor and Clarissa and that would never do. He'd said at first he'd help Andrew, but after consideration in the past week, he decided against it. His sister belonged in Louisiana with her parents where she could marry some local young man and take her place in society.

Not that he didn't like Andrew, but he lived in Texas and that was too far away for Clarissa to move. Besides, she wouldn't have the social standing that she had at home. She'd be taking their mother and grandmother's place in entertaining and keeping their status in the town intact. That had been important to Grandmother Elliot and seemed to be so for his mother as well.

He could deal with Andrew, but what could he do about his own growing feelings for Molly? Hard as he tried to keep their relationship strictly on a friendship basis, his heart refused to cooperate. So as to not be around her so much he'd spent Tuesday, Wednesday, and Thursday at the Gordon ranch with the excuse of learning more about the horses his father planned to buy. He'd even picked out one for himself to take back to Arizona to replace the one he'd lost.

The only times he'd seen Molly had been at the supper table. They'd laughed and talked of anything and everything with their families, but then he'd headed back to the hotel as soon as he could politely leave. Avoiding being alone hadn't helped matters, though. Her red-gold hair and dancing green eyes invaded his thoughts no matter where he took himself.

He'd deliberately stayed in town today, but the time had dragged. Molly deserved an explanation for his neglect, but what could he tell her? He couldn't deny the anticipation and excitement rising in his heart as he approached the Whiteman house.

After their discussion on the porch Monday night, he had grown even more attracted to her, and that wasn't wise. They were too different in their hopes for the future. The main thing they both had in common was their love for the Lord, but was that enough to sustain a lifetime together?

While at the ranch, he'd discovered he truly enjoyed riding with the cowboys. Micah had complimented him more than once on his horsemanship. That shouldn't have been a surprise, since Stefan served as a cavalry officer. He did miss being around horses, and he looked forward to training his new mount.

Andrew stood on the porch at the entrance to the infirmary and waited as Stefan approached. "What brings you out on such a warm afternoon, or should I say hot?"

Stefan stopped at the bottom of the steps and leaned on his cane. "I came to see you, actually. If you're busy, we can talk this evening after the theater."

"It's slow today. Unless it's life threatening, people come early in the morning or late in the afternoon. Come on up here where it's somewhat cooler. I'll let Mrs. Whiteman know you're here and she'll have us a cool drink in a few minutes."

Andrew disappeared into the house, and Stefan climbed the steps to sit in one of the wicker chairs he and Molly had occupied a few evenings ago.

Andrew reappeared. "She'll be out shortly with lemonade." He sat across from Stefan. "What's on your mind? Would it have something to do with your sister?"

Stefan nodded and searched for words to convey his thoughts without angering Andrew or insulting him.

A grin spread across Andrew's face. "I figured as much. I spoke with your father last evening. I wanted his approval to escort her while you all are in town. I must admit I'm quite taken with her, but I realize the distance between our homes would make it difficult to pursue a relationship. I know I'd have the same concerns if it involved my sister Faith."

This young man had more common sense than Stefan had given him credit for. Mrs. Whiteman's appearance with a tray and two glasses of lemonade and a small plate of sugar cookies saved him from having to respond to Andrew.

Stefan stood and greeted her. "Thank you, but you didn't need to go to the trouble for us."

"It was no trouble at all. Your mother and I were having tea and cookies in the kitchen just now, so it was easy to fix you a tray." She set the tray on the table then stepped back with her hands on her hips and tilted her head to the side. "I'm surprised to see you out walking in this heat. The girls are upstairs napping to prepare for the long evening ahead. I suppose you men don't need such rest." She laughed then waved her hand before entering the house.

The song of the cicadas rang through the air and reminded Stefan of those he heard at home in the trees surrounding Oakwood, the family plantation. Although Stoney Creek had plenty of trees, he missed the moss that hung in clumps from the oaks and elms of home.

The streets of town shimmered in the heat, and most folks chose to stay indoors at this time of day. Yet here he sat enjoying a glass of lemonade and Mrs. Whiteman's delicious cookies. All because of two young women now upstairs in this very house resting for their big evening. He sipped the drink and let the cool liquid soothe his throat. At times like this he could very well forget any need for army regiments and drills.

"We discussed my relationship with your sister, but if I may be so bold, I've seen the look of admiration you hold for Molly. The two of us grew up together and she's a special young woman."

"Yes, I've come to realize that in more ways than one." He set his glass back on the table. "The problem is that we have such different points of view on many matters. The one thing we do agree on is our faith, but her ideas about the military and future way of life are directly opposite of mine." He'd spent the better part of the past three days trying to convince his heart to forget a future with Molly and to simply bask in the pleasure of her company.

"I know how Molly feels. She's told me often enough, but then you must remember how hard it was on her father. He spent all those months in a horrific prison camp where many men died every day."

"Yes, I understand that. My mother suffered terribly at the hands of the enemy. If her father had been alive, he'd have killed any man who touched her, and my father would do the same now for Clarissa or Mother. I guess it's hard for Molly to see and come to terms with that."

"I'm not so sure about that. War she doesn't like at all, but defending oneself against an enemy may be different. I'm sure you've heard the story about her mother killing a Yankee soldier who had come into their house during a battle near their home."

Stefan furrowed his brow. Yes, he remembered Molly

mentioning it, but despite what Andrew may believe about self-defense, that killing could well be the reason for her aversion to guns and war. What happened in those four years of hardship and killing on both sides would not be forgotten soon. If somehow he could bring Molly to see the difference between killing for selfish gain versus killing in self-defense, perhaps she'd be more inclined to support his career. However, he wasn't likely to solve the problem in the few days they had left together, and right now he'd settle for having a pleasant time with her without any arguments about war. He'd deal with what his heart wanted later.

CHAPTER 11

UTTERFLIES DANCED IN Molly's stomach in anticipation of the concert at the theater this evening.
Stoney Creek had waited with patience as the theater was proposed then built. Ever since Mayor Gladstone
made the final announcement, Molly had looked forward
to this night.

Prominent citizens of Stoney Creek had been invited
to the reception following the performance, and the
Whiteman family and their guests would be among those
attending. Molly's mind whirled with the names of all
those who would be attending opening night and her
nerves perched on edge.

She smoothed the skirt of her green taffeta gown then
fingered the lace trim at the neckline. Only the slightest
hint of a bustle added to the back of the garment. Mama
didn't care to abide by all the fashion rules. Aunt Hannah
said Mama had complained way back when they were
young girls about corsets and hoops.

Molly grinned and pinched her cheeks to give them
some color. At least she'd inherited that trait from her
mother and aunt. Comfort was much more important
than style. Of course, Mrs. Elliot and Clarissa would be
dressed to suit the occasion in the latest designs, as would
Camilla Hightower and Mayor Gladstone's wife.

Clarissa sauntered into the room wearing a lavender
wrapper that deepened the blue in her eyes and accented
the purple that lurked in them. No wonder Andrew

Delmont was so taken by her friend. Her beauty stole even Molly's breath.

"Oh, I see you're already dressed, and you look lovely in that emerald green. I could never wear that color. Mama chose royal blue for my gown." She headed for the wardrobe and removed her dress.

Molly took the garment and began undoing the buttons while Clarissa removed her wrapper to reveal the corset under it. It pushed her small breasts up into her chemise and gave them a fuller appearance. Molly shook her head. Her bosom needed no such enhancement and gave her another argument against a corset.

"Molly, do you ever wish for a maidservant to help you dress for these special occasions? Mama says that Lettie used to help her and your mother whenever they had a party to attend." Clarissa raised her arms and bent at the waist for Molly to ease the dress over them.

"Not really. Clara and I usually help each other. Our mothers lived in a different time and place than we do here in Stoney Creek. The mayor's wife does have two women who cook and clean for her, as does Mrs. Hightower, but they are accustomed to that style of living."

"I've seen that life in Texas is very different from that in Louisiana, especially in New Orleans."

Molly finished helping Clarissa with her dress and stood back to admire her friend. "I must say that corset does make your waist next to nothing, but how can you breathe?"

"I'm used to it and have learned to take short rather than deep breaths. Miriam took over her mother's dressmaking and she is just as wonderful as Mrs. Tenney."

"Yes, she is. Your dress is beautiful, and the perfect color for you." Molly remembered meeting Miriam Harris on one of their trips to Louisiana. Mama wore a dress Mrs. Tenney and Miriam had made for the wedding of Mama's brother. Miriam and Mama had been good friends, and her husband, Stuart, had served in the war with Papa.

Molly turned to the looking glass at her dressing table and checked her hairstyle. Mama had arranged it in curls fastened with a pearl-trimmed comb at the crown. Only a fringe of bangs swept across her forehead.

Clarissa picked up a pair of long gloves and fitted them over her hands, then pulled them up to cover her bare arms. "Mama said that Stefan came by to visit with Andrew this afternoon. I wonder what that was all about. I certainly hope he didn't come to discourage Andrew from escorting me tonight. It'd be just like him even though Papa already said it'd be all right."

Stefan was here? And she'd been up here sleeping. That was probably for the best. Even though she looked forward to the evening with him, she truly didn't need to spend any more time with him than necessary, or she'd never get her heart to accept the idea they had nothing in common.

"Stefan tells me that after the military, he'd like to live in the country and be a rancher like my uncle. What about you?"

Clarissa laughed and shook her head. "Stefan can be a bore. I prefer New Orleans and the social life found in a city. I could never be happy stuck out in the country somewhere. Even Stoney Creek is better than that."

"I feel the same way and I told Stefan so. My aunt Hannah loves it, but then she's so in love with Micah it wouldn't matter if they lived in a cave." Would her own feelings ever change if she found a love like that? Fat chance of that happening in Stoney Creek. Maybe she needed to visit Clarissa in Louisiana. New Orleans sounded like such an exciting place.

The murmur of voices from downstairs signaled the arrival of their escorts. Molly pinched her cheeks once again then nodded in satisfaction with her appearance. This was one evening she planned to enjoy with all her heart.

Molly preceded Clarissa down the stairs so as not to step on the train of her skirt. In the parlor, her parents waited with Mr. and Mrs. Elliot and Clara. Stefan and Andrew had both arrived. Molly's breath caught in her throat at the sight of Stefan in full dress uniform. He certainly looked handsome in the dark blue trimmed with so much gold braid. If only it didn't remind her of what he did with his life and emphasize the fact that their country still had need for an army.

❧

When Stefan's eyes lighted on Molly on the stairs in front of Clarissa, his heart did a double pump and began a dull thud in his chest. The green of the dress accented the green in her eyes and her hair shone like spun gold. How he longed to see it cascade down her back and run his fingers through its silky tresses.

Her natural beauty captured his attention, and all others in the room vanished. He offered her his hand as she reached the bottom step. "Molly, you are even more beautiful tonight than you were Sunday."

Roses bloomed in her cheeks as she dipped her head. "Thank you, Stefan."

Mrs. Whiteman clapped her hands. "Well, I see we're all here, so let's begin our evening of entertainment."

Stefan offered his arm to Molly and tucked her hand close to him. No matter what he told himself about not caring about her as anything more than a friend, he intended to savor every moment of their time together this evening.

"Mama, where is Tom? Isn't he going with us?"

Mrs. Whiteman turned her head to speak over her shoulder. "He's escorting Faith Delmont tonight." She glanced at Andrew and winked.

Molly's giggle tinkled in the warm air as they stepped onto the porch. "My, I didn't know my little brother had a sweetheart. You might be a part of this family after all, Dr. Delmont."

Laughter spread through the group, and Stefan envied the family camaraderie. He and Clarissa were close but they only had each other. Molly had a passel of brothers and sisters to make her life more interesting.

Outside they boarded the two surreys Dr. Whiteman had procured for the evening. Clara rode with her parents and Mother and Father, which left Andrew and him alone with the young ladies. Andrew offered to handle the reins and Stefan had no objections.

Molly and Clarissa chattered the entire six blocks to the theater, their excitement for the evening causing Stefan to develop more anticipation for the events both now and later.

They found their seats in the center, six rows from the front, and the enraptured faces of Molly and Clarissa increased his pleasure. The program began. The soloist on the stage had a beautiful soprano voice that hit high notes with no vibrato, and that was quite an accomplishment, according to his sister. With the right lessons, she could be every bit as good as the singer performing.

He caught Andrew's glance and smiled. Andrew returned it with an additional nod. Meeting the performer at the reception afterward would be a true serendipity for Molly and his sister. His heart thanked his mother for insisting he accompany them on this trip. Look what he would've missed if he'd stayed at home.

As Miss Cushing's voice filled the air with notes so true they brought chills to his blood, he reached for Molly's hand. Without so much as a glance at him, she clutched it tight, but he didn't mind. The warmth from that small, delicate hand in his sent rivers of delight carving their way straight to his heart.

The hour and a half program passed by in a flash, even with the fifteen-minute intermission. After the applause and standing ovation died down, the audience began making its way up the aisles toward the exits. Stefan placed his hand at the small of Molly's back to guide her through the crowd to the outside. The reception would take place at the hotel on the next block. Stefan anticipated the event as it reminded him of the ones they attended in New Orleans. He could barely wait to see her joy and excitement mixing with the entertainers.

They ambled down the boardwalk toward the hotel with Molly and Clarissa once again dominating the conversation with their exclamations of delight with the program. Clarissa gripped Andrew's arm and smiled at Stefan. "Oh, how I wish I could sing like Miss Cushing."

Andrew patted her hand. "But my dear Miss Elliot, you do sing as well as her. You proved that the other night."

Molly leaned close to Stefan, her words for his ears only. "I do believe Andrew is falling in love with your sister."

Falling in love? That would never do. He glanced again at his sister and Andrew. She clung to him and looked at him with eyes so adoring, Stefan gasped. He must speak with Father right away. A love relationship between Andrew and Clarissa would never do. He and Molly had their differences, but they were merely matters of opinion and attitude. The differences between Clarissa and Andrew were another thing entirely.

He may sound like a snob, but his sister deserved a better life than that of a small-town doctor. She had social obligations that must be fulfilled, and that couldn't happen in Texas. He'd watch them closely the rest of the evening before speaking with Father about the situation.

Molly squeezed his arm. "Stefan, your mind is a million miles away from here. What has you so distracted? Is it Andrew and Clarissa?"

How could he answer her without looking like the snob he didn't want to be? "Um, yes, I was thinking about how pretty she looks tonight." Not the complete truth to his thoughts, but it was the truth about his sister.

"I'm beginning to think she may care as much about him as he does about her. It would be so nice if they become a couple and she moves here to Texas."

Stefan clenched his teeth. That couldn't happen. Clarissa had to stay in Louisiana with Mother and Father. She'd never think about leaving them alone. He most definitely needed to have a discussion with his father concerning this relationship. "I'm not so sure about that, Molly. Louisiana is her home, and our parents will need her while I'm gone. They'd be terribly lonely without her." There, that didn't sound like he thought Stoney Creek beneath Clarissa's station in life.

She bit her lip and glanced back at the couple now lagging behind. "I suppose that's true. As much as I'd like to have her here, your mother probably would rather have her stay in St. Francisville. I've thought about coming out there for a visit since I'm off all summer. I'd get to see my grandmother and uncles, too, as well as my cousins who live there."

"Now that sounds like a good plan. Clarissa could even take you down to Baton Rouge if not to New Orleans. Both are interesting cities, although New Orleans is somewhat more adventurous."

They arrived at the hotel and strolled into the lobby to find a sign directing them to the reception area where a stringed quartet, most likely from the orchestra at the concert, had set up and now played background music for guests as they arrived.

Whatever else they had done, the mayor and town council had certainly gone all out to welcome Miss Cushing and her company to Stoney Creek for the four days she would be in town. He'd never seen so many fresh flowers in one place except perhaps at a wake. Roses, carnations, and lilies in every color of the rainbow filled giant urns as well as short crystal bowls. An area of the floor had been cleared for dancing later, and Stefan looked forward to the opportunity to lead Molly about the dance floor.

"Oh, Stefan, doesn't the refreshment table look lovely? I wonder if Andrew's mother baked that gorgeous cake. She's the best in town as is their bakery. Andrew delivered cakes and things for them when he was younger."

Delmont Bakery, of course. Why hadn't he made the connection before? He'd seen the sign every day as he walked or rode from the hotel to the Whiteman house. How dense could he be not to realize Andrew would be one of them? The discovery served to strengthen Stefan's resolve to speak with his father concerning Andrew and Clarissa.

One thing he must remember for this night, Molly could not by any means learn of his real attitude toward the idea of Andrew and Clarissa as a couple. One slip could ruin everything and make for a most miserable evening.

CHAPTER 12

MOLLY STRETCHED AND opened one eye. Bright sunshine flooded through the lace curtains casting a swirled design across the room. She sat up straight and ran her hands through her hair. How had she slept so long? She glanced over at Clarissa, but she was still curled up sleeping.

They'd come home terribly late last night, but she usually never slept this long. She eased her legs over the edge of the bed and pulled her nightgown down over her knees. She stood with as little moving of the mattress as possible so as not to wake her friend.

She padded in bare feet across the carpet to the wardrobe and pulled it open. The door squeaked and Molly grimaced as a groan cut across the quiet.

"Is it time to get up already?"

Molly peered over her shoulder at Clarissa, who lay with her arms resting above her head on the pillow. "Yes, but I'm sorry I awakened you. I tried to be quiet, but this wardrobe door had to squeak."

Clarissa blinked her eyes and sat up. "That's all right. I need to be getting up anyway. Andrew has off today and is taking me for a ride. He's renting another horse at the livery so we can ride out to the creek. He's going to teach me to ride Western style. His mother is fixing us a picnic basket."

"That will be nice, especially with Mrs. Delmont's cooking." Why hadn't she thought of suggesting something like that to Stefan? Of course their meal would not be near as good as the one Mrs. Delmont prepared, but then Molly did know how to prepare a few things, and with Mama's help, it would have been nice. Maybe it wasn't too late after all.

"That's such a splendid idea. I think I may suggest it to Stefan. Mama and I can fix up a basket for us in no time, but we won't intrude on your time with Andrew."

Clarissa grinned and joined her at the wardrobe. "I didn't expect you would. I've seen the way you and my brother eye each other. Wouldn't surprise me at all if he asked your father if he could court you."

Heat pushed its way to Molly's cheeks, and she bent down to retrieve a pair of shoes. "I don't think so. He'll be leaving to return to regiment in another week, so we won't even see each other after that." Besides, there were too many differences between them that made such a relationship impossible. She had no more plans to marry a man in the army than she had of marrying a cowboy. Of that she was certain.

"Oh, horse feathers, as my grandma says. You can always write to each other, and there are women who marry and move out to the fort."

"I don't think so, Clarissa. I do like Stefan, but not enough to leave everything here and move to some fort out in the wilderness." She drew her night dress over her head and reached for her undergarments. "It's time to get dressed and see if there's anything left from breakfast."

When Clarissa pulled out the dress she planned to wear Molly gasped. "Oh, Clarissa, that's much too pretty to wear riding a horse." She yanked at a hanger. "Here, wear one of my split skirts. You'll be much more comfortable."

Clarissa eyed the skirt a moment then shrugged. "All right, if you say so, but it is rather plain."

Twenty minutes later, Clarissa followed her down the stairs and into the kitchen. Mama and Mrs. Elliot grinned and shook their heads. Mama rose and uncovered two plates sitting on the back of the stove. "I saved these plates for you. Everyone else has eaten and gone on about their business."

Molly accepted her plate and after a quick blessing, plowed into the eggs and biscuits like she hadn't eaten in a month. When she noticed Clarissa's fork simply moving the food around on her plate, Molly stopped and patted her mouth with her napkin. As hungry as she was, she had completely forgotten her manners. Mama's stern frown didn't help either.

Molly leaned over and whispered, "Why aren't you eating? Mama kept it nice and warm for us."

"I don't want to spoil my appetite for the picnic Mrs. Delmont makes for us."

Molly gulped. She'd meant to ask Mama about a picnic basket for Stefan and her, but the sight of the breakfast wiped it clean from her mind. She'd better ask now or she might forget again. "Clarissa and Andrew are going on a picnic this afternoon, and Mrs. Delmont is making up the basket for them."

Mrs. Elliot raised her eyebrows. "A picnic with Andrew? But you were with him only last night. Isn't he busy today?"

"No, Mother. Dr. Whiteman gave him the day off when Andrew asked, so we decided to go down to the creek and have a picnic. He's getting a horse for me, and Molly loaned me one of her riding skirts."

"So I see. Does your father know about this?"

Molly bit her lip and scrunched her napkin in her lap. Why had she said anything? From the tone of her voice, Mrs. Elliot didn't approve of Andrew, and Andrew was the nicest young man around. Then she remembered Stefan's comments, and she realized they were very much like those hinted at by his mother.

"Yes, Father knows. He spoke with me the other day after Andrew asked to be my escort while we're in town. Father wanted to know my thoughts before he said yes."

That was a relief. At least Mr. Elliot hadn't made the decision without speaking to Clarissa herself. Molly had seen relationships forced upon a young woman who had no desire to be pursued by a particular man, and they hadn't turned out well at all.

Mrs. Elliot lowered her voice and leaned over to Clarissa. It gave Molly the perfect time to seek Mama's help. "Would you help me make up a basket so Stefan and I can have a picnic too?"

Mama lifted an eyebrow much the same as Mrs. Elliot had. "Am I detecting an interest in the young soldier?"

"Um, not really." Molly twisted the napkin in her hands out of sight of her mother. "I thought it would be a nice way to spend an afternoon. After all, they only have a week left before they all leave."

Despite her reservations, she did enjoy Stefan's attentions, and once he was gone, she'd have none of that from anyone here in town. And why not have some fun while he was here?

"All right, let's see what we have." Mama opened the cupboard doors and scanned the shelves.

Behind them, Mrs. Elliot's voice rose. "I can't let you go on like this. It can only lead to heartbreak."

Clarissa jumped from her chair and threw her napkin to the table. "I'm sorry, Mother, but I don't intend to discourage Andrew. He's a fine man, and I admire him greatly. I don't want to displease you or Papa, but I must make my own decisions concerning whom I shall allow to court me." She spun on her heel and raced from the room.

Mrs. Elliot's cheeks wore great spots of red. Mama continued with her task, but Molly couldn't help but stare at Clarissa's mother. Was she that afraid something would happen between Andrew and Clarissa that she would ruin their remaining time in Stoney Creek?

Mrs. Elliot did not meet her gaze. "I must go and speak with Mr. Elliot right away. Please excuse me." With a swish of skirts and a firm step, she left the kitchen.

Molly could only offer up a brief prayer that nothing would spoil the day for her friend. Then she turned to help her mother prepare a picnic with Stefan, but now her anticipation waned and her enthusiasm for a picnic all but disappeared.

Stefan approached the Whiteman home with Andrew, who carried a basket from which enticing aromas drifted. "If the food tastes half as good as it smells, you and Clarissa are going to have a fine picnic." If it was anything like the spread at the hotel last night, it would be delicious.

"Ah, yes. My parents know how to make foods irresistible. Pa learned his skills from his father. Men in our family have been great chefs at some of the finest hotels in Europe, but Pa chose to come to Texas after he and Ma met. They figured the 'Wild West' needed some taming with good eats."

Every time Stefan passed by the bakery in town, he had to resist the temptation to stop and indulge in one of Mrs. Delmont's cinnamon rolls. Even their cook back home didn't make them that good. A picnic today would be nice. He'd have to ask Molly about having one.

"I say, do you think your mother would fix up a basket for Molly and me? I'd offer a nice sum for whatever she wanted to fix."

"I'm sure she would, but I imagine Mrs. Whiteman would do the same. She's a wonderful cook herself."

That might be good idea. From what he'd seen already, most of the women in Stoney Creek were excellent cooks. He hadn't dined on a bad meal yet. "I'll ask when I see her in a few minutes."

Clarissa called out from the porch and waved then hurried down the steps toward them. She glared at Stefan before grabbing Andrew's arm. "Are the horses saddled and ready? I want to go right now."

Andrew raised his brow. "Why, yes, they are at the livery waiting for us. Is there a problem?"

She glanced at Stefan again but didn't speak to him. "I'll tell you about it later. Let's just go get those horses now."

"Whatever you say." Andrew grasped her arm and they headed back toward the livery at the edge of town.

Stefan stood for a few minutes staring after them. Clarissa's demeanor disturbed him. Something had happened, but why was she angry with him? He shook his head and proceeded up the steps to the porch and knocked on the door.

His mother flung open the door and moved her head

to see behind him. She grabbed his arm and pulled him inside. "Stefan, I'm so glad you're here. Did you see Clarissa run out of the house?"

"Yes, she and Andrew are headed for the livery to get their horses for their picnic. Why? Did something happen?" Anger and concern flashed in her eyes. Whatever had caused it must have come from Clarissa. He led her back to the parlor.

His mother sank down onto the sofa. "Clarissa and I had an argument. I warned her not to get too close to Andrew as she was only going to be here for another week. I didn't like what I saw between them last night. A relationship with him would never work for her."

Stefan sat down beside her and grasped her hand. "Is that what you told her?" If so, then Clarissa's anger didn't surprise him. His independent sister had a mind of her own.

"Yes, and I see that was a mistake. She let me know in no uncertain terms that she would decide about any relationship she'd have with any man. I...I pushed her toward him rather than away. Now what am I to do? Your father has already left to visit the ranch again today, so I haven't been able to discuss it with him."

"Mother, Clarissa is a smart woman. She's not going to do anything rash. She's angry now, but she'll cool down and see the futility of a relationship with someone who lives so far away."

As the words left his mouth, Molly invaded his thoughts. The words must apply to his relationship with her as well. *Enjoy the next week, but don't expect more to come.* The distance between them was too great, and he didn't mean in miles only.

Molly appeared in the doorway. "I thought I heard a man's voice in here."

Stefan jumped to his feet. Even in her riding dress, she looked beautiful. Her hair was caught up at the crown with a large bow and the rest hung down past her shoulders in a cascade of waves and curls. He swallowed hard before greeting her.

"Mother and I were talking, but Clarissa and Andrew have already left."

"I thought they might. I asked Mama to fix us a picnic basket so we can have a picnic at the creek as well. I do hope you're pleased."

Pleased didn't begin to describe what went on in his heart at the moment. They thought alike in so many good ways, but their differences would soon drive them apart. Why must he keep reminding himself of that?

"That sounds like a very good idea. I envied Andrew his picnic basket and entertained the thought of asking your mother to do the same, and here you already have it done."

"I'll be back in a moment with the basket." The suede fabric of her skirt whispered its softness as she pushed through the door to the kitchen.

"Ahem, Stefan?"

He turned to find his mother staring at him with her eyes open wide and her brow furrowed. "I detect the same desire in your eyes as I did Andrew's. As much as I like Molly and would love to have her in the family, you know it won't work, don't you?"

His heart groaned. "Yes, I do, and I'll remember that." But his feelings didn't want to be buried and forgotten.

"Do you prom—" She stopped and smiled beyond his shoulder.

He spun around to find Molly with her basket in one hand and her mother right behind. He prayed he'd remember what he must do, but he'd make no promises to that effect.

He held out his hand and Molly grasped it. "Our horses await us at the livery." He turned to Mrs. Whiteman. "I'll be sure to have her back in time for this evening's supper."

A smile graced her lips. "Oh, take your time and have fun. There's enough food in there to satisfy your hunger now and later."

Despite his mother's frown and warning, he planned to do just that. Molly grabbed her hat and they made haste to the livery to pick up their horses. They waved at Andrew and Clarissa as they passed. His sister looked much happier now with a smile aimed at Andrew. She didn't even glance his way, riding astride the saddle as if she'd done it all her life.

Let Mother and Father worry about her. He had enough worries of his own to be concerned with what his sister did or didn't do.

He gasped as Molly swung her leg up over the horse and settled astride in the saddle. Her skirt was one that allowed her to ride full in the saddle, but he hadn't expected her to be so competent and confident. She must have noted the surprise in his face because she laughed and pulled back on the reins and turned her horse toward the street leading from town.

"I've been riding since I was a young girl, and this is the easiest way to get around. I would never be comfortable riding any other way, so don't look so shocked. Come on, we're wasting a beautiful day."

Yes, they were, and he didn't intend to let it slip by. He

swung up into his saddle and followed her up the street. At her side, he slowed to keep pace with her. "I will say you are a good horsewoman. You handle him like a born rider."

He admired so much about this lovely woman riding next to him with a wide-brimmed hat shielding her face from the sun. Now if he could keep his emotions in check and simply enjoy her company this afternoon, all would be well.

CHAPTER 13

SOMETHING OR SOMEONE had angered Clarissa, but Andrew had no idea what or who, and he didn't know what to say, so he said nothing. If she wanted to share, she would. Otherwise he'd stay quiet and let her sort things out on her own.

When they reached the edge of town, he turned their horses away from the main road and started off across the meadow. Clarissa sighed and headed toward a clump of trees. Andrew shrugged and followed her. This was her day, so they'd go wherever she wanted and do whatever she desired.

Clarissa stopped her mare and dismounted. She waited for Andrew to do the same. Once on the ground, he noted the troubled look in her eyes and grasped her hand. "I know something is bothering you, and if you want to share, I'll listen."

Moisture dotted her lashes and she blinked. "I'm upset with my mother. She seems to think I'm still a child and can't make decisions for myself."

Andrew nodded, still holding her hands. He fought the desire to bring her to his chest and wrap his arms around her. She peered up at him from under the brim of a straw bonnet trimmed in purple to match her shirtwaist and deepen the blue in her eyes. He could drown in those pools of color.

"Andrew, my mother seems to think our seeing each other is not a good idea. We only have another week, and then it's back to Louisiana and our life there. She believes we are growing to care too much about each other."

Her mother was right about that much. In one week he'd grown to care more about Clarissa than he had any girl in his life. To say he loved her might not be right so soon after meeting her, but that's exactly where his heart was headed.

"I do care about you, Clarissa, but I also understand your mother's concern. She doesn't want you to be hurt or disappointed."

"Oh, how could I be hurt or disappointed by your caring about me? You've been wonderful this past week, and I care about you, too." She moistened her lips and squeezed his hands. "None of us knows what the future may hold. All we can do is enjoy the time we have and let God take care of the rest. Even if we never see each other again, we'll have these two weeks as a wonderful memory."

Two weeks became as nothing when he considered a future without Clarissa. When had he come to that conclusion? He swallowed hard in an effort to speak without ruining all that had been built. "And they will be the best two weeks ever, and who's to say that we'll never see each other again? Louisiana isn't that far away."

She leaned toward him. "You always know just what to say. I'd like nothing better than to have you come to Oakwood for a visit."

"Then that will certainly be a part of my plans for the future." He lowered his head toward hers, but snapped back. No, a kiss was the last thing that should happen today. He reached for the reins of the horse behind her. "Here, let's get you mounted, so we can continue on our journey toward a pleasant afternoon."

Disappointment filled her eyes, but she shifted so he could help her into her saddle. Once she sat securely, he mounted his own and led the way across the grassy field to open country. Keeping his emotions in check for seven more days would take all the strength he could muster, but he'd do it. If he didn't, Mrs. Elliot may well forbid him from ever seeing Clarissa again and that's the last thing he wanted to happen.

Although Molly smiled and chattered about the picnic and the creek where they were headed, Stefan still sensed an underlying worry. When they reached the creek, he helped her dismount then untied the picnic basket from his saddle. "Where do you want to set this?"

She reached for the blanket folded up behind her saddle. "Right over there under those trees near the creek."

Stefan nodded and headed that way. After she spread the dark green blanket across the grass, she sat and removed her hat and shook her head to loosen the curls. He used every ounce of will power in his body to keep from reaching over and running his hands through the silky mass on her shoulders.

"Stefan, I'm worried about Clarissa and Andrew."

His name from her lips broke the spell. Her words voiced his concerns, especially since his conversation with his mother. "I am too. Their relationship appears to be headed for much more than friendship."

"I think it would be wonderful, but after what your mother said this morning, I'm not sure she or your father would ever accept Andrew as a suitor for Clarissa."

He didn't either, but for reasons he wasn't sure Molly would understand much less accept. "That may well be true simply because he lives here and we must return to Louisiana. Such a distance wouldn't bode well for a relationship."

"If they love each other, that shouldn't matter. After all, Mama and Papa were separated for many months, but their love stayed true. And she wasn't even sure if he was dead or alive."

"That was an entirely different circumstance." Why were they discussing his sister's life when he wanted to know more about Molly? This wasn't going the way he wanted.

She narrowed her eyes and quirked the corner of her mouth. "You don't approve either, do you?"

This was not good. He didn't plan on having any arguments about Clarissa. "Whether I approve or disapprove has no bearing on what Clarissa will or won't do. I say that's between her and our parents. After all, God is in control, and He will help take care of such matters of the heart." Had he really uttered those words? If what he said was true for Clarissa, then it most certainly was the same for him.

A broad grin spread across her face and lit up her eyes with merriment. "I do believe you're right. We can't go meddling with other people's lives. We have to let God take care of things and know that His plans are really best after all."

His sentiments exactly. Now he had to remember that as far as he and Molly were concerned as well. *Lord, it'd be nice if You could change her mind about soldiers and living in the country. I'm falling in love with her, but without some work on Your part, I don't see her returning that love.* Seeing how

God answered that prayer would make for an interesting time ahead.

⁂

If only Molly could make her heart believe the words she'd spoken to Stefan. She'd been smitten with him as a young girl, and to see him now revived all those old notions she'd had of being his wife someday. However, his profession as a soldier did not appeal to her in the least.

As handsome as he was sitting across from her, she had to control her feelings and do what she'd advised for Clarissa and Andrew. Instead of his uniform, he wore brown pants and a cream-colored shirt that set off his sandy hair and blue eyes so like his mother's. She could almost forget his usual attire was army blue and gold. As he continued to observe her with a slight smile, heat filled her cheeks. Seemed every time she was near him, her face turned red, and that couldn't be attractive. She jumped up and headed for her favorite rock at the creek bank.

A moment later he followed and pulled up to sit beside her. "I can understand why you love this place so much. The water babbles along with its gurgling song, but the air is as still as a church mouse on Sunday."

His masculine scent along with the heat of his arm pressed against hers created a longing she didn't quite understand. She cast a sidewise glance at his face and settled on his full lips. How would it feel to have those lips pressed against hers? She blinked and focused on the fields across the creek. She couldn't let her thoughts go there.

When she turned her head toward him, he gazed at her with those deep blue eyes that shone with a desire she had never seen in a man's eyes. Was this what it was like to be in love? She pulled her knees to her chest and hugged them close.

Dear Lord, no, please don't let me fall in love with him. I couldn't bear his being so far away, especially in the army. Still my heart and calm my nerves.

Why had she suggested something like a picnic where she'd be alone with him? She slid from her perch on the rock and ran back to the blanket. She had to get control or no telling what she might say or do.

She smoothed out the wrinkles on the blanket and reached for the basket. Stefan sat beside her and peeked as she removed the cloth covering the food.

"Mmm, whatever you brought smells delicious." He leaned close and lifted the corner of a napkin covering the ham.

She slapped at his hand. "No snitching. You'll wait until I have the plates ready." Her hand trembled as she removed the plates and silverware.

He laughed and sat back. "All right, m'lady. You're in charge of the food."

Silence ensued while she arranged pieces of ham and thick slices of homemade bread on the plates. Mama had included some of her homemade pickles and a jar of her canned peaches. When it was all arranged, she set a plate in front of Stefan and herself.

"I will say the blessing for us." Stefan grasped her hand and bowed his head. "Dear Lord, thank You for this beautiful day, delicious food, and delightful company. Bless the food to serve our bodies and us to serve You. Amen."

At the last word, she jerked her hand away. The heat from his hand raced through her nerves to her heart, searing it with what she didn't want to feel. The next seven days were going to be the most difficult of her life.

If Stefan noticed her quick withdrawal, he didn't say anything. Instead he opened the jar of lemonade and poured two glasses. "Is that cinnamon I smell?"

Grateful for the distraction, Molly removed the napkin-wrapped bundle from the basket. "Yes. Mama made cinnamon sugar cookies this morning. They were still warm when we wrapped them."

All she wanted to do now was to get this picnic over with and head back to town. There she could at least gain some control over the emotions that threatened to undo all her resolve about Stefan. She was not going to fall in love with him no matter what happened in the next few days.

CHAPTER 14

A FTER HER EXPERIENCE on Saturday Molly avoided being alone with Stefan for the next several days, but with meals and family gatherings that was next to impossible. Being near him was simply too dangerous for her resolve. Their goals in life were much too different to make a relationship work. Even though prospects in Stoney Creek itself looked dismal, she had to keep her heart away from someone like Stefan.

On Sunday Hannah and her family had stayed in town to have dinner at the Whitemans'. Although Molly had chosen to sit with Grace between her and Stefan, she found his gaze on her whenever she glanced his way. After the meal, Andrew had to take care of any emergencies in the clinic, so that meant he and Clarissa could not be alone, but then Stefan made no effort to be with Molly either and that created anxiety about whether he had reservations about her as well.

At least they had talked to each other, even if it had been in a conversation with other members of the family both Sunday and at supper last evening. Why did she avoid him so when she really desired his company? Well, if she had the answer to that, all her problems would be solved.

Today she planned to do a little shopping with Clarissa, who had managed to spend more time with Andrew on Monday when they went out to the ranch with her father and Stefan. Clarissa had enjoyed riding with Andrew so much that she had asked her father to buy a horse for her as well, and Stefan worked with Micah to ready a horse for travel back to Arizona.

Everything appeared to be fine yesterday when the group left even though she sensed an undercurrent of uneasiness as she stood on the porch and waved good-bye. Stefan had politely asked her to join them, but she begged off with the excuse that she wanted to stay behind and help Mama with the extra laundry and the party coming up on Friday night.

With Stefan and his father back at the ranch to make payment and arrange for getting the horses to Louisiana and to Arizona, folding clothes from yesterday's wash gave Molly the opportunity to consider what she would do about Stefan at the dance. She'd already consented to let him escort her, and backing out was not an option. But how could she spend an evening that close to him and keep her emotions in check?

Alice pulled up a chair beside Molly. "Why do you look so sad? You get to go to a party Friday night, but Juliet and I have to go stay with Lettie again." She sighed and hugged her doll. "I'll be glad when I'm grown up and old enough to go to the parties and dances."

Molly reached over and cupped her hand on Alice's head. Her green eyes, so like Mama's, peered back at her. "Honey, I'm not really sad, just thinking about all I have to do. You have plenty of time to play and enjoy what you're doing now. Going to parties and dances will come soon enough, and I bet you'll have all the boys standing in line waiting to dance with you."

Alice frowned and bit her lip. "You really think so?" She pulled at one of her carrot-colored braids. "If my hair was a pretty red like yours or Mama's, it wouldn't be so bad. Mine's more orange, and I hate it."

"Oh, dear sister, your hair is perfect, and one day you'll be glad it's the color it is." Molly reached over and hugged her sister. "Please don't grow up too soon. I like having two little sisters who still play with dolls and have tea parties."

"Humph, that's all I ever get to do." Her shoulders sagged and her chin dropped to her chest.

Molly remembered those days of wanting to do things the older girls did, but now she almost longed for the time when she didn't have to worry about boys and relationships.

Clara pushed open the kitchen door and whirled into the room. "You'll never guess what happened."

"No, probably not, so why don't you quit spinning in circles and tell us."

"Ted Gladstone asked if he could escort me to the party Friday night." She sighed and clasped her hands to her chest. "I think he's one of the most handsome young men in town."

Molly had to agree with that. The mayor's son was a little less than a year older than Clara and had completed his first year in college. "That's wonderful. I know you've liked him for a while so I'm glad he's taken notice of you."

"Will you and Clarissa fix my hair and make it as pretty as yours for Friday night?"

Clarissa appeared in the doorway, a twinkle lighting her eyes. "What's this about doing your hair for Friday night?"

The glow in Clarissa's face caused a lump to rise in Molly's throat. Her friend was in love, and envy filled Molly's heart. She swallowed hard to dispel the lump and envy before she could speak.

Clara hugged Clarissa. "Teddy Gladstone asked to be

my escort for the party on Friday. I asked if you and Molly would do my hair for me."

"I'd be delighted." She fingered Clara's sandy curls. "We'll find a style that will make you even prettier than you are."

"I wish my name was as pretty as yours. Clarissa is so much better than plain old Clara, and my hair is so drab."

Alice planted her hands on her hips and scowled. "Well, at least it's not orange like mine."

Clarissa laughed. "You girls have lovely hair, and it will be fun to do yours, Clara, and that's a fine name by the way." She glanced around the kitchen. "I actually came down looking for Mother. Have you seen her, Molly?"

"Yes, she and Mama took Juliet and went to the bakery, and then they were going by town hall. I suppose they're checking things for Friday night."

"Well, then, if you're finished here, can we go to town?"

"Yes, I just need to freshen up a bit. Clara, will you stay with Alice until Mama returns? Danny is with the men out at the ranch, so there would be just the two of you here."

Clara looked like she wanted to say no, but she sighed and grabbed Alice's hand. "C'mon punkin'. Let's go see what we can find to do."

Molly hated to leave Clara out of the shopping trip, but someone needed to stay with Alice. She'd be sure to make it up to her sister next week. Molly had had her share of foregoing activities to take care of her younger siblings, so she understood Clara's sigh and resignation that she had no choice.

Twenty minutes later she and Clarissa walked toward town, their parasols shielding them from the sun's rays.

June in central Texas meant temperatures well into the ninety-degree range, and sun like that could ruin a girl's complexion mighty fast.

Clarissa linked arms with Molly. "I'm glad we're doing this alone. I have some things I want to talk with you about, and your house has so many ears."

That was true, and the walls weren't all that solid. Privacy was a rare commodity with a family as large as hers. "What do want to talk with me about, as if I didn't know? It's about Andrew, isn't it?"

Clarissa only nodded as they stepped up to the boardwalk at the edge of the business area of town. "I like your town. Stoney Creek people have been so friendly toward our family, and I'm looking forward to the dance on Friday night. Your mother told me that almost everyone invited will be there."

"Yes, they will, and you'll have a grand time." Whatever Clarissa wanted to say about Andrew would come about eventually. All this small talk about Stoney Creek acted as a bridge to what was really on Clarissa's mind. Molly would be patient and let her friend decide when she wanted to share.

They stopped in front of the dress shop and eyed the display in the window. Several hats in the latest style sat atop cushion-topped posts for all to see. A mannequin stood in one corner wearing a dress of the prettiest yellow silk she'd ever seen. She'd love to have it, but her budget wouldn't allow it, and she didn't want to ask Mama for such an extravagance. She turned to say something to Clarissa, but the tears glistening in her eyes stopped Molly cold. "What in the world is the matter? Has something happened between you and Andrew?

Once again Clarissa only nodded. She blinked her eyes before speaking. "Let's go over to the bakery and have tea and cake. I saw our mothers leaving, so we won't run into them."

"All right." Molly followed Clarissa across to the bakery shop. All types of scenarios paraded across Molly's mind. Whatever had happened was enough to make her friend cry, and that didn't bode well for anybody.

Faith stood behind the counter and filled their order for pound cake and herb tea. She grinned and came around to place the plates of cake and cups of tea on their table. "I can see why my brother is so smitten with you. I don't think I've ever seen anyone with eyes the color of yours. They're beautiful."

Pink filled Clarissa's cheeks. "Thank you, Faith." She wrapped her hands around the teacup and Faith headed back to the counter to help another customer.

Molly reached across and grabbed Clarissa's hands. "Now, please tell me what has you so troubled."

With a glance over her shoulder to make sure Faith was not in hearing range, she said, "It's Mother and Father, and even Stefan. They're all against my having any relationship with Andrew."

Molly had suspected as much, and her heart ached to see Clarissa in tears because of her family's attitude. "I see, and just what are your feelings for Andrew?"

"Oh, Molly, I love him. He's been so wonderful. I know we only just met, but I can't stand the thought of never seeing him again. He...he asked if he could write to me after we return home and I said yes, but I'm afraid Mother and Father will frown upon that and forbid it."

Molly had heard of love coming quickly, but she wasn't

prepared to hear this from Clarissa. Why, Andrew and Clarissa barely knew each other.

"I don't know what to say, Clarissa. From what I've observed, Andrew loves you as well. I'm sure your parents will let him at least write to you."

"But we want more than that. I'd be willing to stay here in Stoney Creek if he asked me to marry him, but after what Father said last night, he wouldn't let me."

"What did he say?"

"He said he could never let me leave home and live in a place like Stoney Creek. He said..." She blushed and looked down. "He said that we have far too much social standing in St. Francisville and Baton Rouge for me to give it up to be a small-town doctor's wife."

"What do you feel?" Molly asked.

"I like Stoney Creek well enough, and I think it would be interesting to be a doctor's wife."

"You say that now, Clarissa, but think about all the friends and activities you'd leave behind. Marriage isn't something you enter into lightly. It's for a lifetime."

"I know that, and that's what I want with Andrew, a lifetime of love and having a family together. But I love my parents, and I can't dishonor them by leaving them alone in Louisiana. What am I to do?"

"I don't know, Clarissa. Has Andrew declared himself?"

Clarissa sighed. "No. And I don't know if he would if he knew how much against this match my parents are. Isn't that unfair?" She gripped Molly's hand. "What about you and my brother? Surely your parents wouldn't be against the match, and I know my parents adore you and your family. As do I!"

Molly smiled faintly. "I do like Stefan very much, but

Clarissa, I just don't know if I like him enough to give up my home and everything I know. Being a military wife would be so different—and difficult."

Clarissa sobered. "I can't blame you. It looks like a hard life. And if I marry Andrew and live in Stoney Creek, I would want you to stay here anyway!"

Molly smiled and reached for her tea, but her mind was elsewhere. If Clarissa could give up her family and the only life she had ever known for the sake of love, shouldn't Molly be able to do the same? At least Molly's parents weren't likely to stand in the way of a relationship with Stefan, so why was she so hesitant? She cared about Stefan a great deal, but the life of a military wife held no appeal to her. And for that reason she needed to make sure her feelings for Stefan didn't grow any deeper, or like Clarissa she'd be in a terrible dilemma, but for different reasons.

After securing a bill of sale and method of transport for the horses, Stefan rode beside his father with Danny back to town. As much as he'd like to talk with his father about Clarissa and Andrew, he didn't want Danny to hear the conversation. Danny chatted with Father and pointed out his favorite trails and places for hunting.

The boy's enthusiasm reminded him of Molly, and that presented a question as big as the one about Andrew and Clarissa. He'd seen through the tactics to avoid him since Saturday afternoon. The impossibility of their situation loomed even greater than his sister's with Andrew.

How could he be satisfied with being only friends when her very presence ignited a fire in his belly that he couldn't ignore? If she'd allow him to write to her after he returned to his regiment, perhaps he could help her to see that being in the military didn't always mean fighting and killing, and that whenever that happened, it was to protect innocent people.

She loved her work as a teacher, and she loved her town. Those were obstacles that rivaled her distaste for war and meant he'd have to come up with a plan to entice her away from here. That would take all the genius planning he could muster in the weeks and months ahead.

Danny's high-pitched voice on the verge of changing to a much deeper one broke into Stefan's thoughts. "Mr. Stefan, when are you going back to the army?"

"After I get back to Louisiana I'll see the doctor and he'll tell me. I think it'll be very soon." The Whiteman boys certainly didn't share their sister's point of view about the army. Both Danny and Tom had questioned him at length about what army life was like. If not for the promise to his parents to finish his schooling, Tom most likely would have joined the military.

"Do ya every get lonely and wanna be back home with your ma and pa?" Danny's brown eyes held sincere interest in whatever Stefan had to say.

"Yes, son, I do. But then we get busy and I get a few letters from home and it's all okay."

"I think I'd miss my ma and pa somethin' fierce." With that he rode on ahead a few yards.

To be honest, the post in the desert did get lonely. Sure there were lots of other soldiers around, but they were from all over the country. He could have stayed with the Louisiana 4th Regiment where his father had served, but the lure of the cavalry was stronger. He'd made his choice and ended up out in Arizona.

Asking Molly to leave Stoney Creek, her family, and her beloved students for the desolate Arizona desert was more than unfair, and he couldn't do it to her, no matter how much he loved her. He blinked and gulped at that idea. He did love her, and now there was no denying it. He'd need all the strength the Lord could give him to get through the remaining days of their visit.

CHAPTER 15

OLLY'S HEART HUNG heavy in her chest. Tomorrow Stefan would be leaving, and she most likely wouldn't see him again for a very long time. Clarissa's mood over Andrew didn't help to make things any better either. At least they had the party tonight, but even that dimmed in light of reality.

Clara ambled into the room in her pink wrapper, ready for Clarissa to do the magic on her hairstyle for the night. Molly squared her shoulders and breathed deeply. In no way would she ruin her sister's happiness with an evening in the company of Teddy Gladstone. And Tom would again escort Faith Delmont, so at least her siblings would enjoy the evening. Only she and Clarissa would face the evening with bittersweet feelings.

Clarissa smiled and waved her hair brush. "Let's get on with making you the most beautiful young lady at the party tonight."

Molly pasted a smile on her lips to match that of Clarissa. "She'll work her magic on you just like she did for me last week. Which dress did you choose to wear?" Molly could guess, but small talk about clothes might help to get her mind off Stefan's being her escort tonight.

"The lavender one. Mama says it makes my hair look lighter and shinier. I hope she's right, but I love the dress anyway."

"So do I. It makes your complexion absolutely creamy." Clara had worn the dress once before to a tea at Mrs.

Gladstone's home and, from what Mama had said, received many compliments on it.

While Clarissa worked on Clara's hair, Molly removed her own yellow-gold dress from the wardrobe. This one didn't have a bustle, but several layers of fabric attached with a large bow to the waist in the back. She tied her petticoats about her waist then sat on the edge of the bed and pulled white silk stockings up over her legs.

Alice and Juliet raced into the room and plopped on the bed. Alice tilted her head and peered at Clara. "Oh, my, Clara, you are beautiful."

Clara's cheeks turned pink, but she smiled at her reflection in the mirror. "Thank you, sweet Alice." She turned and hugged Clarissa. "I can't believe you did this. I love it." Clarissa had woven lavender ribbons through her hair, then pinned it into a glorious mound on top of Clara's head. Tendrils of hair kissed the nape of Clara's neck and danced against her cheeks.

"It does look nice even if I say so myself." Clarissa swished her hands. "Now shoo, and go get that dress on. Alice, Juliet, why don't you go help her?"

Alice bounded off the bed. "Oh, can we, Clara? Can we?"

At Clara's nod the two little girls scampered from the room, their giggles filling the air. Clara shrugged then grinned and followed them.

Clarissa sank onto the dressing stool, the hair brush still in her hand. "I wish I felt as happy as they sound."

"I know. I do too. I've been so foolish to avoid being alone with Stefan this past week, but I just don't trust my heart right now." The thought of his leaving tomorrow brought chills to her blood and regret to her heart. How could she feel this way about someone like Stefan? A soldier of all things.

Clarissa sighed in sympathy. "Andrew did ask Father about writing to me, and I couldn't believe he agreed. I shall look forward to and cherish every letter I receive from him. Mother warned him that his letters must be friendly without any other nuances, whatever that means."

It meant declarations of love or any other such sentiment, but no sense in telling Clarissa now and spoiling everything. Her mother would most likely read those letters, so she could tell if Andrew was getting too amorous. Molly breathed a prayer of thanks that her own mother wouldn't pry like that. But would Stefan even want to write to her after the way she'd all but snubbed him the past week?

While Clarissa finished her preparations, Molly strolled over to the window in her stocking-covered feet and stared at the street below. A number of Stoney Creek citizens wandered about either at a leisurely stroll or at a determined pace to reach some destination. A figure below caught her attention. Tom raced down the sidewalk and to the buggy Papa had arranged for tonight.

Oh, dear. If Tom was headed to pick up Faith, then Stefan and Andrew would be on the doorstep very soon. She whirled around and searched for her slippers. They didn't have time to spare. "Hurry, Clarissa. Stefan and Andrew will be here any minute. I just saw Tom leave to go get Faith."

Clarissa stood and moved to the bed and the velvet jewelry case there. "I'm all ready, but I need your help to fasten my necklace."

After securing the pearls at Clarissa's neck, Molly

checked her appearance. She reached up and positioned the tendrils falling in front of her ears. Everything had to be perfect tonight.

A few minutes later Mama opened the door to announce the young men had arrived. Molly gasped at her mother's beauty. Ordinarily her hair was twisted into a bun on the crown of her head, but tonight red gold curls trailed down from a coiled mass at the crown. Two green jeweled pins matched the emerald green of her dress, and Mama's eyes glowed with joy. Molly stood speechless, admiring her mother.

Mama tapped her ivory fan on her fingertips. "Come, girls, no time for any more primping. You don't want to keep them waiting." Her taffeta skirts swished and crackled when she turned and headed back downstairs.

Molly blinked her eyes and shook her head to clear it. Papa would be the envy of every man at the party tonight. Then one glance at Clarissa reminded her that Andrew would be the same with her on his arm. Well, Stefan would just have to be stuck with plain Molly.

She and Clarissa hooked arms and headed to meet their escorts for the evening. At the bottom step, Stefan stood gazing up at Molly with such intentness her breath caught and tightened her throat. The sight of him again in full military dress, his sandy hair perfect, and eyes the color of sapphires, made her resolve melt like ice in the June heat.

He reached for her hand to assist her on the last step. "You are beautiful this evening. Heads will turn with you on my arm."

Her heart skipped a beat then pounded. Almost the exact words she'd used for Clarissa and Mama. She'd never measure up to them, but as long as Stefan looked at her like that, she'd be happy.

Everyone began talking at once and gathering up shawls and hats before strolling out to the carriages waiting on the street. Stefan assisted Molly up into the backseat of the surrey Andrew borrowed from his father for the evening. The ride would only be six blocks but the men had insisted they didn't want the ladies to walk that far in their finery, and that suited Molly fine.

The silence between her and Stefan became awkward, but she could think of nothing to say. Her tongue may as well have been cut out for all the good it did her at the moment. Being near him and feeling the warmth of his body next to hers threatened to unnerve her. Emotions she'd buried for almost a week pushed through to send heat racing through her veins. Tomorrow he'd be on a train back to Louisiana and then on to his regiment. This may well be the last time they'd be together for many years, and she'd do well to remember exactly where he'd be spending those years.

Stefan helped Molly down from the surrey. All during the ride, he'd kept silent for fear of saying the wrong thing. He wanted this last evening to be perfect, and the wrong words could ruin it. He'd never seen her as beautiful as tonight in the yellow gold that served to intensify the gold in her hair. Being around his mother and sister had given him an eye for fashion, and Molly's dress tonight didn't fit into any style he'd seen them wear, but it was perfect for Molly, and that's all that mattered.

He tucked her hand under his arm and escorted her up the steps and into the town hall that had been transformed into a gardenland of beauty on this June evening. Where could they have possibly found so many flowers in this town? They were everywhere the eye could see and all in a rainbow of colors.

"Your mother did a wonderful job with the decorations."

"Thank you. I think she and the ladies at the church must have stripped every garden in town for this many flowers. One thing I do know though, Mrs. Delmont and her cooks did the baking and cooking, so it's going to be delicious."

"If it's anything like the reception at the theater last week, I look forward to it." He led her to a table set up against the walls where guests would sit and eat around the perimeter of the floor cleared for dancing later.

Molly sat and arranged her skirt to minimize wrinkles. "I remember coming here for a party for my aunt Hannah when she first arrived in Stoney Creek. I was almost twelve, and Uncle Micah danced with me. I thought he was the most handsome man in town, and so nice to dance with a little girl when he could have his pick of the ladies."

Stefan sat next to her, content to listen to her voice all evening, but then of course he'd enjoy having her in his arms for a dance as well.

His situation with Molly had given him more empathy toward Andrew and his feelings for Clarissa. He didn't want Andrew to bring his sister to Stoney Creek so far from her family, but his desires would do the same thing with Molly. He'd be taking her away from her home and the family she loved to live on an army post away from most civilization. True, many of the forts had towns springing up around them, but not the one where he served in Arizona. If the territory ever became a state, it wouldn't be a densely populated one.

More guests arrived and filled the tables. Their greetings and further chatter rang in the air, adding to the festive atmosphere. A raised platform served as a stage for the three men who would perform the music for the night.

By the time Dr. Whiteman proclaimed the food line to be open, it seemed as though everyone in town had stopped by to say their good-byes and wish the family well on its trip back to Louisiana. A few even wished him well and thanked him for his service to his country. He never tired of hearing those words. They served as fuel when he faced tough situations.

When the music finally started, Stefan whisked Molly to the center and held her a little closer than the dance actually called for, but he'd waited this long to have his arms around her and he didn't intend to waste a minute.

Molly grinned up at him. "I'd say you were anxious to get on the floor."

"It's my first chance to have you to myself for a few minutes. We've been surrounded by people all week. I had begun to think you were avoiding me."

Her eyes opened wide, and her back stiffened, but that gave him the answer. Had the idea of his being in the military been so repulsive that she could no longer bear to be near him? The idea chilled his heart. If that were true, then all hopes of courting her and hoping she'd change her ideas were lost.

"I've...I've been...um...busy with helping Mama with the party and taking care of the younger children."

He stared into eyes that lacked the excitement and joy

of the days before. He wanted to see that joy and sparkle again before he left, but how to manage that escaped him now.

She pulled her gaze from his and glanced around the room. "Everything looks so nice. Your mother was such a great help to Mama. And it looks like everyone is enjoying the effort."

Everyone but the girl in his arms who caused his heart to do all sorts of crazy tricks and sent his thoughts sailing to places they had no business being.

As soon as the music ended, he grabbed her hand. "We need to talk, Miss Molly Whiteman." He headed for the door and forced her to follow him by holding tight to her hand.

"Stefan Elliot, let me go this minute. You don't have to drag me, I'll come with you."

Something in her voice stopped him cold. People all around the room stared at them. He'd embarrassed her in front of her friends. He dropped her hand. "I'm sorry, I didn't mean to hurt you, but we do need to talk, please."

She rubbed her hand that had turned red from the pressure he'd put on it. Remorse filled him and he wished he could take back every second of the past few minutes. When he stepped through the doors to the boardwalk beyond, she followed like she said she would.

Once they were at the corner of the building and away from the crowd, Stefan grasped both of her hands and held them to his chest. Words jammed in his throat as he searched her face for some indication of her feelings for him. Finally, he took a deep breath then exhaled. "Molly, this has been a difficult week. Every time I tried to get close to you, you'd find some excuse to move away. There's so much I've wanted to say, but now we have so little time left for me to say all the things I wanted to."

He strained to hear her answer, barely above a whisper.

"I'm sorry, Stefan. My head has been in turmoil all week with all the things going on. I do care about you, but you know how I feel about the military."

"Yes, I do, but I hoped that somehow you might be able to change your mind about that and see the reality of the world. As long as there are men who want what others have, there will be some kind of war. Whether it's one nation against another one or a man robbing a bank, guns will be used and people may get killed. We don't live in a perfect world."

She looked down. "I know that, but I don't have to like it."

"No, you don't, but you do have to accept it." If only she could understand good men, Christian men didn't want to kill others, but sometimes had to do so to save other lives.

"This is so hard. Mama waited for Papa for so many months not knowing if he was dead or alive. I don't think I can do that, and I don't think I could live at the fort knowing that every time you go out, you might not return."

"Molly, all those wars and battles are about over. It's much safer there now that the Indians are contained." That much was true, but out where he was, danger still lurked in the badlands where lawless men tried to take what didn't belong to them all the time.

"I know, but it's still the army and dangerous."

He lifted her chin with his fingers so that their gazes locked. "Molly, I love you and want to spend the rest of my life with you, but I can't ask that of you until you can accept what I do. You are the most precious thing in the world to me, and I'd do anything, anywhere to protect you." He bent his head and touched her lips with his. When she responded by pressing into him, he deepened the kiss.

A fire began in his belly that surged and roared its way through his body. He held her tighter and let the heat wash over him. He wanted her now and forever.

She pushed hard on his shoulders and stepped back. "Oh, Stefan, this can't be. It hurts too much." Moisture glistened on her eyelashes in the bright light spilling through the windows. Her fingers brushed her lips before she turned and fled back to the noise and gaiety inside.

He slumped against the building, his nerves still flaming, and his heart pounding. He should never have kissed her, but it only proved how much he loved her. He had less than fifteen hours remaining, and he saw no hope of her returning his love before he boarded that train back to the life he loved, but she hated.

CHAPTER 16

MOLLY WRESTLED DURING the night with her feelings for Stefan and her hatred for wars and killing. He wanted her to face reality. Reality for her was the fact that he could easily be killed fighting outlaws, Indians, or whatever else might be facing the cavalry of the west.

She stayed as still as possible so as not to awaken Clarissa. The first quarter moon barely shed light into the room, but it was enough for Molly to see her way to the window. There she sat with her head resting on her hands, staring at the night sky. All the stars in the heavens that usually gave her peace as she gazed at God's creation now twinkled as though to mock her sadness.

Her fingers touched her lips, and once again Stefan's kiss burned there. She had wanted it to never end, and a deep emotion she never knew could exist had pulled her toward him. Oh, how it had hurt to break away, but she couldn't accept his love. He wanted an entirely different life than she did, and that only served to prove she didn't love him enough if she couldn't change her desires to mesh with his.

Tears slid down her cheeks. Tomorrow she'd say goodbye, and she may never see him again. Why did life have to be so hard?

A hand grasped her shoulder. "I can't sleep either, Molly. I can't bear the thought of leaving Andrew tomorrow. Are you feeling the same about Stefan?"

Molly blinked her eyes to repress the tears. "Yes, but I

don't want either of you to leave tomorrow. I'm so sorry your parents feel the way they do about Andrew. He's a fine man and a dedicated doctor. I can see how he loves you." Stefan had gazed at her the same way last night, and she had no doubts about his love, only her own.

"And I feel the same for him. If only Mother and Father would understand that I'm no longer a child. A young woman of twenty is able to make up her own mind in matters of the heart."

Clarissa spoke true, so why should it be so difficult for Molly to do the same? She was two years older but her heart wavered with so much uncertainty she may as well be a child, like Alice.

"As long as you and Andrew can correspond, perhaps you can make up a secret code that will make your true feelings known when you write. That way, if your mother happens to read them, she won't think he's going against your father's wishes."

Clarissa gasped. "Molly, how can you suggest such a thing?"

"I'm sorry. You're right. You must honor your parents and abide by their wishes for you." Molly bit her lip. Why couldn't she keep her mouth shut?

Then Clarissa giggled. "I love the idea." She jumped up from the floor. "I'm going to write a list of code words right now and give them to Andrew tomorrow. This will be such fun."

Molly groaned and laid her forehead against the windowsill. What had she started? What if Mr. and Mrs. Elliot discovered the code and then forbade them to even write each other? She glanced over to where Clarissa had lit the lamp and begun making her list. Such joy shone in her face that Molly didn't have the heart to remind Clarissa of what could happen if she and Andrew were discovered.

Even though Molly's heart broke because she couldn't be the wife Stefan deserved, she prayed he would write to her. No matter what else, she did want to know what happened in his life.

She sighed with a heavy release of breath and headed back to bed. Tomorrow would come too soon, and being tired and looking peaked was not the way she wanted Stefan to remember her. She turned to face the wall and closed her eyes to shut out the light.

Stefan awakened after a night of restless sleep. The sun's rays spread light throughout his hotel room. He groaned and turned over. Not only did he not want to get up, but he did not want to say good-bye to Molly. Several times during the night he awakened with the memory of her kiss still on his lips. He should never have let that happen.

His body warmed with the memory of her next to his heart last night. The emotion had gone as deeply for her as it had for him when she had leaned toward him.

With another groan and grunt, he pushed back the covers and swung his feet to the floor. He may as well dress then eat breakfast here at the hotel instead of down at the Whiteman house like he usually did. Seeing Molly at the train station would be hard enough, let alone sitting across from her at the table this morning.

After shaving and dressing in his uniform, he swung his satchel up onto the bed and began packing. His mind tumbled with images of Molly at various times during the past two weeks. Her voice with its charming accent and her musical laughter rang in his ears. She had captured his heart and he'd remain a prisoner, praying that somehow God would change her mind about his being a soldier.

He picked up his cane then slammed it on the bed. It hadn't even been used the past three days, but it represented the excuse for this trip. If not for that stick of wood, he wouldn't have been here in Stoney Creek in the first place. He'd be with his regiment in training and preparing for whatever duty called. He would never have seen Molly again, and never have fallen in love.

He had come and he had fallen in love, but it shouldn't have to hurt so much. His cane clattered to the floor. Too bad it hadn't shattered like his heart.

The satchel yawned open, reminding him of what he had to do. Packing must be finished before he went down for breakfast and checked out of the hotel. If on time, the train would roll into the station in a little over two hours. His teeth clenched as he stuffed the remainder of his belongings into the satchel then closed it with more force than necessary, almost breaking a clasp. Suddenly he didn't want to waste one minute of the remaining time with Molly. Forget the hotel, he'd rather sit across the table with her for even a little while this morning.

After checking out and taking care of his bill, Stefan carried his satchel and strode toward the Whiteman house. Even if he was late for breakfast, he'd be there in the same house with Molly.

When he reached the gate, he paused and read the sign bearing both Dr. Whiteman and Dr. Delmont's names. Stefan's fingers curled to make fists of his hands, and he winced with the sudden realization that Andrew must be experiencing the same pangs with having to say good-bye to Clarissa as Stefan was with Molly.

The satchel handle cut into Stefan's tight fist, but he didn't loosen his grip. He deserved the pain after the way he'd convinced his father that Andrew was not a good choice for Clarissa. He couldn't deny the love he'd seen in both their eyes when they didn't think anyone would notice.

The truth of the matter hit Stefan like a blow to the stomach. Andrew and Clarissa would be perfect for each other because she was so much like their mother and Mrs. Whiteman. They cared about people. For that reason, Clarissa would be an excellent doctor's wife.

He'd make amends and let Andrew know he had Stefan's support. With that settled he headed up the steps where the aroma of bacon and fresh cinnamon rolls greeted him, and sent his stomach to rumbling in anticipation.

Clarissa and his parents sat with the Whiteman family around the table. "Good morning. I hope I'm not too late to enjoy that wonderful breakfast I smelled on my way in."

Danny grinned from ear to ear and patted the empty seat beside him. "This is your place. I get to sit next to you this morning. We've had the blessing, so we can go ahead and eat."

Stefan would much rather be next to Molly, but with her straight across the table, he'd be able to observe more easily, so perhaps this was better after all. "I'm honored, Danny, and happy to sit with you." He glanced to his other side where Juliet grinned up at him, exposing the gap left by two missing teeth. "And you too, Miss Juliet. You look very pretty this morning."

He swallowed a chuckle as a pink blush spread over her

face and she returned her gaze to the plate of eggs and bacon before her. Stefan kissed his mother's cheek then sat down and glanced across at Molly and Clarissa. Red, puffy eyes gave evidence their night had been as restless as his had been. They barely glanced his way when he greeted them.

So much for having a conversation with Molly or even having eye contact. If she'd look at him, he could tell then whether the kiss last night had meant to her what it had to him.

His mother sipped her coffee and eyed him over the rim of her cup. She set it down and said, "I trust you brought your satchel all packed and ready to board the train."

"Yes, Mother. I left it on the front porch to take to the station later." He should have taken it to the station when he left the hotel, but he had been so anxious to see Molly that he'd forgotten.

Father placed a cinnamon roll on his plate. "I see you're without your cane again this morning, and I don't detect a limp. I'm assuming that means you're ready for duty once again."

"Yes, sir, I am. All the pain is gone, and I feel very good." From the corner of his eye he noticed the frown on Molly's face. Even a mention of where he was headed appeared to bother her.

"Very well, I'll send a wire to your commanding officer to let him know you'll be on your way the beginning of next week. You'll need to check the train schedule and make arrangements for the trip."

Stefan only nodded. He'd grown tired of protesting his father's taking charge as though Stefan had the sense of a child. He couldn't blame Clarissa for complaining about the decisions made for her.

As Stefan placed the last bite of eggs into his mouth, his gaze caught Molly's staring at him. This time she didn't jerk away, but allowed her gaze to lock with his. What he saw dismayed him even more than her words last evening. Emotion filled her eyes, but the set of her mouth said it would be controlled and out of his reach.

Why couldn't Molly understand the reality of life? Not since the fall of Adam and Eve in the garden had there been true peace in the world. Sin had entered the hearts of man through that first couple, and now good men would die if they couldn't or wouldn't defend themselves. The Quakers had shunned the war between North and South, but he believed even they would defend their own if necessary.

Molly pushed from the table and tossed her napkin to the table before turning and running away with Clarissa fast on her heels. Mrs. Whiteman bit her lip and shook her head.

"I'm not sure what has taken hold of my oldest daughter. I apologize for her rude behavior."

Mr. Whiteman reached for her hand. "Now, my love, it's only natural that she be upset with our guests leaving today. She and Clarissa don't want their visit to end."

"That may be true, but it's not an excuse for rude behavior." She peered across at Stefan. "Is there a problem between the two of you?"

Stefan swallowed hard and paused to get the words he needed to speak as much truth as he dared. "She would prefer that I not return to my regiment at Fort Apache."

"I see, and I'm sorry, but I do understand why."

"But the cavalry is your life, Stefan. I'm so disappointed." His mother clutched her napkin in her hand then reached over to grasp Father's arm. "Our son was born for the military."

"Yes, he was. West Point graduates have a duty and honor to serve their country just as Manfred and I and so many others did." He turned and beamed at Stefan. "Our son will do us proud in the United States Cavalry."

Leave it to his parents to remind him of his obligation to the family. After what happened to Mother during the war, he couldn't understand why she too was so adamant about his serving.

One thing for certain, it may be his role in life, but he had no right to force that life on Molly. He loved her too much to see her living with him and hating what he did. Until he or the Lord changed her mind, he'd have to learn to live without Molly Whiteman.

CHAPTER 17

ANDREW COMPLETED THE notes on his last patient and checked his pocket watch. Almost time for the train. Clarissa had sent a note asking him to meet her a few minutes early because she had something for him. His heart ached with the thought of her leaving, but her father had made it clear he wanted no courting of his daughter.

A door closed and footsteps headed his way. He shoved the chart notes into his desk drawer then hurried to meet Dr. Whiteman. The doctor turned the sign on the door over and posted additional information about their whereabouts and time of return.

He dusted his hands together and grinned at Andrew. "There, that should take care of anyone seeking our aid in the next half hour. Come, let's go see our guests off on their journey."

Andrew followed him to the foyer of the main house where everyone gathered. He noted Stefan standing off to the side alone. Molly must not have come down yet, but Clarissa rushed to Andrew's side and pulled at his arm.

"Come over here where I can speak with you in private." She led him to a corner of the parlor and stopped. "I have something I've worked out so that we can say what we really want to say without Mother or Father being suspicious."

She handed him a folded piece of paper. He opened it to find two columns of words. One heading indicated words to use and the other the true meaning of the word. Andrew furrowed his brow. "What is this?"

"It's our code." She leaned over and pointed to the first column. "See, these are the words we can use in our letters and the other column is what the first ones stand for."

He read through the list. "I still don't understand exactly."

"Well, if you talk about the things we did while I was here and the fun we had, you're telling me how much you miss me and wish we could be together. When you tell me about what you're doing, it means you love me and want me to be here with you. Talking about your family is the same as talking about our future."

It looked complicated, but the sparkle in her eyes and the enthusiasm with which she spoke led him to smile and agree to the plan. He'd figure it out later. Right now he had no desire to let anything interfere with these last minutes together.

"That's a grand idea, Clarissa, and I'll study it in full later today." He stuffed the paper into his pocket then grasped her hand and tucked it under his arm. "Come on, your mother is looking this way, and her frown doesn't look good for either of us."

When they approached her parents, Mrs. Elliot's scowl remained, but she joined her husband with the doctor and his wife to head out to the carriages. Molly had finally made an appearance, but without the smile and greeting she usually gave everyone. Stefan stepped toward her, and they engaged in a conversation inaudible to others.

Andrew led Clarissa to the carriage they were to use for the trip to the station and helped load her baggage. When it was secured to the colonel's satisfaction, Andrew assisted Clarissa up onto the front seat then climbed up beside her.

"I don't know why your father is allowing me to drive you to the station, but I'm thankful for it. Every moment I have with you until the train leaves is precious." He placed his right hand on the seat between them and Clarissa grabbed it.

She squeezed his fingers. "So am I, and the minutes are precious to me, too." She leaned forward. "Here come Molly and Stefan, and neither one of them looks very happy. I feel so bad about what is happening between them."

Andrew understood all too well how much Stefan loved Molly and hated to leave. From his conversations with Stefan, love and courtship for him and Molly would not be possible until Molly accepted his career in the military. Andrew regarded the misery in Molly's face and made a commitment to take up the challenge of convincing her of the necessity of what Stefan was doing. That's the least he could do.

Doubt and uncertainty tore Molly's heart in half. Everything she firmly believed had been tested these past two weeks, and she was no closer to the truth now than she was then. Stefan had created turmoil like none she'd ever experienced.

Her body ached not only from lack of sleep, but from the pain of separation. If only she and Stefan had more time to hash out their differences, perhaps a compromise or understanding could be reached. Her stubborn will had prevailed in the past, but now it did nothing but obstruct her future.

Stefan grasped her arm to assist her onto the carriage seat, and fire raced through her arm straight to her heart. When he released her to climb up beside her, she blinked her eyes to ward off any tears. This was not the time for weeping, although every bit of her wanted to cry out for him to stay with her in Stoney Creek.

He leaned toward her. "Molly, will you allow me to write to you in the coming weeks? I want you to know what I'm doing."

For a moment she couldn't respond. Did she really want to know what he was doing at the fort? Of course she did. She wanted to know everything about him. She nodded her head. "I...I would like that."

The grin that spread across his face tore at her soul. His letters would only emphasize the agony of not being with him. Forgetting him and getting on with her life would be the much better choice, but she couldn't do it.

In front of her, Andrew and Clarissa spoke in quiet tones, the love they shared so evident in their eyes and gestures. In one way she envied them because they could express their love, and if the code Clarissa made up worked out, the two of them would continue in their love.

Stefan leaned forward and grasped Andrew's shoulder. "Before we get to the station, I want you to know that I understand now how you feel, and I'll do everything I can to help your relationship along." He glanced toward Clarissa. "I promise you that I will try to convince Mother and Father of what a good man Andrew is and how you'd be the perfect wife for him."

A tiny squeal burst from her lips and she reached back

to take Stefan's hand in a tight squeeze. "Thank you, Stefan. You're the best brother a girl could ever have."

A lump rose in Molly's throat at the change in Stefan's attitude. He was a man of honor and integrity, so he'd keep his word to both Andrew and Clarissa.

An image of Stefan on the battlefield emerged to block out the scene before her, and a chill coursed through her veins. What if something happened to him? She couldn't bear the thought of him fighting and killing, but that was his life. He didn't love her enough to give up the military, and she didn't love him enough to support him in it. They had sure made a mess of things these past two weeks. Nothing could ever come of their relationship without a miracle, and she didn't see one of those in her immediate future.

The train's whistle split the morning air with its shrill blast. Dread like he'd never experienced filled every part of Stefan's body and soul. At least she had given him permission to write to her in the coming weeks.

Andrew drew the horses to a stop at the hitching post. When he stepped down to the ground, he waited for Stefan to do the same then leaned in to whisper, "Thank you for being willing to help Clarissa and me. In return I'll speak with Molly and try to make her see the necessity of what you're doing."

"Thank you. I need all the help I can get." One good turn had resulted in another. His hopes soared. Maybe the future would be brighter after all.

With his hand at the small of her back, Stefan led Molly

over to the platform where the train hissed and squealed as iron grated against steel and the engine came to a stop. Mother and Father stood with Dr. and Mrs. Whiteman saying their final farewells, so Stefan pulled Molly aside for one last good-bye.

He grasped her hand and pulled her behind the depot. "I will look forward to hearing from you. The return address will be on the letter, so you'll know how to reach me." He held her hands close to his chest. "These past two weeks have been the best in my life, and I pray they've meant something to you as well."

She said nothing, but the expression in her eyes was all the answer he needed. The urge for one last kiss over-whelmed him. He reached out to pull her head toward his. She didn't resist and when their lips met, warmth and love mingled to seal the emotions stirred in the last few days. Molly leaned against his chest, and he wished the moment would never end.

Another ear-splitting blast from the train and the con-ductor's "All aboard" intervened before Molly pulled away.

Her lips quivered and her eyes glistened with moisture. "Good-bye, Stefan. I'm sorry." With that she turned and raced back to the carriage.

Sorry for what? For loving him? His loving her? Somehow, in His own time, God would work out their dif-ferences. Stefan had to believe that or be the most miser-able man on earth. With a heavy heart and a heavy step, he boarded the train to begin the journey back to the future set out before him.

With her heart broken, Molly climbed into the carriage to wait for Andrew. She sat in the back once again to avoid any conversation. He may be a good friend, but she had no desire to share her private thoughts or feelings with him.

The train began its departure, chugging away with Clarissa and Stefan, taking them back to their lives in a different world than the one in which she and Andrew lived. She spotted him coming toward the carriage followed by Clara.

Clara climbed up beside Molly. "I couldn't let you go back to the house all alone looking as sad as you do."

Perhaps being alone wasn't the best thing after all. "Thank you. I welcome your company."

Clara grasped Molly's hand. "I know you love him. I can see it so plainly in the way you look at him. And he loves you, too." Then she smiled. "I saw you slip behind the building with him. He kissed you good-bye, didn't he?"

Molly didn't answer, but heat filled her cheeks.

"Oh, he did. That's so romantic." Her eyes sparkled with glee then dimmed. "It'll be hard to be separated, but if he writes to you, it'll bring him closer."

"I don't think so, but thank you for caring." Molly blinked back tears. Reading his letters would only make her sad, but not nearly as miserable as not hearing from him at all.

"Life gets complicated in matters of the heart. I hope you and Teddy have much smoother sailing with your relationship."

Pink tinged Clara's cheeks. "He asked Papa if he could call on me, and Papa said yes. I like Teddy a lot, and maybe we'll fall in love and be married someday. He has to finish school first, but then he'll return and become a partner with Mr. Hightower in his law firm. With Mr. Murphy taking over the position of county prosecutor, Mr. Hightower told Teddy he'd have a spot when he graduated. Isn't that wonderful?"

"Yes, it is. It looks like his future is secure and you might be a part of it." She was happy for her sister, and Molly vowed to do nothing to take away from Clara's joy. Her sister continued to chatter, but Molly tuned her out. It had helped for a few minutes to fill the void left by Stefan, but now the emptiness returned.

She breathed in relief as Andrew stopped the carriage at her house. If not for the need to help Mama with the noon meal, she'd prefer to run up to her room and be alone, but that would have to wait.

Clara reached over and hugged Molly. "Things will get better, and you'll be getting letters, so please don't be so sad." Then she hopped down and raced up the steps to the house.

Andrew helped her down from the carriage and held her hand a moment longer than necessary. "I understand your feelings, Molly, but we do need to talk about Stefan, Clarissa, and all that's happened these past two weeks."

She peered up at him. "Exactly what is it we need to discuss?" They both knew how the other felt, so why talk about it.

"I know you too well, Molly Whiteman, and your beliefs about guns and war are tearing you apart from Stefan."

Molly blinked her eyes, but said nothing. She'd let him have his say then go on her way.

"I'm sure Stefan told you about the necessity of having

protection for our country. Nations need to have a powerful military to defend themselves. Stefan is playing an important role in building that military and defending our country."

"But why does it have to be with guns and wars? Why can't they just talk things out and make peace?" That seemed the logical thing to do. Papa had always made her talk things out when she and her brothers and sisters disagreed and got into arguments.

"Because some men don't want to talk. Some men want whatever someone else has and think the only way to get it is by force. If someone came in and threatened your family and tried to steal things from you and your home, wouldn't you want your father to defend you with every means available?"

"Well, yes, but…" She hesitated. But what? How would Papa defend them? He'd shot at men before. Would he do it again? A shudder coursed through her. She shook her head. "I don't want to think about this now."

"You need to, Molly, and think long and hard." He stepped away from her. "I'm going to open the infirmary now, but maybe we can find some time to talk more later."

He tipped his hat and headed to the office he shared with Papa. Molly lifted her shoulders and breathed deeply. She'd get through this day and tomorrow and all the tomorrows to come. She had to, or she'd live the summer in misery over what might have been. Her future lay right here in Stoney Creek, not off at some fort in Arizona Territory. With that resolve, she trudged to the house and the duties that called.

CHAPTER 18

MOLLY EXCUSED HERSELF from the dinner table and scrambled upstairs to her room. She closed the door behind her and sprawled across the bed, not caring whether her dress was rumpled or not. Stefan and his family would be almost across Texas to the Louisiana border by now and in St. Francisville by tomorrow evening.

The room she'd shared with Clarissa for two weeks lay silent without the giggles of two friends comparing notes and getting ready for parties and fun. She'd done the right thing in spurning Stefan's love, but she didn't have to feel good about it.

A soft knock was followed by her mother's voice. "Molly, may I come in? We need to talk."

Molly sighed. Seemed everyone wanted to talk with her. First Clara this morning, then Andrew, and now Mama. She had avoided talking at length with the other two, but there would be no denying Mama, and perhaps that was best.

"Yes, Mama, come in." She sat up and straightened her clothes.

Mama joined her on the bed. She reached out her arms and Molly fell into the embrace. "Oh, my dear child, this has been so hard for you." She ran her hands over Molly's back, using only her fingertips in the soothing gesture she'd used so many times on Molly to give comfort.

"I saw the looks that passed between the two of you this

morning, and know you care deeply for each other. When Stefan told us you didn't want him to return to his regiment, my heart broke."

She pushed Molly back from her and held Molly's shoulders. "Sweet child, you mustn't let what happened to your father and me keep you from loving Stefan. The months we were apart were almost more than I could bear, but the years since have been worth every minute of waiting."

Molly blinked back tears. "It's not so much being apart as it is that he's in the military and trained to fight and kill. I can't accept that. People shouldn't be killing other people."

"I understand your feelings. It sickened me when I shot that poor boy so many years ago, but I'd do it again if it meant protecting my family. I may be more careful now and make sure there is a threat, but if there is, I'd do it."

"How can you say that? That's so cruel." How could Mama talk like that after killing a man?

"Molly, it's time to face reality. I'm sure Stefan told you the same thing. There are evil men and even women who want what isn't theirs, whether it's money, land, or possessions. They use guns to get what they want, and decent, law-abiding citizens must defend themselves against such cruelty, especially if the law isn't around to give help."

The words held truth, but Molly couldn't wrap her mind around shooting and killing a person on purpose. "Stefan and I discussed it. He is not willing to leave the military, and I am not willing to support him in it." As far as she was concerned, the military could get along just fine without Stefan.

Mama hugged Molly again. "War is terrible, but sometimes it's necessary. I don't understand it very well myself, but I know we need men like Stefan to defend and protect our country."

Mama stood, but her hands remained on Molly's shoulders. "I'll pray for you, and I want you to pray for God to help you understand. You may not like or approve of what Stefan is doing, but we need him and others like him to keep our nation safe."

A lump rose in Molly's throat and threads of fear wove themselves through her heart. Mama's and Andrew's words made sense, but even if she did believe the military was necessary, she couldn't bear the idea of the danger facing Stefan every time he left the fort. She could only nod in reply to her mother.

Mama patted Molly's shoulder then left the room. Molly flopped back on the bed, her gaze riveted on the ceiling. She wanted understanding and acceptance, but the words for prayer wouldn't come. God knew her heart and He'd show her the way without her having to utter a single word.

An ache began in her toes and flowed upward to fill every fiber of her being with a longing she didn't quite comprehend, but if it was love, it hurt too much to let it continue. She balled her hands into fists and pressed them against her eyes. Letting go of that love may end up hurting even more.

"Lord, I need You now more than I ever have before. Help me, please." Her whispered words floated in the stillness of the room, but the answers she sought eluded her.

After a light meal on the train, Stefan sat staring at the countryside flowing past his window. As they neared the

Louisiana border and the Sabine River the pine forest grew thicker with the tall, slim trees crowding each other for space. Each mile drew him closer to home and then the return to Fort Apache and the 1st Cavalry. Unless a major uprising occurred with the Apaches in the area, the only duty Stefan would likely see would be escort and scouting details. Not much danger in those unless he ran into a band of outlaws.

If only he could make Molly see he was safe at the fort, and she would be too. The past week had not been enough time to do that, but would more weeks have made that much difference?

Clarissa nudged his arm. "Are you thinking about Molly like I'm thinking about Andrew?"

"Yes, I have to admit I am. How is it that both of us fell in love with a man and a woman with lives so different than those we have?"

"Oh, I don't know about that. Andrew and I like the same things, we both love God, and we both like to take care of others. It's the distance in miles between us that has Mother and Father worried. I don't think they object so much to Andrew as a person."

"Maybe not, but they do want you to maintain your place in society in St. Francisville. You couldn't do that as a doctor's wife way off in Texas." Even as he said the words, he doubted Clarissa's place in the social circles of home would change her love for Andrew.

As if to prove his point, Clarissa swatted at his arm and said, "Pooh, I don't care about teas, balls, and concerts or anything else Mother wants us to do. I care about Andrew." Then she giggled. "I made up a secret code for us so that when we write we can express our feelings without Mother or Father knowing."

He had to grin at her news. "Now that was a clever thing to do. You don't think Mother and Father will figure it out?"

"Oh, dear, I hope not. I don't want to go against their wishes, but I do love Andrew, and I'm hoping that maybe with time, they'll think differently."

Stefan laughed at that and shook his head. What dreams his little sister had for the future. A stern glance and furrowed brow from his mother stopped his humor dead in its tracks. If she did discover the ruse, she'd go to great lengths to see no more correspondence between Clarissa and Andrew.

Despite his mother's troubles as a young woman, she'd never given up the ways of the Southern belle she was before the war. Things that were not important to him or perhaps even to Clarissa ranked high on Mother's list of living up to her heritage. Living in the plantation home of his grandparents helped her maintain that image. He'd made it clear that the plantation wasn't for him. If something happened and he inherited it he'd sell it before he'd quit the military and oversee a crew of laborers.

Clarissa nudged his arm again. "Mother's not happy, but you'd think that she'd understand. After all, Mrs. Whiteman married her doctor and went off to live in Texas. Mother sees nothing wrong in that."

"It's a little different for us. We have the plantation to maintain. Since I've made my desires clear to stay in the military, I'll bet they're hoping you end up with a young man who can take over the plantation for them someday."

Clarissa sighed and slumped back against the seat. "I

never thought of that." She elbowed him. "You should quit the military and take over the plantation to leave the way clear for Andrew and me. Maybe then Molly would accept you."

He stiffened. "The military is my life. I've made a commitment."

"I know," Clarissa said, her tone more compassionate. "I wish things could have worked out differently for the two of you."

"So do I." He turned his face again toward the window and the pine forest. One thing for sure, he was not a quitter. Until Molly completely rejected him and someone else claimed her heart, he'd never give up on doing everything possible to win her.

🙟

Andrew ambled into the parlor where Faith sat playing the piano. The evening now loomed long and lonely with Clarissa gone. When he sat on the sofa and picked up a book, she stopped the music and came to sit beside him.

"You look so sad since Clarissa left. Do you miss her that much?"

"Yes, I miss her with all my heart." Only a little over ten hours had passed since her departure, but it may as well have been ten days or months or years what with the ache in his heart.

"I'm sorry, Andrew. I know she cares about you, but she's in Louisiana or soon will be again and you're here in Texas. What can you do?"

"We're going to write of course, and that makes me appreciate Mayor Gladstone making sure we have a decent post office and are on the east-west route." He hadn't thought much about it when the mayor had announced the changes last winter, but with the new building and the train coming through regularly now, he realized how much sooner his letters to Clarissa would arrive.

"I guess Molly is in the same predicament as you are. Clara told me how much Molly cares about Mr. Elliot."

"And he cares about her a great deal. The problem is that he's in the military, and you know how Molly is about wars." For a girl as smart as she was, Molly could sure be ignorant about some things.

Faith knit her brows together and bit her lip. "Oh, yes, I've heard her complain about guns and gunfights often enough. I don't understand it. I'm glad we have a sheriff and lawmen who carry guns and will protect us if outlaws or Indians or whatever come in to rob or hurt us."

Andrew reached over and laid his hand on top of his sister's. "I am too, and I'm glad Pa taught me how to use a gun if I have to. I carry it with me when I make calls out in the country so I'll have protection." Mostly against wild animals, since he couldn't wrap his mind around shooting a person.

"I'm glad Tom lives right here in Stoney Creek. He may be off to school for the next year, but I know he's coming home, and I'll be here waiting for him."

Andrew raised his eyebrows and peered at his sister. "Oh, has he declared his intentions in that direction?" How could his little sister suddenly be so grown up? He'd been away at school and she'd become a very attractive young woman.

Pink tinged her cheeks, and a smile graced her mouth. "Not in so many words, but we have talked about when he comes home and what he will do. Mr. Anderson at the newspaper has already told him he'd have a place waiting for him there. I think Clara and Ted Gladstone will marry when he finishes school, too."

Love sure had been busy around town right under his nose. Clara and Faith had been friends since childhood, and now both had young men interested in them. All the talk about love and marriage deepened his determination to share the rest of his life with one Clarissa Elliot.

He leaned toward his sister until their foreheads touched. "Little sister, you and I have some tall praying to do. We need God's help to get the Elliots to change their mind about me, and even more praying to get Molly to support Stefan in his calling as a soldier."

Two mighty tall orders for the Lord, but then God was bigger than any problem that may face Stefan and him. If Molly and Clarissa belonged in their futures, God had already worked out how to make that happen, but it sure would be nice if He'd let Andrew in on any such plans.

CHAPTER 19

TEN DAYS AFTER his return to his regiment, Stefan posted his first letter from Arizona to Molly at the post office on the fort grounds. He had written her a brief note when they arrived in Louisiana, but then he was caught up in the whirlwind preparations for the journey back to the fort. The return to military routine had been harder than he'd expected, and last night was the first time he had found the time or energy to sit down and write. The stage would be through today to pick up the week's mail. He had no idea how long it would take for the letter to go across Arizona and New Mexico then into Texas, but it would get there eventually. He left one for his parents as well so his mother wouldn't worry.

The hot sun bore down, and most everyone had retreated to the indoors where the shade made the temperature a few degrees cooler. No drills on afternoons like this, and in the summer they didn't have to wear full uniform on the fort grounds, but it would be expected of them if they went on patrol or had escort duty or visitors came to the fort.

He passed by the family units on his way to the officer quarters, but all was quiet. Children usually napped this time of day, and the women stayed indoors sewing or taking care of household chores. His imagination took flight, and he could almost see Molly on one of the porches, broom in hand, waiting for his return. For the first time in all the years since West Point, loneliness nudged its way to his heart.

He may be surrounded by men and some women, but none filled the void left by Molly. Stefan closed his eyes and her face filled his mind. He wanted to sit next to her, hold her hand, and perhaps steal a kiss like that one at the dance. His breath expelled with a swooshing sound. Seeing her again was not likely to happen anytime soon if ever. Andrew had promised to talk to her, but with her strong convictions and opinions, he may as well be talking to a stone wall.

He'd written about life here on the fort and how dull his routine would be for someone accustomed to the hustle and bustle of a town like Stoney Creek. He also wrote of the time they'd spent together, his new horse, and the trip back to Louisiana. He'd know from her response whether or not she cared to hear anything more personal.

Inside the officer quarters, men either lay on the beds resting or sat at the table in the corner jawing and playing cards. He could join in the conversation, but had no desire to sit in on the card game. He'd seen too often how card playing could take over a man's life.

The bed assigned to him beckoned even though the mattress was not the most comfortable. Sitting on the side of his cot, he stretched his arms upward and moved his head in a circle to loosen the muscles.

One of the officers turned from his conversation and addressed Stefan. "Saw you writing a few letters earlier. Did you find yourself a girl while on leave?"

The smirk with which he delivered his question exposed his true intent. Stefan breathed deeply to avoid an angry retort. "I met a number of people while I recuperated at home. We visited old family friends in Texas, and their hospitality deserved a thank you."

The man snickered, winked, and returned his attention to his friends. "If you say so, if you say so."

Stefan shook his head and reclined on his cot. The officers were a good group of men, but he didn't care to share with them the details of his furlough. The morning had been rough as he had ridden harder and worked harder than he had in months, but it tested his strength and found him in better shape than he hoped. Now he'd be ready for the next patrol or escort duty that may come along.

With July 4 coming up next week, the officers' wives had planned a special dinner and dance for the officers in the main hall, and a separate dinner would be served to the enlisted men in the barracks. Major Rawlins's two daughters would be in attendance and carefully guarded as to who their dance partners would be.

Stefan didn't mind that as he had no thoughts for either of the girls. Even though they were born to the military and had lived on posts most of their lives, nothing about them attracted him to them. He may have entertained the idea at one point, but after meeting Molly again, the old spark he'd had for her returned with a force he had not anticipated.

The young lieutenant in the bed next to Stefan sat down. With his elbows on his knees he peered across at Stefan. "Did those old family friends happen to include a pretty young woman?"

Stefan blinked and then knit his brows. "What makes you ask something like that?"

Red flooded the man's face. "I...um...I happened to see

one of the envelopes was addressed to a Molly Whiteman in Texas."

Seeds of anger sprouted in the pit of Stefan's stomach. Nothing was private or sacred around this place. "I don't believe that's any of your business, Callahan." Sharing any information about Molly would be the last thing he'd do around these men.

"Sorry, I miss my girl back home, so I thought maybe you might be missing one too."

The young man's sincere look of apology softened Stefan's anger. "It's difficult being so far away from those we care about. Are you planning on marrying her?"

Again Callahan's face flushed red. "I'd like to, but this is no place to bring a new bride. Yes, we have other wives here, but it's hard on them way out here in this desert-like country. It isn't even a state, just a territory, and we're so close to Mexico."

That was true, and the threat of Mexican renegades coming in to raid and attack was real. The United States had taken much away from Mexico, and some rebels wanted the government to pay.

"I understand that. Unless a woman is as committed to the military as we are, bringing her out here is not a smart thing to do." And once he'd returned, he realized even more so that this was no place for a woman like Molly. No matter her feelings and attitude toward his way of life, she'd never be happy in so remote a place without all the frills and extras provided by a town like Stoney Creek.

Molly checked the mail and sighed. At last a letter from Clarissa had arrived, but nothing from Stefan. "Mama, the mail's here. I'm leaving it on the hall table."

She tucked Clarissa's letter into her pocket and climbed the stairs to her room with a heavy heart. A week had passed since she'd received his brief letter from Louisiana, and two weeks since their departure from Stoney Creek. She closed the door behind her and plopped across the bed. She hadn't encouraged Stefan to write as much as she could have, but still, she'd expected something just to let her know if he'd made it to Arizona.

May as well read what Clarissa had to say. With the letter spread out on the bed, Molly propped herself on her elbows and read of two parties Clarissa attended and then a long narrative of how much she missed Andrew. Only one brief sentence mentioned Stefan and that they had not heard from him since his return to his regiment, but they weren't worried because they knew the mail carriage only came through the fort once a week or so.

After the last word, Molly folded the letter and flipped over to her back and stared at the ceiling. Letters from Arizona Territory would take a long time to get to Central Texas, so she'd have to be patient. Although she couldn't be the person Stefan needed for a wife, she still cared a great deal for him and wanted to know how he was doing.

She prayed daily for God to keep Stefan safe, but she wouldn't know whether he was or not until she heard from him. Her imagination conjured up all sorts of situations in which he could be injured or even killed. She pushed off the bed and stood. Those thoughts would not invade her life today. Stefan was fine. If not, they would most certainly have heard from his parents.

Even with the window open, and a slight breeze stirring the curtains, the afternoon heat of a Texas summer bore down. No rain had fallen for weeks, and the grass as well as flowers had wilted and dried out. Some parts of the state had flooded from heavy rains, but not here. This was one of those days when she would love to shed her petticoats and wear only her skirt, but Mama would frown on that for sure.

The annual Independence Day celebration would be in four days. All her cousins and aunts and uncles would be in town, and Mama had a big family picnic planned. Of course Aunt Hannah and Ellie as well as Margaret would help, but Mama wanted to do most of the work, and she expected Molly and Clara to help. That was fine with Molly, but Clara had already complained to Mama about wanting to spend more time with Teddy Gladstone.

A knock on the door was followed by Clara's voice. "Molly, come on downstairs. It's a little cooler in the parlor and Mama made cold lemonade for us."

Cold lemonade sounded heavenly. Molly opened the door just as Clara started to knock again.

"My goodness, I almost knocked on your nose." She giggled then lifted her eyebrows. "Are you coming down?"

Molly hooked her hand on Clara's elbow. "Most definitely. I hope Mama has some of her sugar cookies to eat with the lemonade. I love you, Clara-Beara, and I can't believe you're all grown up and having a young man courting you."

A frown crossed Clara's face at the use of her childhood

nickname, but Molly loved the name and liked to use it occasionally even if it did irk her sister.

When they entered the parlor, Mama sat on the sofa with the tray of lemonade and a plate of cookies on the table before her.

"Oh, girls, I'm so glad you're both here." A frown creased her brow and caused Molly's heart to jump.

"What's wrong, Mama? You look so worried." Molly dropped down beside her mother on the sofa.

"Walter Braden just delivered a telegram from my brother. Mama took a fall and is in poor condition. She's been confined to her bed. Tom says a letter will follow, but he wanted us to know right away."

That couldn't be. Grandma Dyer was so active and led a busy life in St. Francisville. She practically ran the ladies' mission group at her church singlehandedly. There must be a mistake. "But Mama, she's so healthy and busy."

"I know, dear, and I'm worried about her, but we'll have to wait for Tom to write and give us more information." Mama lifted her handkerchief to wipe away a tear.

After Grandpa died, Grandma Dyer stayed in St. Francisville to care for her mother until she passed on, and also because both Uncle Tom and Uncle Will had chosen to live there too. Mama would want to go see about Grandma Dyer, but with all the family to take care of, she'd say she didn't have time to go away. Molly reached for Clara's hand.

"If she's not doing well, then you should go to her. Clara and I can handle things here. I'm off for the summer so we can watch after Daniel, Alice, and Juliet. We both know how to cook and take care of a home because you've been such a good teacher."

Clara quickly joined in with Molly. "Alice and Juliet will be no trouble at all, and Tom will be working and Dan could go out to the ranch like he's always begging to do, so we'll all be fine."

Mama's hands dropped to her lap. Her gaze flitted from one daughter to the next. "You'd do this for me? I really must go and check on her condition."

Molly wrapped her arms around Mama's shoulders and Clara did the same from the other side. "We love you, and we're old enough to share the responsibility. Papa will want you to go as well, and he can take care of getting you a ticket on the eastbound train."

"I'm so lucky to have daughters like you two girls." Mama sat back and blinked. "No, I'm not lucky. God gave you to me and your father to take care of and nurture through your childhood, and it looks like the Lord helped us to do a fine job. Luck had nothing to do with it."

She swiped at her cheeks once more then leaned forward and picked up the pitcher of lemonade. "Now, it's time for us to enjoy a bit of refreshment and talk about the celebration next week."

That was Mama, soon as one problem set itself right she turned to another task at hand. One thing for certain, she wouldn't have to take care of this one all alone either. With as many womenfolk as they had in the family, everything would be handled to perfection. Nothing would mar the family picnic. Molly would bet her life on that.

CHAPTER 20

SALLIE WIPED HER brow and made sure the food she'd prepared for later was covered and ready. A hot July Fourth was nothing new, but a little cooling breeze would be nice. This was the last family get-together before she boarded a train for Louisiana to see about Mama, so she wanted it to be extra special for everyone.

The laughter of her children drew her to the hallway where they jostled and teased in their excitement about the holiday festival. Manfred kissed her cheek and handed her a parasol. "You'll need this today. Everyone's ready to go. Tom's gone on ahead to meet Faith, and Ted and Clara have also gone on."

Molly grabbed Alice's and Juliet's hands. "So that leaves me to corral the girls. C'mon, let's go have some fun." She glanced at her youngest brother. "Okay, Daniel, you come with us."

His bottom lip dragged down. "There's just too many girls in this family. When we get to town, I'm gonna find my friends." He stomped out the door ahead of them.

Sallie had to stifle a chuckle at her youngest son. At twelve he wasn't quite a man, but he had grown so much this past year that he wasn't a little boy anymore. Why did they have to grow up so fast?

The girls skipped down the sidewalk then slowed their pace to walk up toward town. Manfred held Sallie's hand. "Shall we go have some fun, too?"

"I'd be delighted." She laughed and then opened her parasol when they stepped into the sunlight. With so many people being in town today for the festivities trying to find a place for the carriage didn't appeal to either of them, so she and Manfred walked the few blocks to Main Street.

While they walked, she kept her eyes trained on the three girls not far ahead. As much as she trusted Molly to look out for her sisters, Alice and Juliet could break away and disappear in the blink of an eye.

Manfred squeezed her hand. "I want you to enjoy today. Tom and Will are taking care of your mother and she'll be fine. You'll get there soon enough to see to her needs."

"Thank you, my love." Waiting those months to hear from Manfred during the war had been worth every moment of agony to be married to this man today.

Others joined them in heading to town so that by the time they reached the area where booths and concessions were erected, people milled about by the droves.

"Land sakes, where did all these people come from? They must have come from the next county, or else the area around Stoney Creek has grown much more than I knew about." Never had she seen this many people in town at one time. The crowds were even larger than last year, and Mayor Gladstone said they set a record then.

Red, white, and blue bunting and flags decorated every storefront, railing, and post visible all along the street. With all the concessions and attractions gathered at one end of town around the courthouse square and park, the noise created quite a din.

Molly joined her with Alice and Juliet in tow. "I didn't

realize we'd have this many people around. I think we'll stay here near you and Pa. Danny went off with his friends."

That was fine with Sallie. Danny could take care of himself, but she liked having her two younger ones near. She waved to Hannah and Micah coming into town with Micah's mother and their children. Grace rode Starlight into town for the first time, and she sat proudly in the saddle with her father on Midnight beside her. Hannah lifted her basket to show she'd brought her food to add to Sallie's.

Micah helped Hannah and his mother down from their perch, and Joel scrambled from the rear. Micah kissed Hannah's cheek. "I'm taking Midnight and Starlight over to the livery so they'll be out of the heat. I need to keep Midnight ready for the race."

Of course Micah would be racing today. He had raced every year since he'd come back to Stoney Creek, and usually won. "I'm glad to see both of you. After you see to your horses, Micah, will you take your basket and put it on our back porch or in the kitchen with mine?"

Hannah shook her head and shooed Micah off. "I see Levi and Ellie have also arrived. You go take care of the horses, and we women will look after the food."

Micah nodded. "After I take care of business at the livery, I'll be over at the gun contest booth."

Levi waved, jumped down to unhitch his horse from the back of the wagon, then rode out to join Micah on the way to the livery.

Ellie dismounted from the wagon, watching as her three boys met up with Joel and ran off together. "We finally made it. Those boys of ours are going to either give me gray hair or an early grave." She held little Sarah tightly by the hand.

Manfred spoke up. "I'll take care of the driving soon as we've loaded everything from Hannah's wagon."

Hannah hitched her wagon to the post near the bank where they began unloading. She shaded her eyes against the sun. "While you and Manfred take care of the food, Ellie and I can take the children over to the church for the children's activities. Will that be all right, Sallie?"

"Of course. You go ahead and get them entertained."

Grace grabbed Alice's and Juliet's hands and followed Hannah and Ellie. Molly glanced down Main Street. "Margaret isn't here yet. I'm going to run down and help her get ready."

After Molly left, Sallie and Manfred clambered aboard Ellie's wagon for the short ride back to the house. They unloaded the food and stored it in the kitchen, then Manfred unhitched the wagon and led the horses to the stable. At last they once again set off to town on foot.

As they neared the church, Manfred scanned the crowd. "Where is everyone? Aren't Ellie and Hannah supposed to be here? I don't see them."

Sallie glanced down the street and glimpsed her oldest daughter. Molly had stopped to talk to a man outside the livery and was shaking her head and frowning. What in the world was her daughter doing talking to a stranger like that? She was supposed to be with Margaret. Suddenly the man grabbed Molly's arm and yanked her into the livery.

Sallie gasped and grabbed Manfred's arm. "Some man just grabbed Molly and dragged her into the livery!"

Manfred jerked around and peered that way, but the

street and boardwalks were empty on that end. "I don't see anything. You say they were at the livery?"

Sallie squeezed tighter. "Yes, I saw him take her inside. Do something!"

Manfred's jaw tightened. "I'll get the sheriff and we'll see what's going on." He ran in the direction of the sheriff, who stood with both Levi and Micah at the gun booth.

She called after him, "Hurry!" At least the sheriff and the Gordon brothers would know what to do.

Sallie squeezed her eyes shut. *Oh, Lord, take care of my child.*

That awful man had grabbed her and covered her mouth before she had a chance to scream. Why hadn't she walked on by after leaving Margaret instead of stopping when she heard those unfamiliar voices coming from inside the livery? Curiosity had landed her in trouble before, but not this bad.

The man shoved her inside and pushed her to the floor. He trained a gun on her and said, "Keep quiet, little lady, and you won't be hurt."

Two other men came from the back where all the horses were boarded. They held the reins of Micah's horse, Midnight; Grace's horse, Starlight; as well as several others. The taller and heavier of the two said, "What's all the ruckus? You're supposed to be outside keeping watch." Then his gaze fell to the floor and to Molly. "Clem, what's she doin' in here?"

Molly froze. They were stealing horses! She opened her

mouth to yell, but the one called Clem poked the gun at her head.

"I warned you, little lady. Scream and I'll shoot."

Her heart thundered in her chest as the cold steel pressed against her temple. Molly gulped and closed her mouth. Bile rose in the back of her throat, but she swallowed hard. She had to keep her composure. Help would come soon. She stared at the two men to memorize their features. The one behind her kept the gun pressed close.

"Sorry, Mort, but she was wanting to know what I was doing here. I was afraid she'd yell and have the whole town looking this way."

The man glanced behind him. "We don't need no witnesses." He pulled a bandanna from his pocket and threw it at Clem. "Here, tie this around her mouth, and use that piece of rope to tie her hands."

Clem caught the scarf and grabbed the rope to do as the other man said. She almost gagged at the foul odor and taste of the dirty fabric. He tied the rope so tight around her wrists she couldn't move her hands. She pressed her tongue against the bottom of her mouth behind her teeth to keep it from touching the awful scarf. At least she could breathe, and he had tied her hands in front of her, but what would they do with her after they finished their job? With all the people at the other end of town for the festival, no one would even realize horses were being stolen right under their noses. She hated to see them take Starlight from Grace, but what could she do?

If only she had a gun hidden in her skirt, she could defend herself.

An icy chill skittered down her spine. Where had that thought come from? She hated guns and killing, but right now she'd like to see this man dead. Her eyes squeezed shut. *Oh, Lord, please forgive me. You know I hate guns, but a friendly face holding one on these men would be mighty welcome.*

The three men conversed in the corner, but she couldn't make out their words. They kept glancing her way before the one called Clem went back outside. He stuck his head back through the door. "Everyone's still at the other end of town."

"Good. We're done here. We took the best-looking horses. It's time to go." Clem still pointed his gun toward her. He leaned over her and yanked her head back until it hit the post behind her. He twisted his hands in her hair. "Don't try any funny stuff or think about runnin' out that door. We're taking you with us just in case we're spotted."

He pushed her again, and her head slammed against wall. She all but lost consciousness and her head hurt. Tears welled but she blinked them away. All the things Andrew and Mama had spoken in regard to defending oneself came back in a rush. But there must be some other way. Killing for any reason was wrong. Now faced with her own threat of death, doubt crept into her soul. How could she defend herself against these horrible men? What if they killed her? Her heart thudded with the realization that if they did, she would never see Stefan again.

Andrew spotted Micah Gordon and Sheriff Bolton slipping into the alley behind the businesses lining Main Street. He furrowed his brow then frowned even harder as Levi followed after them. What was going on with those three?

Dr. Whiteman rushed up to him. "Andrew, Sallie saw a man drag Molly into the livery. I told the sheriff, and he and the Gordons are investigating."

Terrible scenarios filled Andrew's head, ranging from a simple explanation to assault to an all-out robbery of some kind. But why the livery? Then it dawned on him. Some of the finest horses in the county were there waiting for the big race this afternoon.

He turned to head for the livery. Dr. Whiteman grabbed his arm. "Be careful, Andrew. You're not armed and that man could be dangerous."

Andrew started down Main toward the livery, but it looked quiet. He mimicked Micah's path and went up another block before shifting and heading for the alleyway. If Molly was in trouble her uncles and the sheriff would take care of it, but the more help the better.

When he neared the block with the livery, he spotted Micah and the sheriff inching their way along the back wall. Levi had disappeared. Staying as quiet as possible, Andrew quickened his step until he was right on their heels.

When Micah saw Andrew, he motioned him to stay back against the wall. Levi reappeared.

"Looks like there may be two or three men in the livery. The only reason they could be there is the horses. After Micah and I left our horses there Willie left with us to enjoy the fun for a bit. That's when they must have gone in. Don't know how long they've been in there, but it's only been about five minutes since the doctor came to get us."

Micah nodded his head and asked the sheriff, "What now?"

"If they're stealing the horses, and Molly is inside, then we have to make sure they don't take her with them."

Andrew swallowed hard. Or leave her dead on the floor. A man could kill a woman in a minute without firing a shot if he was strong enough to snap her neck. Cold chills ran through him. They wouldn't let that happen to Molly.

Sheriff Bolton pushed Andrew into the shadow of the building. "You stay here. We'll need you if anyone gets hurt. Micah, Levi, and I are going to position ourselves on either side of the back doorway and catch them as they come out. If they have Molly with them, we'll have to be careful with our aim."

Andrew hunkered down behind a stack of crates and waited. In only a minute or two, which seemed like an hour, the back door flew open and three men barreled out, one on Midnight holding the reins of Levi's horse. The second one rode Starlight, and the third one raced out with Molly on the saddle in front of him.

Andrew peeked around the crates. Molly kicked up a storm, but a cloth covered her mouth and ropes secured her hands. The sheriff fired a shot of warning as did Micah, who also called out to his horse. The black stallion stopped and reared up, causing the horses behind him to swerve out of the way. When the other two men didn't stop Levi fired and hit the middle man, who fell from the saddle. Starlight fled out of harm's way. The man holding Molly pushed her from the horse and raced off, almost trampling the sheriff. The rider atop Midnight dropped the reins of the other horse he led but couldn't gain control of Midnight.

Micah grabbed the reins and kept his pistol trained on the thief. "Whoa, Midnight." With a jerk of his gun, he forced the man to dismount then sent Midnight back into the livery with a brisk slap on his hindquarters. Meanwhile, Levi raced after the fleeing man, firing shots as he went.

Andrew's heart skipped a beat and then thudded against his ribs. He ran over to Molly while the sheriff arrested the man who'd been shot. He could assess the man's wound later.

He knelt down beside Molly and pulled off the bandanna. "Are you all right?"

She coughed and nodded, then indicated her tied hands. As soon as the rope was loosened her anger spilled out. "How dare they treat a lady like that? Who do they think they are stealing horses? Hanging is too good for them." She glared as she watched the sheriff and Micah start down the road toward prison, guns trained on their prisoners. The wounded man held his arm, which apparently had been merely grazed by the shot.

"To think they almost got away with Grace's precious new horse." Molly grabbed Andrew's arm, then her face crumpled and she fell against him. "I was so scared." She blinked back tears and raised her eyes to his. "I . . . I actually wanted a gun to shoot them. How could I have wanted that?"

Andrew gathered her to his chest. Now was not the time to remind her of their talk about the necessity of using force in self-defense. She needed time to process what had happened. Maybe this was the breakthrough she needed to help her understand and support Stefan's role in safeguarding his country.

CHAPTER 21

MOLLY LAY TREMBLING in her bed. Papa had checked her over, and she had assured him that everything was okay. The truth of the matter was the total opposite. Never had she been as afraid as she'd been today. Even now her heart raced at the memory of the evil in the eyes of those men.

With nothing to defend herself, she'd been at their mercy. When they rode through that back door and found Micah and Sheriff Bolton waiting, she wanted to shout to her uncle to shoot the man holding her. Even now the thought brought cold chills to her body.

Images rose then spun away like water in a whirlpool leaving nothing but confusion in the swirls. How could something she believed so wrong be justified? None of what Mama and Andrew had said truly registered until today. Killing was so wrong, but she'd wanted that man dead. The idea went against everything she believed and preached. *God, forgive me for even thinking I wanted him dead, but I was so scared. Thank You for sending Micah, Sheriff Bolton, and Levi to rescue me.*

The voices of her mother and aunt drifted up the stairway from the kitchen. No words were discernible, but they must still be preparing everything for the picnic. The family get-together had always been the highlight of the festival, but now it was ruined. How could she go to the pavilion and eat and have fun with so much turmoil in her head?

"Molly, may I come in?" Aunt Hannah spoke from the hallway.

"Yes, come on. I'm not asleep." Who could sleep after what she had experienced?

Hannah entered and then sat on the bed beside Molly. "That was quite the scare you had this morning. Micah said you were very brave."

Molly snorted. "Scared to pieces is more like it, and mad." She sat up and peered at her aunt. "Have you ever been in a situation like that?"

"No, I can't say that I have, but do you remember the bank robbery when I first came here? Micah's father had a heart seizure and died, and Camilla Swenson was shot in the shoulder, so I've seen what can happen. You were very fortunate to have good men so near."

Molly nodded, and Aunt Hannah slipped her arm around Molly's shoulders.

"The best way to forget all of this is to come with us to the picnic grounds. The band will be playing patriotic music you love and we'll sing and have lots of fun. Your cousins think you're the bravest person they know right now, and you're Grace's hero because you saved her horse from being stolen. So you may as well bask in their adoration while it's here. May even help when school rolls around again."

The grin on her aunt's face did cheer Molly. Maybe she was right and the picnic would help her forget the morning's ordeal as well as all the doubts playing tag in her head. Besides, Mrs. Gordon's chocolate cake was too good to miss, and if she stayed in her room, most likely she'd never get a piece.

Molly swiped her cheeks then pressed her hands against

her hair. "I think you're right. I love the music and the food, and it'd be much better than sitting up here thinking about what happened. After all I'm not hurt, only shaken." Even if her head did still ache where she'd bumped it.

Hannah laughed. "Now that sounds like my Molly. Come on, let's get down to the park before everyone eats all the food." She grabbed Molly's hand and pulled her toward the door.

Molly shook off the remaining strands of fear from earlier and followed her aunt down the stairs. She'd think about all the confusion it caused later.

Nothing was going to mar the rest of this day for her. Right now Mama's fried chicken and biscuits called her, and she'd have the biggest slice of that chocolate cake she'd ever had.

Stefan lay on his cot, his belly full from the feast prepared by the army wives. After a few weeks of camp rations by the army cook, home-cooked food always tasted like a bit of heaven. Later this evening a dance would be held with the wives and older daughters of the officers serving as dance partners. Most of the men enjoyed the events, but since he'd met Molly, everything paled in comparison to the time they had had together.

Still, he would attend as a good officer should as a courtesy to the commanding officer's wife and family. First he'd get some rest. Although healed, his leg gave him problems after he'd been on it too long. The drills yesterday had been rough, and dancing tonight wouldn't help it any if he didn't give it some time elevated.

For the next hour he dozed and listened to the murmur of his fellow single officers who played cards or simply conversed with the topic of conversation most likely about girls back home. The fort had been quiet for the past few years since the Indians had relocated on the reservation and quit their raiding. The fort had even enlisted a number of them to be scouts. Arizona was still wild territory as far as terrain, but the Indians were quiet.

His cot mate, Tom Slater, sat down and picked up a neckerchief. "Can't decide whether to wear this tonight or not."

Stefan shook his head. "Don't think you'll need it. We're to be in full dress tonight, and that doesn't include the neck scarf."

"I suppose you're right." He bent over with his elbows on his thighs. "What do you think about the rumors of those Mexican bandits coming up here, rustling cattle, and robbing folks on the stage?"

"I think they're more than rumors. We're not in much danger since we're pretty well protected by the mountains. Of course we may be called on to go down toward the border and defend the territory there. If you ask me, we have more danger from the outlaws right here in Arizona. It hasn't been that long since the Earp brothers and the Clanton clan had their shootout. Outlaw cowboys are still said to roam the territory."

Tom laughed. "I don't think they're any match for the US Cavalry, but I wouldn't want to have a run-in with them." He reached for his jacket. "Time to get dressed up for this dance tonight."

When they entered the main headquarters later, the room had been cleared of all furniture but a few tables covered with checked cloths and laden with food. Several men sat at one end tuning instruments they would use to play dance music later. Decorated with red, white, and blue, the room had become festive and invited celebration.

After the first several numbers, he danced with the colonel's wife, a middle-aged woman with several grown children. She peered up at him with that motherly look he'd seen so many times in his own mother's eyes. When the music stopped she still held his hand. "Come talk with me a spell."

He lifted his brow, but followed her to the refreshment table heaped with platters of cookies, pastries, and a large bowl of fruit punch. Whatever she had to say must be important for her to detain him like this, and he really wouldn't mind having a cup of the punch. After securing cups for both of them, Mrs. Sanford retreated to a corner where he joined her.

"What is it you wish to discuss, ma'am?"

"I've noticed a difference in you since your return from medical leave. Have you changed your mind about the military?"

Stefan gulped. He didn't know what he'd expected to hear, but it hadn't been this. "No, ma'am, I was more than ready to return." And he had been, except for not wanting to leave Molly.

"I see. Then you must have met someone while on leave. Someone you didn't want to leave behind."

Heat rose in Stefan's face. How did she know something like that?

"Don't be embarrassed. I've seen it far too often. Love changes a person, and you have that look about you now.

Remember, I have four grown children, and I've seen them all through various stages of love and courtship."

The kindness in her dark eyes and the gentle smile on her lips touched his heart. He wanted, no needed, to talk with someone, and Mrs. Sanford would be the perfect one to trust. "Her mother and mine are childhood friends, and our family visited in Stoney Creek, Texas, where Mother's friend now lives. I've known their daughter since we were children, but this was the first time I'd seen her in ten years or so."

"And so you fell in love with her, but I sense there's more to the story than that or else your eyes would be shining bright with love."

She *was* like his mother, who recognized every mood of Stefan's and sensed any uneasiness or unhappiness in his soul. "Yes, I fell in love with her, but she hates the military and anything that involves shooting or killing. Her mother and father had some bad experiences in the war, and Molly wants no part of it."

"Oh, dear, that does present a problem." Sympathy filled her face, and she frowned. "I suppose you've discussed this with her."

"Yes, I have, and a friend did the same, but she is adamantly against the military. Besides that, she loves living in town around people and teaching the children at the school there."

"That makes for a difficult situation." Then she smiled and patted his arm. "I'll pray for you both to find what God's plan for you is. Now tell me about your father. I understand he fought bravely under General Lee."

Stefan's head jerked back. How did she know that? "Yes, ma'am, he did. He served as an officer under General Lee not long after the war began, but he returned to the 4th Louisiana regiment and served with them until he was taken prisoner at Port Hudson. I have a big pair of boots to fill." And he'd fill them the best he could to make his father proud, even if it was an obstacle in his winning Molly's heart.

The music once again stopped, and Mrs. Sanford set her punch cup on a nearby table. "I see my husband coming for me." She grasped his arm. "Lieutenant, remember, if it's the Lord's will for you to be together, He will work things out for you. Be patient and trust Him."

"Thank you again, Mrs. Sanford. I will do that." He saluted his commanding officer then stepped back for the couple to proceed to the dance floor.

Mrs. Sanford's words rang in his heart. God would provide and take care of the situation with Molly, but He wished God would be a little more direct and clear as to how that would happen.

CHAPTER 22

O N FRIDAY AFTER almost two days of wrestling with her doubts and confusion, Molly had no clear answer as to what she should do or believe. After breakfast she helped her mother with household tasks downstairs while Clara and the younger girls worked in the bedrooms upstairs.

After Mama laid down her dust rag and removed the scarf from her head, she headed for the kitchen. "I believe it's time for a break and some of my herb tea."

Molly followed her and bit her lip. Mama hadn't said a word more about what had happened day before yesterday. Now Molly wanted her advice. This was something she couldn't handle on her own. Even after praying about it yesterday and this morning, she'd found no peace.

Once they were seated at the table in the kitchen, mint tea filled the room with its sweet aroma. Molly inhaled deeply of the fragrance then sipped from the china cup her mother loved to use for tea time. She held the cup with both hands, admiring the rose pattern painted on it. Mama had such pretty things she'd brought with her from Louisiana.

This room had been her haven for more years than she could rightly remember. The pale yellow walls, maple table with eight chairs, black iron stove, and shelves holding Mama's dishes all gave her great comfort. The kitchen was her favorite room in the house, and it always had wonderful smells filling the air.

Someday Molly wanted hand-painted china cups and a teapot like Mama's. She set her cup back on its saucer and breathed deeply. After exhaling, she leaned toward her mother. "Mama, we must talk about what happened to me. I have so many questions flooding my mind and heart. My feelings are all confused."

"I sensed the whole ordeal still troubled you, but I wanted to wait until you were ready to talk before saying anything."

How blessed to have a mother who stayed in tune with her children. Never had she loved her mother more than at this moment. "I've been praying about my feelings and how I wanted to kill that man with anything I could get hold of, even my bare hands."

"Those feelings are perfectly normal when your life is threatened."

Molly ran her fingertip around the rim of her cup and chewed the corner of her lip. "Is that the way you felt when you shot that young soldier?"

Her mother's expression didn't change, but her eyes flickered for a moment as though remembering a deep pain. "Yes, it was. He was the enemy, and he was in our kitchen. I didn't know why and all I could think about was protecting my mother and Hannah." She squeezed her eyes shut. "It is something I will never forget."

Molly waited for her mother to compose herself before speaking again. When Mama finally opened her eyes, Molly leaned forward. "Would you do it again?"

Mama's eyes opened wide and her mouth gaped. Finally she shook herself and stared straight at Molly. "If it meant defending my family against a threat to their life, yes, I think I would."

Molly slumped in her chair. That was the answer she expected, but it still didn't satisfy her own doubt. Mama reached across the table and covered Molly's hands with her own.

"My dear child, feeling as you do about guns, I imagine you are shocked at my answer."

Tears filled Molly's eyes. "Yes, I am. The Bible tells us not to kill."

"I believe in that instance it meant murder. Obviously God allowed for war, because the Old Testament is full of battles. God gave David the strength to kill Goliath when the giant threatened to destroy the Israel soldiers. He also sent leaders into battle to conquer the lands He promised them. Yes God said not to commit murder, but the evil deeds of others caused God's people to defend themselves and even sometimes to attack and wage war in order to eliminate evil. I know it's difficult to understand, and it's difficult for me to explain, but sometimes we have to commit violent acts in order to guard our lives."

The words sounded right, but they brought no comfort. "So what I wanted to do at the livery and what Stefan does now and what Papa and Colonel Elliot and even you did wasn't a sin?" That had become her sole worry, and it ate at her heart, tearing it to pieces.

Mama didn't answer but sat holding Molly's hands. Concern washed across her face. Finally she said, "I don't have all the answers you need. I only know that when circumstances demand drastic actions, God understands because He loves us and forgives us. It took me a long time to accept the fact that God forgave me for shooting those two young men, but when I finally did, my heart was at peace."

Molly longed for that peace. Maybe she'd been praying for the wrong thing. She needed to talk with God about this some more.

"Do you love Stefan?"

Molly jerked her head back. "Yes, but it hasn't been enough to keep me from hating what he does and worrying about what will happen to him."

"We all worry about those we love, but worrying doesn't change a thing. What you feel now may be no more than concern for him and where he is. When your love is strong, deep, and true, you'll want to be with him no matter what he does or where he is, and you'll do everything you can to make sure you are, just like I left my parents and home to come to Texas with your father."

Maybe that was the problem. Maybe she didn't really love Stefan, but if she didn't, why did her heart ache so for him? She withdrew her hands from Mama's and pushed back from the table. "I think God and I have some serious things to talk about, and I have a lot more thinking to do."

She pushed through the kitchen door and greeted her sisters, who were headed into the kitchen to find Mama. Then she trudged up the stairs to her room. *God, I really need some answers. I'm going to trust You to speak to me and show me what I need to do.*

In all her twenty-two years, God hadn't failed her yet. He already had her future planned, and now she had to make sure she listened and didn't miss what she should do in the days ahead.

Molly stayed up in her room even through the noon meal. Later Mama brought up a tray with soup and homemade bread. She set it on the table beside the bed and gazed down at Molly.

"Are you ready to talk again?"

Molly squeezed her eyes shut. "No. Please keep praying for me."

Mama bent down to kiss Molly's forehead. "Of course I will. God will give you the answers you seek if you will listen." After those words of wisdom, she left the room.

Of course Mama was right, but she'd been trying to listen to God ever since the conversation downstairs this morning. She had spent the rest of the morning scanning every passage in the Old Testament that mentioned wars and battles. She'd reread Romans 13:4, which spoke of rulers who bear the sword as God's agents for punishing evildoers. And she'd read Hebrews 11:34, which clearly stated that God blessed His faithful servants with success in battle. Would God have blessed them if He was against war? She thought not.

The rich aroma of the homemade soup reminded Molly of her hunger, but she didn't want to eat until she'd come to a decision.

Although she'd been with Stefan only two weeks, he had become a part of her life and she missed him now. What if she never saw him again? No, she didn't want to consider that. She sat up on her bed and grabbed her Bible again. "All right, Lord, I've seen from my reading that wars and violence are sometimes necessary and You use them for Your purposes. I think I can understand that now. Mama had to defend herself just like I wanted to defend myself at the livery." Still, the longed-for peace eluded her.

She placed the Bible back on the table and picked up the slice of bread spread with a thick coat of butter. She nibbled a bit and let her mind wander back over the past few weeks. She swallowed a bit of the bread and lifted her fingers to her lips. The memory of Stefan's lips against hers remained vivid in her memory.

The room had become stifling with its heat. She had to get out of there now. Out on the porch, she stood at the railing under the shade of the elm spreading its branches across the yard. Molly gazed up the street toward town. Why did it hold such an attraction for her? Especially after what happened on Wednesday.

She went back in and grabbed her parasol. A walk would do her good and get rid of the pent-up energy coursing through her body. People greeted her and smiled as she walked along the boardwalk past the bakery shop, the dressmaker's store, the hotel, and then the livery.

A shudder shook her body as the memory of the attack came flooding back. She bit her lip and turned away. She could have lost her life that day and never have seen Stefan again.

Her breath caught in her throat and a new under-standing flowed through her veins straight to her heart. She whirled around and almost ran the distance back home. Life was short and could be over in an instant, whether on a battlefield or in a town like Stoney Creek. Where she lived didn't matter, it was who she lived with that made the difference.

When she reached the steps to her home, she stopped,

panting and out of breath. Andrew stood at the top peering down at her.

"It's a little warm to be running, isn't it?" He held out his hand. "Come, I think you need something cold to drink."

Molly grabbed his hand and let him pull her up to the porch. Once beside him, she grabbed his arm. "I need to ask you something."

"All right. Let's sit here in the shade." After they were seated, Andrew leaned forward. "Now, what's on your mind? I can see those wheels spinning in your head, so tell me, what sent you out in the heat of the day?"

After a deep breath to calm her nerves and give her time to form an answer, she said, "You told me how much you love Clarissa, but do you love her enough to leave everything here and go to Louisiana for her?"

"Yes, I do and I've already spoken to your father about that. He's willing to give me a recommendation at the hospital in New Orleans. That's not so far from Clarissa and a place her parents enjoy visiting. If I'm there, maybe they won't protest Clarissa's relationship with me."

"You'd actually do that?" Clarissa had already told her she'd leave Louisiana in a minute if it meant spending a lifetime with Andrew.

"Of course, and it's all arranged. I'm to accompany your mother tomorrow on the train to Louisiana. While she is seeing to her mother, I'll be at the hospital in New Orleans finding my way around and deciding if that's the place for me or if I should have my own practice."

Andrew and Clarissa had their future coming together, and Molly's heart filled with happiness for them. However good that was, it wasn't the most important matter at hand.

Stoney Creek was a great town and a wonderful place to live, but it was just another town without Stefan there.

She leaned toward Andrew. "I've decided I want to be where Stefan is no matter where it is. God showed me that my attitude towards war was a bit unrealistic. He showed me story after story in the Bible where armies were used to accomplish His purposes, and He reminded me that He is in control and uses earthly rulers to fight and punish evil."

Andrew reached over and hugged Molly. "That is the most wonderful news I've heard in weeks."

"I want to let Stefan know, but I haven't heard from him yet, so I don't know where to send a letter." Excitement built in her heart, and she had so much to tell him about her discoveries. A letter had to come soon, or she'd burst.

Mama stepped out to the porch. "I thought I heard voices out here. I have fresh tea made if you'd like a little cold refreshment to—" She stopped and stared at Molly. "What has happened? You're positively glowing."

Molly jumped up and hugged her mother. "God showed me the truth and helped me figure it all out. I do love Stefan with all my heart and I want to be with him no matter where he is."

Mama returned the hug with her arms tight around Molly's back. "Oh, my sweet child, that's the best news I've heard today."

After a moment, she held Molly at arm's length. "Did Andrew tell you he's going with me to Louisiana tomorrow?"

"Yes, he did, and I'm excited for him. Of course I'll miss him around here, but if it all works out, he'll be with Clarissa."

Andrew laughed. "Oh, it's good to see you so happy

after everything that's happened the past week." Then his expression sobered. "I'm sorry, Mrs. Whiteman. I forgot about your mother."

"That's all right. I know what you mean, and besides, Mother is in good hands. Tom and his wife are taking good care of her. Seeing her will ease my mind, so that's why I'm going."

That may be true, but Molly had overheard her speaking with Papa only last evening. Mama was much more concerned than she let on, but she depended on the good Lord to take care of Grandma.

How Molly wished she could be going to Louisiana too. She had so much to tell Clarissa, but staying here would be a bigger help for Mama. Her happiness wouldn't be complete until she could tell Stefan how much she loved him and wanted to be with him wherever he was, even on an army fort.

CHAPTER 23

STEFAN GLANCED BACK at the soldiers following him. Now back into normal routine after the holiday, his unit escorted the mail, payroll, and supply detail back to the fort. So far the trip had been without incident as it usually was, but recent rumors of an outlaw band hiding in the mountains had brought concern for his men.

The sun bore down and shimmered across the desert before them. Sparse vegetation in this region gave little concern for an ambush, but doubt skittered across Stefan's thoughts. He'd seen groups of bandits come out of the foothills so fast they left no time for planning, only instinctive reaction. Those mountains and foothills loomed ahead of him, their peaks and valleys offering beauty to the blue skies overhead.

Coming as he did from a coastal state with mostly flat lands and only a few hills, the mountains had impressed him with their majesty. He'd been told that these were nothing compared to the Rocky Mountains in Colorado, but to him these were impressive enough.

Ten men rode under his command and he had utmost confidence in their abilities and awareness of their surroundings. The wide brim of his hat shaded his eyes as he peered into the distance. The men would need a rest break soon. With so little shade to offer relief he'd take time only for refreshing drinks of water for his men and the horses.

In another two hours they'd be near enough to the fort

that if anything happened they'd hear the bugle sound of battle and send help immediately. Getting through the next two hours became his prime goal.

At his signal the small supply train of wagons came to a halt. Canteens were passed around, refilled from the water barrels, and passed again. Each man made sure his horse had water before remounting in preparation to continue their journey.

"Lieutenant Elliot, the men are ready to depart." A corporal saluted then stepped back to await instruction.

"Thank you, Evans." He returned the salute and the man turned to rejoin the group, who were mounted and ready.

Stefan swung his leg up over the horse he'd brought back from the Gordon ranch. So far he'd been the perfect mount and took to the drills as if he'd been born to do them. Stefan raised his arm then moved it forward as a signal to resume their march.

Several times he pushed the image and thoughts of Molly from his mind. He had to stay alert and ready for trouble if it came, not daydream about a girl who couldn't be his without some miracle or intervention from God. At least they no longer had fear of an Indian attack. With both Geronimo and Cochise captured, that danger no longer existed.

When they picked up the supplies he'd left his letter to Molly and one to his family to be posted on the next mail run. He hadn't heard from her, but he wouldn't until she had news from him. Even then he had no guarantee she'd respond.

His scout, Running Cloud, came galloping up and reined in next to him. "Looks like trouble ahead. A large band of outlaws is hunkered down up in the mountains.

They were packing up and mounting like they were fixing to head out. Don't think they saw me, sir."

Stefan whipped out his binoculars and peered in the direction the scout pointed. A dust cloud formed in the distance, still too far away for the naked eye to see. "How many were there?"

"I counted at least eight, maybe ten, sir."

Stefan gazed at the terrain around them. Nothing but hills and scrub bushes and a few boulders. Nothing to hide behind to wait. He had enough men, but if they didn't have a place to hide and attack as the men approached, they'd have to fight in the open. Even if he rode his men hard from this point, they'd never make it back to the fort in time, but they could get closer.

After issuing orders for them to proceed to the fort with all haste, Stefan sent his men forward. "Running Cloud, ride to the fort and get help."

"Yes, sir." The Indian raced off toward the fort and Stefan could only pray he'd reach it in time to send more troops. He stopped and trained his binoculars on the terrain behind. This time the dust cloud loomed much closer. He lowered the glasses and could make out the dust rising in the distance.

The heavily loaded wagons didn't make as much progress as he'd like. He raced ahead of the unit but, when he realized the gang was getting closer, he called for them to halt. When all were stopped and gathered round, Stefan gave instructions. "Running Cloud says there are eight to ten men in the band, so we're in for a fight. Get the wagons secured, and take your places. You know what to do. I sent Running Cloud back to the fort for help. Man your positions and pray he makes it back in time."

In only a few minutes the men had formed a battle station and the cloud grew larger and closer. Now the thunder of hooves in the distance roared in his ears. They'd come in with guns raised and firing. He warned his men to wait until they had the targets well in sight then shoot to kill.

Stefan's heart pounded loud and hard, his hands steady on his rifle. This is what he'd been trained to do but would it be enough?

Then the band was on them and the shooting began. Bullets whizzed past his head as he fired back then reloaded and fired again. Gunfire blasted the air around him as his men shot it out. The wagons offered some protection but not enough with this many attacking. Pain seared his cheek as a bullet whizzed by but he continued to shoot.

The screams of men as they fell stabbed his soul and renewed his determination to fight. An object flew past him, but before he could react, flames shot from the wagon protecting him. Stefan tore off his jacket and flung it again and again over the orange fingers now racing toward the sky. *Dear God, help us.*

He kept battling the fire until the heat seared his flesh and something blasted into him from behind with such force it pitched him forward against the side of the wagon. Pain like he'd never experienced slammed through his body. He hit the wagon side, dropped the jacket, and fell over, sprawled on the hot sand, unconscious.

Sometime later he was roused when something nudged his cheek. He raised his head from the grit and opened his eyes, but only one worked. The sun's glare almost blinded him but he could make out the shape of his horse's head poking his face.

"Warrior, you're still here." He placed his palms on the sand and tried to lift himself from the ground, but the pain was more than he could bear as his left arm gave way and his chest plummeted back to the gritty sand. He breathed deeply before attempting to move again. More pain radiated from his chin to his forehead. Not again. He'd only been back a few weeks. He sensed movement near him and reached out, thinking he'd grab Warrior's reins. Instead a hand grabbed his arm and turned him over.

"Colonel, Lieutenant Elliot's alive!"

A shadow blocked the sun, and Stefan once again opened his eyes. Through his one good eye, he recognized the face of Sergeant Major Grimes. Two others joined Grimes as they examined his wounds.

"He's burned and has a bullet hole in his shoulder, but I think we can move him." As hands lifted him from the ground, excruciating pain laced his body with knife-like sharpness. Then he rested on the bed of a wagon. A glance to his left had him staring at one of his men also lying in the wagon. Stefan breathed in relief when the young man's chest rose and fell. He was alive. How many others had survived? What had happened to his men?

He yelled, "Sergeant Major!"

"Yes, sir, right here."

"Where are the rest of the men?"

The soldier blinked his eyes and looked up then back down. "Three are dead, sir: Smith, Andrews, and Little. The rest are wounded or okay and are being taken back to the fort. We got here too late to save the cargo. Those outlaws took the payroll and are already high-tailin' it back to the mountains. Colonel Sanford sent a unit after them, but I'm not sure it'll do much good."

Three of his men dead. How could that be? And why couldn't he see out of one eye? He grabbed Grimes's arm. "What's wrong with my eyes? I can't see."

"Sir, one of them is swollen shut, but the other one looks okay. We'll get you back to the fort and into the hospital right away." He pushed a canteen of water against Stefan's mouth. "Here, you need fluid in you."

Stefan gulped the tepid liquid that soothed his parched throat. He laid his head back down. "Thank you, Grimes, that helped." If only the pain would stop, but he'd bear it until they made it back. He had to. Then darkness gripped him again.

He awakened to the fresh, clean scent of the pillow and sheets. For a moment he thought he was home, but the weight on his chest and head told a different story. He opened his mouth, his burning throat crying for water.

In the next few seconds, a hand lifted his head and pressed cool water against his lips. Once again he drank to slake his thirst and cool his throat. When finished, his head went back to the pillow. His gaze went down to his chest. The weight was caused by his heavily bandaged right arm and hand resting there. He raised his left hand only to find it also swathed in bandages. Still he used it to explore his head, and once again detected thick bandages. These covered the left side of his face and his head.

A figure in blue loomed over him. Doctor Curtis reached down and placed his fingers at Stefan's throat and stared at his pocket watch. He smiled then stepped back. "Your pulse is good considering your injuries, young man."

"My men..."

"They're being cared for. Only one, Sergeant O'Riley, is critical. The others will be all right."

Stefan groaned. Still, he'd lost three. Men he'd trained and worked with for months gone. He peered up at the doctor. How could he face their families with news like this? Then he remembered his horse. "What about Warrior? Is he all right?"

"Yes, he is. He was fine after he had some water and oats. He's a strong horse. Stayed right by you and protested when we moved you to the wagon."

"Thank you." He closed his eyes as the pain diminished. His faithful horse had not left him. *Thank You, Lord.*

"Don't you want to know the extent of your injuries, Lieutenant?" The doctor held a chart in his hands.

Stefan nodded. May as well get the bad news out of the way now.

"I've given you laudanum to lessen the pain. A bullet grazed your cheek, and you were burned on your face and hands. Your left eye is swollen shut as a result of the burns on your face, but I don't believe any permanent damage was done. Another bullet entered your back about half an inch above your heart and lungs. There's tissue damage and it nicked a bone, but those will heal."

A bullet wound he could deal with, but burns on his face and hands were another matter. "How...how bad are the burns?"

"Serious enough that we're going to send you to a hospital in New Orleans. I know that's a long way, but you'll be closer to your family, and they have an excellent burn unit there to take care of you."

Stefan clenched his teeth. Being sent to a major hospital didn't look good. They only did that when nothing else could be done at the fort. He stared at his right hand. Severe burns could ruin his fingers…his gun hand. This could mean the end of his career. All thankfulness of a minute ago was swept away with the tide of anger swelling in his chest. Why had God let this happen? Why hadn't He sent help in time? Good men lost all because of the greed of a few evil men.

He turned his head to the wall. He wanted to scream but no sound came from his throat. The anger burned like acid in his gut. He directed his fury at God and let all the rants he could remember pass through his mind before the laudanum did its work and he slipped into blessed sleep.

CHAPTER 24

On Saturday, after seeing Mama and Andrew off on the train to Louisiana, Molly hurried back home to write a letter to Stefan and pour out her love for him. She and Mama had sat up late last night talking about Stefan and what it meant to be a military wife. All the things Mama said didn't shake her faith, but the advice had given her something to truly think and pray about all night.

Being the wife of a military officer would not be easy. The fort where Stefan was assigned sat in the White Mountains of southern Arizona Territory and was cut off from civilization by its remote location. He had told her a bit about the fort, but then it hadn't really concerned her. Now she wanted to know every little detail.

After a session of prayer in which she'd turned her entire future over to the Lord, she had fallen into peaceful sleep. This morning had been busy with breakfast, listening to last-minute instructions for her and Clara, getting to the station, and then saying good-bye. Molly had no time to think about her decision, but had told her mother just before boarding the train that all was well. Mama had understood and hugged Molly in a tight embrace.

Now Molly sat at her writing desk with a fresh sheet of vellum and her pen poised. How should she start? She bit her lip, her heart overflowing with words and phrases, but no idea how to put them together to make sense. If only she could see him and tell him what was on her heart.

Words on paper could never convey what she wanted to say.

She stared out the window of her room that overlooked the street in front of the house. People went about their business as usual on a Saturday morning. Papa was downstairs in his office to see to patients who lived out a ways and could only make it in for a visit on Saturdays. Juliet and Alice played on the front porch, their voices drifting up to Molly through the open window. Both had taken Mama's departure quite well and had promised to listen to any instructions given by Molly or Clara.

Everything about her followed a routine, even to the Claremont sisters driving by in their wagon on the way to the general store. They waved to the girls on the porch then stopped. The elder Claremont sister, Miss Emily, leaned out from her perch.

"With your Mama gone for a while, if you or your sisters need any help with anything, you be sure to let Molly know she can call on us. We'll be glad to do whatever you need." Then she sat back and the wagon proceeded on to town.

Molly smiled at the scene. One of the best things about Stoney Creek was the friendliness of the people living there. Of course, everyone usually knew everyone else's business, but that meant they'd be on the spot to help if the need arose.

Juliet ran out onto the street to greet Mrs. Olson and her daughter Melissa. Juliet shaded her eyes and peered up at Molly. "Can I go with Mrs. Olson and play with Melissa?"

Molly leaned out and waved at Mrs. Olson. "If it's all right with you, Mrs. Olson."

"Of course it is. Alice, you come too. We'll have us a tea

party." She moved her little boy to her other hip and beckoned to Alice to join them.

Alice ran out to the street and the three girls made their way toward the Olson home.

Molly sat back at her desk and tapped her pen against her teeth. Oh, how she'd miss this town and all the wonderful people who lived in it, but her heart swelled with love for Stefan. Anyplace would be her home as long as she could be with him. Stoney Creek would always be here, and she'd be welcome anytime she returned.

Her memory drifted back to when her family first came to Stoney Creek. Mama had left all her family back in Louisiana to travel to Texas to be a doctor's wife in a town she'd never heard of until Papa was offered the practice here. Her memories were vague as she hadn't been quite four years of age at the time, but her first impression had included lots of horses and a lot of noise.

If her mother had been able to leave her family and childhood home behind to follow Papa, then most certainly Molly should be able to do the same with Stefan. She grinned and straightened the paper on her desk. She had just the words to write.

As she wrote, her love poured out through the pen and flowed onto the paper like silk. Her heart grew happier and lighter with each written word.

> Dear Stefan,
> So much has happened in the days since you left. My heart overflows with the love I hold in my heart for you. On the Fourth of July, I was held at gunpoint in an attempted horse theft at the livery. I wasn't hurt, just scared and angry, but, Stefan, I

wanted to kill that man who was holding me. I actually wanted a gun. Suddenly I realized that guns are very necessary for self-defense. Thank God that the sheriff and my uncles were nearby and were able to rescue me and stop the theft. Two of the men are now in custody and they have high hopes of catching the third.

As I sat there with my life being threatened, all I could think about was never seeing you again. I couldn't bear the idea. Stoney Creek is nothing without you, and my desire is to be with you wherever you are. God has opened my eyes and my heart to see the great gift you are to me. My prayer is that you will feel the same about me.

I pray you are well, and bid you Godspeed with whatever duty you must fulfill as you serve our country.

Forever Yours,
Molly

Satisfied with what she'd written, Molly folded the paper and slipped it inside a matching envelope. Now came the hard part, waiting to hear from him so she'd have an address to send the letter.

Agonizing, throbbing pain coursed through Stefan's body. Nothing seemed to alleviate the constant burning of the skin beneath the bandages. With his left arm immobile and his right hand bandaged, he could do nothing for himself.

Humiliation washed over him as a nurse tended his

wounds and fed him broth. Even when propped against the pillows, he found it hard to breathe.

Sleep offered no comfort as it brought on dreams of the attack and the image of his men lying strewn about like rag dolls. Sergeant O'Riley had made it through the night, which improved his chances of survival. Stefan mourned the loss of the others in his unit. He'd let them down. God had let him down.

He opened his uncovered eye and turned his head to gaze about the room. The long room held ten beds, but only five were now occupied, with two of his men having been treated and released. His heart filled with thankfulness for that but still grieved the three who died.

Fading sunlight sent orange beams through the windows. The door opened and the nurse came through to light the lanterns for the evening. She'd stay with the three men through the night and tend to any needs that arose. A desk sat against one wall, and she lit that lamp first. Charts and papers were stacked there, and she checked papers before coming to check on him and the two others.

The cots had been padded, but even that wasn't enough to be comfortable. He longed for his bed in the barracks. Even though it wasn't much softer it was longer and wider and fit his tall body with room to spare.

Finally the nurse stopped by his bedside. He peered up at her with one good eye. "Miss Harrison, did I understand the doctor say he's sending me to Louisiana?"

"Yes, and as soon as you're able to travel we'll get you on a train. He's wired Charity Hospital in New Orleans, so they'll be expecting you." She moved her fingers over the bandages with such a light touch that he could barely tell her hands were on him.

If his wounds were serious enough for him to go back to New Orleans, this would be no simple rehab assignment like before. The doctor here had treated him, and then he'd been given a furlough to exercise the leg and retrain the muscles. Charity was a huge hospital, and he'd get the best of care since it was a teaching hospital as well, but it didn't bode well for his military future.

"I'm giving you something for your pain. It should help you to sleep. You need plenty of rest and fluids to heal."

He watched as she prepared the medication in a syringe with a beastly looking needle. He closed his eye and bit his lip to absorb the pain, but all he felt was like a pin prick to his skin. He blinked his eye and grinned at her. "That was easy. I was expecting it to hurt."

Nurse Harrison returned his grin and winked. "That's what I've been trained to do. I'm glad to know I did it well. You've been asleep the other times I've given it to you."

As she turned to leave he lifted his arm as though to grab her, then realized he couldn't. "Please, stay a minute or two longer." Although other beds were occupied, the two men with him remained unconscious. He didn't want to be left alone in the dark. It gave him too much time to think.

"All right, but you'll be asleep as soon as the morphine takes effect." She stood beside his bed, the warm glow of the lamp behind creating a halo of light around her head.

His angel of mercy used a cool, damp cloth to wipe the exposed part of his face. If only it would ease the burning of the part hidden under bandages, but the drug could do that. Shadows danced against the walls, creating an effect that soothed his soul, but the extent of his injuries plagued his curiosity.

"How bad are the burns?" He stared steadily with his one eye. "Please tell me."

She sighed and dipped the cloth back into the cool water. "About 5 percent of your body is burned, and it's confined to your face, neck, arms, and hands. The bullet wound will heal, but the rest will take a while."

Even worse than he'd feared. "Thank you." He'd seen burns from battle before, and scars were not pretty. His career would be over and his face scarred for life. He closed his eyes, anger against God for allowing this to happen rising like bile in his chest. He dreaded the disappointment that would fill his father's face, and the fear he'd see in his mother's eyes.

The nurse touched his shoulder. "I'm leaving now. You'll soon be asleep, but I'll be back to check on you and the others in an hour or so." The *tap, tap* of her shoes on the wood floor faded away as she left him alone. He pictured the days ahead and shuddered at the looks of horror that would fill the faces of those who would see his scars. The pain subsided, and his muscles began to relax, but anger and despair still filled his soul.

"God, how could You do this to me? You know the military is my life. It's all I ever wanted to do. Three of my men are dead, and I'm scarred forever." His words echoed off the walls, but did little to bring relief to the anger building in his heart.

What would Molly think? He couldn't bear the thought of her seeing him so ugly. She'd been right to hate what he did. His parents must swear to never tell her about his condition. She'd have no reason to come to Louisiana except to visit family, and then she never needed to know he was there. Her attitude about his military life would keep her away. As much as he longed to see her, he didn't want her to see him like this. Even if she answered his letter, he wouldn't write back. As uncertain as his future stood, she had no place in his life.

CHAPTER 25

NERVES FINALLY CAUGHT up with Sallie as she stared through the train window when it pulled into the Baton Rouge station Monday afternoon. When they had changed trains in Houston, she'd managed to send a wire to Tom to let him know when they would arrive. Now she prayed he'd be there to meet her and Andrew. She didn't relish the idea of spending the night in Baton Rouge when she was so close to home.

Butterflies flitted about her stomach as what-if scenarios raced through her head. What if Tom didn't get her wire? What if Mother was worse? What if she died? What if she had to stay longer?

The train screeched to a stop and Sallie steeled her spine. No more questions. The Lord would help her handle whatever may come.

Andrew stood and smiled down at her. As if reading her mind, he said, "Don't worry, Mrs. Whiteman. Everything will be all right." He extended his hand and helped her to stand.

"Oh, my, Andrew, I'm so glad you came with me. I don't know what I would have done without you. This has been a much longer trip than I anticipated." This time she'd had too much time to worry and fret over what she might find at her mother's.

"It's been a pleasure, and I will check on your mother just as I promised. I hope Tom and Marissa won't mind."

"Of course they won't. It'll be good to have another

opinion." She reached for her travel bag. "Now let's get on with this visit."

She strode down the aisle toward the door and stepped down to the platform. As soon as her foot touched ground, a shout drew her attention.

"Sallie! Sallie! We're here."

Tom and Laurie rushed toward her through the throngs of passengers. Tom stopped in front of her and then reached out to hug her. "We're so relieved you're here. Mama's been asking for you ever since we told her you were coming. I'm so sorry you had to travel alone."

"Oh, but I didn't. Dr. Delmont, Manfred's associate, came with me. He has an appointment with a doctor at Charity on Thursday to see about a position on the teaching staff there."

Tom extended his hand in greeting. "Thank you, Dr. Delmont. We appreciate your coming with her."

"I was glad to do it."

Marissa hugged Sallie and spoke in low tones so only Sallie could hear. "Tom has been worried sick that you wouldn't get to come after all. He was so thankful to get your wire."

Of course she'd come, what was Tom thinking? "I hope he doesn't mind, but I asked Dr. Delmont to check Mama and give his opinion."

Marissa nodded then stepped back as Tom motioned to his driver to load Sallie's larger bag onto the carriage that waited at a hitching post. "Tompkins will take care of getting the luggage loaded. We'll eat before we head back to St. Francisville. Even then we should be able to get back home before dark."

Although it was another delay, she did need to eat to

keep up her strength. "All right, but you must fill me in on everything while we eat."

She followed her brother to the carriage he'd brought from St. Francisville. Andrew and Tom talked for a few minutes outside the carriage after she and Marissa had been seated. From the grim expression on Tom's face, Mama's condition must not be good. She twisted her handkerchief in her fingers and bit her lip.

Marissa leaned over to cover Sallie's hands. "He'll tell you everything in a few minutes."

Sallie only nodded, but a chill skittered through her as the fears she'd experienced earlier resurfaced.

Andrew climbed in and seated himself beside her then Tom sat next to Marissa across from them. Once the carriage began to move, Tom cleared his throat.

"Sallie, Mama is not well at all. The fall didn't break anything, but what caused the fall has left her somewhat incapacitated." He hesitated, reached over, and squeezed her hands in his. "She can still speak and she recognizes us, but her left side is useless and her right side weak. The doctor has her confined to bed for most of the time. We have a wheeled chair for when she wants to move about. We moved her to our home but she'd much rather be in her own."

Sallie's heart grew heavier with each word he spoke. She wished she could have been here sooner, but now that she was, the best was not too good for Mama. "We can arrange for that, and I can take care of her as long as she needs me." Molly and Clara would have to understand and be willing to assume responsibility at home for a while longer. Manfred had already told her to take all the time she needed.

Tompkins drove them to a restaurant where they had a quick meal of shrimp creole and beignets before heading for St. Francisville. Sallie hadn't realized she even missed the flavors and sights of Louisiana until now, and she soaked them all in as they rode. Moss hung from huge trees like her grandfather's beard. Magnolia trees graced the area with their waxy green leaves, and the crepe myrtles were in full bloom. The pink crepe trees reminded her of her favorite house, The Myrtles, so named because of the flowering trees in abundance around the French-style home.

Andrew and Tom discussed the hospital and why Andrew had chosen to move from Texas. "I'm not sure of the move yet. It will all depend on Clarissa Elliot and what her parents have to say. I knew they wouldn't want her to come to Texas with me, so I decided I could come to her. She doesn't even know about this visit because it happened so quickly after Mrs. Whiteman received your news."

Tom grinned and winked at Sallie. "Clarissa Elliot, you say. We've known the family for years, and Clarissa is quite the talented and lovely young woman."

Andrew's cheeks flamed red. "Yes, sir, I know. She sang for us when they visited and she has a beautiful voice. Since she doesn't know of my coming, I'm hoping she will welcome me."

"I'm sure she will, and we'll have to invite them for dinner one evening while you're here. When did you say you are to go to New Orleans to meet with the doctor there?"

"On Thursday, and I'm not sure how much time I'll have for socializing once I get there. If Dr. Sutton is agreeable, I will work with him for a week or so and get the feel of the hospital. If all goes well there and with Clarissa, then I will make plans to remain in New Orleans."

Sallie listened, but didn't contribute any more to the conversation. Her mind could not rid itself of the images of her mother in the past. A vibrant, active woman, she had been the rock that steadied Sallie so many years ago when things were so bad during and after the war. Even after the damage to her own home she remained positive and happy. To think of her ill and bed-ridden was almost more than Sallie could bear.

They finally arrived at Tom's home in the heat of the early evening. One other thing hadn't changed. The humidity was as bad as it ever had been. Sallie's shirt-waist stuck to her back as Tom helped her down from the carriage.

"Mother is in the library at the back of the house. It was too difficult for her to be upstairs, so we made the library into a bedroom for her."

"I'll find it." She rushed up the steps and into the house. How thoughtful of Tom to think of Mama and make her comfortable downstairs. She paused in the parlor and shook her head. Not a thing out of place. The lamps sat squarely on crocheted doilies and not a spot marred the upholstery of the sofa and chairs. How nice it must be to have servants take care of things.

Double doors opened into a room lined with shelves of books. A bed had been set against one wall with a table and lamp beside it. The desk, chair, and reading table she remembered from the past must be stored away.

At the sight of the slight frame lying under a sheet on the bed, Sallie gasped and fell to the floor beside her mother. "Mama, it's Sallie, I'm here."

Eyelids fluttered before finally opening. When they focused on Sallie's face, a broad smile formed on Mama's lips. She tried to lift her hand, but it rose only an inch or so. Sallie clasped it and kissed the gnarled knuckles. "Oh, Mama, I'm so sorry you're ill. I came as quickly as I could, and Hannah will come later."

"You're here…that's all…that matters…now." She blinked away a tear.

Her faltering speech brought tears to Sallie's eyes. From the looks of things right now, this was going to be a difficult visit, but she planned to spend every moment of it making her mother comfortable and happy.

Stefan swallowed the moan that filled his throat when he tried to move. The ride over rough terrain in the medical wagon had created a few new aches and pains, but nothing like the burns on his face and arms. The doctor had said that his hat was the only thing that had kept the fire from searing his scalp too.

His wounds had been cleaned and protected once again before leaving the fort. Nurse Harrison had ridden with him to the town where he'd been loaded aboard a train headed east. He'd lost count of the days because of the medications that kept him sedated most of the time.

Seats had been arranged to give him ample room to lie down, which he did most of the time. A soldier about Stefan's age accompanied him on the train and now sat beside him. Most of the other passengers had stared at first then averted their gazes.

Stefan spoke to the young man. "Corporal Dennis, what day is it?"

"It's Tuesday morning, July 10, sir. We should be arriving in Baton Rouge on Thursday morning. From there they'll transport you down to New Orleans and Charity hospital."

Another two days of this swaying and screeching across the countryside must be endured before he could sleep in a real bed. This time was so different from the trip he and his family had taken to Texas. Then his anticipation for seeing Molly filled his thoughts, but now his heart grieved that he'd never see her again. She deserved a man who was whole and could provide for her, not a scarred cripple like himself.

The corporal touched his shoulder. "Sir, are you all right? Are you in need of more pain relief?"

Stefan shook his head and the pain caused him to wince. "No, I'll be okay. I'll try to sleep." No matter how much he may hurt, he'd stand the pain as long as possible. He'd heard too many stories of wounded men becoming addicted to pain drugs. He vowed to never let that happen to him. It was bad enough to be scarred for life, but to have that hanging over him too would be more than he could bear.

Prayers for relief had reached closed ears. After all his cursing and blaming God the past few days, his soul was as empty as a creek bed in a drought. Why would God listen to him now? He'd ignored all of Stefan's requests in the past days, so no answers now did not come as a surprise.

Someone touched him again, and he opened his eye to find a woman standing over him. "Young man, my name is Helen Barnes. I've been watching you and can see that you're in a great deal of pain. Do you mind if I pray for you?"

Stefan stared at her. The last thing he wanted was some stranger taking pity on him. He'd take care of himself without the meddling of any do-good Christian. But Mrs. Barnes's eyes held such sincerity that Stefan's resolve slipped a notch. "Thank you, ma'am."

He closed his eyes and let her words rain over him. Would God listen to her pleas for mercy and healing? He doubted it, but he wouldn't stop her from trying.

After she said amen, Mrs. Barnes patted his arm again. "You get some rest now. God will take care of you." Her skirt swished as she turned and walked away.

Sure God would take care of him, just like He had for the past few months. If that was God taking care of him, he didn't need His care. All Stefan wanted was for God to leave him alone.

CHAPTER 26

A FTER ANDREW EXAMINED Mrs. Dyer Monday evening, he agreed that the diagnosis by their family physician, Dr. Collins, appeared to be correct. The paralysis on one side and the slurred speech were indicative of bleeding on the brain or what her physician called apoplexy. Her doctor was treating her with everything he had available for such problems, but the prognosis did not look good.

Today Tom and several of his servants, as well as Dr. Collins, would be moving Mrs. Dyer back to her home, where she'd be under her daughter's care. After arriving at the Dyer home last night, Andrew had spent his time helping Mrs. Whiteman prepare a room downstairs in what had been Judge Woodruff's private study. Bookshelves lined the walls but the desk and other furnishings had been removed, and a bed with a side table and a chest for supplies and clothing had been moved in with the help of Tom and George, the man who took care of the outside work of the Dyer home.

Mrs. Whiteman met him in the downstairs hall. "Good morning, Andrew. Flora has breakfast ready for us." She led him into the dining room where two places had been set. The sideboard held a steaming bowl of eggs, a platter of ham, and a cloth-covered basket of biscuits.

Both helped themselves then sat at the table where Andrew returned thanks. The dining room was much more elegant than the one in the Whiteman home in

Stoney Creek, but the warmth of past years of enter-taining and family meals prevented it from being cold and impersonal.

After the prayer, Mrs. Whiteman placed her napkin on her lap and peered at Andrew. "Do you think it's wise not to let Clarissa know that you are here?"

As much as he wanted to see her, that would have to wait until his visit with the hospital and Dr. Sutton. He had no desire to build up her hopes only to have them dashed if the job at the hospital didn't work out.

"Yes, I do believe it is. Colonel and Mrs. Elliot did not approve of our seeing each other so frequently in Stoney Creek, and I don't believe they would appreciate my visit here."

"Well, I don't see why not. You came with me to check on my mother, and you're a fine young man and a good doctor as well." She buttered a biscuit then set it on her plate. "Andrew, Laurie told me last evening of some prob-lems with the sugarcane crop at the Elliot place. The drought hasn't been kind to the crops this year."

"All the more reason not to upset him with a visit. If and when my affairs are in order and all is finalized with the hospital, I will again approach Mr. Elliot with a request to call on his daughter." Until then he'd have to be satisfied with reading the one letter he'd received from her before leaving Stoney Creek. Clarissa's ultimate happiness con-cerned him more than any visit.

If he could not gain her parents' approval, he would not pursue the matter. If Clarissa went against her parents' wishes and moved to Texas with him, they would never have the peace needed for a successful marriage. How could God bless a union marred by disrespect to one's parents? Until such time as he could seek her affections openly and with approval, he'd avoid pursuing anything other than her friendship.

Mrs. Whiteman reached across and grasped his hand. "I know you will do what is best for both you and Clarissa. I will pray for good results." Then she nibbled at the corner of her mouth. "Now if only things would work out for Molly and Stefan."

Andrew chuckled at the memory of Molly's joy at declaring her love for Stefan. "I'm sure he'll be elated when he gets the letter she planned to write. God does work in strange ways to accomplish His purposes, especially in that relationship." He'd never forget that look of fear in Molly's eyes when he untied her. Too bad she'd had to experience evil before she could understand the necessity of force to restrain it.

After breakfast, Tom and his servant Tompkins arrived with Mrs. Dyer. They brought her into the prepared room and laid her on the bed. Her pallor sent warning signals through Andrew. As soon as they had her settled, he checked her pulse. Satisfied to find a steady beat, he stepped back and let Mrs. Whiteman arrange the pillows and sheets for Mrs. Dyer's comfort.

The ashen appearance must be caused by the stress of the trip from Tom's home. If so, a little nourishment and rest this morning should restore the color to her cheeks.

After the men left, Flora brought in a bowl of broth and a cup of herb tea for Mrs. Dyer. Andrew only stayed a few minutes to see that Mrs. Dyer downed a few sips of the broth. When he left the room and closed the door behind him, Flora waited in the hall.

"Mistuh Andrew, she don't look good to me. Is what the doctor been telling us true?"

The concern in the dark eyes of the servant reflected her respect and love for Mrs. Dyer. "Yes, Flora. She's had a type of brain injury that causes bleeding. She needs rest and plenty of fluids to keep her hydrated. Also, we need to keep her slightly elevated so pneumonia won't develop."

"I can do that. I's shore glad Miss Sallie is here to see to her. I didn't like one bit for her to be off to Mr. Tom's. Not that he's not a good son, but Miss Sallie, she knows what her momma needs."

She turned to leave then whipped back around. "Mr. Andrew, tell me about Hannah. Is she happy?"

Andrew grinned and patted Flora's shoulder. "She's as happy as she can be with her two little ones and living out on the ranch. Micah Gordon is good to her and loves her more than you could imagine."

"What about my Lettie? Is she doing okay, too?"

"She sure is. She promised to come over and help Molly if she needed it. Burt is a good blacksmith and the town has fully accepted them both as fine, upright citizens."

"That's good. I shore do miss seeing her young'uns. They's about all growed up now."

"They are, and it would be nice if you could come to visit with them sometime. Yancy's as strong as his pa and has started helping in the smithy shop. He has a way with horses, too, and Mr. Gordon was talking to him about coming to work at the ranch."

Flora's face beamed with delight as he told her more about her family. He'd always liked Lettie and Burt Sanger, and after meeting Flora, Andrew could see where Lettie came by her kindness to others.

"Thank you, Mr. Andrew. That does ease my mind a bit. Don't know that I'll git over that way, but iffens I do, I hope I see you."

"I'm sure Lettie and Burt would be more than happy for you to visit, and I'd like to see you too, if you come."

She grinned, her smile flashing pleasure with his report. Then she tucked her hands into the folds of her apron and hurried back in the direction of the kitchen.

The way of life in the South was certainly different from anything he'd ever been around in Texas. From what he'd heard, the Negroes still had trouble making a life for themselves outside of slavery. Flora and her husband George were the only two servants here at the Dyer home, and from Mrs. Whiteman's story, they'd been around ever since she could remember, and they weren't slaves but freed household help.

If the Elliots owned a sugarcane plantation, did they have slaves to do all the work? He'd never thought to ask that of Clarissa or Stefan. He'd assumed all slavery had stopped, but apparently some still went on with the larger farms. Andrew shook his head. He definitely had a lot to learn about the way of life of people in the South. Strange how Louisiana bordered his own home of Texas, but could be so completely different in culture and way of living.

"Molly, Molly, I have the mail, and there's a letter for you!" Clara burst through the kitchen door with the mail in her hand.

"Land sakes, I could hear you coming a mile away." Molly grinned and reached for the stack of envelopes.

"Only one you'll be interested in. It's from a place called Arizona." Clara held the letter high with a wicked gleam in her eye.

Molly grabbed it and held it close to her chest. The letter she'd been waiting for had at last arrived. She waved toward the stove. "Watch the stew and the biscuits in the oven. Don't let them burn unless you want cold jelly on bread for lunch today."

"I suppose I can do that for you." The gleam still shone in her eyes. "If my beau was that far away, I guess I'd be excited to hear from him."

Molly flipped the dishtowel toward Clara, who ducked and laughed but grabbed her apron. "Go on now. I can take care of this."

With the letter still clasped to her chest, Molly raced up the stairs to her room, where she could read Stefan's letter in private. She flopped on her bed then tore open the flap and pulled out a single sheet of paper written on both sides.

After reading it through once, she propped herself on a pillow against the headboard of her bed and commenced to reread the letter. He talked about being back at the fort and taking part in drills as well as how much he liked Warrior, his new horse. He was perfect for the army and followed orders like a regular soldier. He mentioned Clarissa and how she missed Andrew and how he'd pray for them to work out their lives.

Then she stopped to read more slowly and devour the parts about their time together.

> Molly, I treasure the time we spent with one another in Stoney Creek. Your laughter still rings in my

head when I think of you. I also remember the glow about you when you talked about the children in your classes. I pray you enjoyed our time together as much as I did.

She frowned as the remaining words reminded her of how stubborn she'd been in her attitude toward the military and Stefan's chosen career. How could she have been so mule-headed?

Life here is hard, Molly. I've watched the other women, and they have so much to take care of each day as their men leave on duty patrols. It's a lonely life confined within the fort walls, and the terrain around us is barren and dry and hot. I wouldn't even think of asking you to come here to live now that I've come back and really see what life is like here for the military wives. I do miss you, but I love you too much to ask you to give up your life there in Stoney Creek for me, especially knowing how much you dislike the military. I will always keep you in my heart and pray that someday we see each other again.
Ever Yours,
Stefan

Tears welled in her eyes and blurred the words but joy filled her heart. He didn't know of her change of heart. Of course he wouldn't ask her to come to him with the attitudes she'd displayed while he'd been with her. She had to get her letter to him right away so he'd know how much she'd changed and how much she wanted to be with him.

She jumped up from the bed and searched in her writing table drawer until she found the letter and an envelope. Seated at the table, Molly took up her pen and copied Stefan's address onto the blank paper. After sealing the envelope and placing a stamp in the corner, she sat back to revel in her thoughts and feelings for Stefan.

The mail wouldn't go out until tomorrow's train, but then it would streak its way on the rails to Arizona and into Stefan's hands. Then he'd know how much she loved him and wanted to be with him no matter where he lived or what he did.

CHAPTER 27

On Thursday morning Andrew checked to make sure he had the papers he needed for introduction to Dr. Sutton at the hospital. He secured them in the inside pocket of his suit coat, picked up his satchel, then made his way downstairs to Mrs. Dyer's room. In the past few days he'd heard numerous stories of the days when Sallie, Hannah, and their brothers lived here. He could understand why they loved it so much. His room opened onto a balcony above the front porch. Several plants decorated the space along with a white wicker chair. He'd spent last evening reading in that very spot.

At the foot of the stairs, voices drifted in from the back room where Mrs. Dyer lay. He recognized Sallie Whiteman's, but not the man's. Not wanting to intrude, he stopped at the doorway and found a man in a black suit with a white clerical collar speaking to Mrs. Dyer.

Mrs. Whiteman turned to see him at the door and motioned for him to come in. "Andrew, this is the rector from our church, Reverend William Douglas."

Andrew extended his hand in greeting as Mrs. Whiteman continued. "Dr. Delmont is Manfred's associate in Stoney Creek. He accompanied me on the train and is going down to New Orleans on the morning boat to see about a position at Charity Hospital there."

The rector gripped Andrew's hand with a firm hold. "I'm pleased to meet you, and so glad you were able to come with Mrs. Whiteman. I will pray that all goes well on your visit to Charity."

"Thank you." He reached down and held Mrs. Dyer's hand. "I'll be back to see you as soon as I return from New Orleans, but that may be several days." Her color this morning appeared even paler than it had earlier, but that could still be a result of the move.

The older woman smiled but did not attempt to speak. Mrs. Whiteman bent over and kissed her mother's cheek. "I'll see Andrew out and then be back. The rector will stay with you until I return."

She escorted Andrew outside where she hugged him. "I do pray all goes well. We would miss you in Stoney Creek, but if this is where God wants you and it will bring you closer to Clarissa, then this is best for everyone."

The more he'd thought about it the more determined he became to win Colonel and Mrs. Elliot's approval. Andrew would never expect Clarissa to defy her parents' wishes for her, but if she still loved him as she claimed, with God's help, they would find a way to gain consent from her parents.

Down at the steamboat landing, he met two of Manfred's brothers, Edwin and Theo. They had taken over the shipping company after the death of their parents and kept it going as a thriving business in Bayou Sara. After exchanging news of the family in Stoney Creek, Andrew boarded the steamboat to take him down river to New Orleans. He leaned over the railing and gazed at the banks of the mighty Mississippi River and the town of Bayou Sara. He'd read about the river in geography books, but to actually see the expanse of water took his breath away.

A shrill blast from the boat signaled they would be

underway, and the gangplank was lifted and stored. The activity brought to mind the story Mrs. Whiteman had told him about the day the war stopped for the burial of a Union Navy captain who was also a Mason and desired a Masonic funeral service and burial. All fighting ceased that day to carry out the man's wishes.

The memory served to reinforce Andrew's belief that war didn't have to take away man's concern for others, and true courage came when enemies showed compassion and cared about one another. Maybe others called it a fantasy, but it was the United States he wanted to see.

An hour after a late lunch on board the boat they landed in New Orleans. Andrew stepped onto the dock and searched the crowd. Dr. Sutton had arranged for a buggy to pick him up and take him to the hospital, and in minute, Andrew spied a sign held high with his name printed on it. He strode toward the man and stopped.

"I'm Dr. Delmont. I believe you have a buggy waiting for me."

The man nodded. "Yes, sir, right this way." The driver led him to the waiting vehicle tethered in front of the steamship office.

A short time later, Dr. Sutton greeted him in his office. "Come in, come in, young man. Dr. Whiteman has told me much about you in the wire he sent me."

Andrew shook the man's hand and followed him into his office. Dr. Whiteman had told Andrew that the Sisters of Charity had taken over the hospital in the 1830s and still ran it, but it was also one of the finest teaching hospitals in the South.

After going over what was to be expected in the next few days, Dr. Sutton informed Andrew that he'd be staying in the resident quarters at the hospital. With that said, the doctor stood and motioned for Andrew to follow him. "Let's take a tour so you can see what we're all about here. After that I'll show you to your quarters."

The tour lasted an hour with visits to all of the departments in the hospital. Andrew's head swam with so many details and the magnitude of the services offered, from emergency treatments to pathology to a burn unit in addition to a well-equipped, fully up-to-date surgical unit. Despite the abundance of what he had to retain from the tour, Andrew determined to learn everything he could and be worthy of the trust Dr. Whiteman had put in him.

With a squeal of iron wheels on the tracks and a hiss of the engines, the train pulled into New Orleans, where an ambulance wagon waited to transport Stefan to the hospital. His escort from Fort Apache stood by his stretcher before the attendants loaded him onto the wagon.

"I have enjoyed these few days with you, Lieutenant Elliot. We all will be praying for your quick recovery." He saluted then stepped back. "Have a safe trip."

Stefan returned a somewhat clumsy salute with the bandages on his hands. "You have a safe trip back to the fort too, Corporal Dennis. I appreciated your company."

The young soldier nodded then turned and headed for the train that would take him back through Texas and New Mexico to Arizona Territory.

Two attendants picked up the stretcher and placed it in the back of the ambulance. One stayed with him and the other climbed up front to drive them away. As much as

Stefan loved New Orleans, this was not the way he would wish to visit.

Charity was a good hospital with its connection to the university and medical school. No doubt he'd get excellent care, but he'd much rather be at his home in St. Francisville. Mother could nurse him back to health and take care of his wounds, but it would be best to wait until he'd healed some before giving her that responsibility.

The short trip to the hospital turned out to be less stressful than the train ride. The road lay smooth beneath the wheels without the bumping and jostling usually expected with a wagon ride. After a dose of his pain medication, Stefan drifted off to sleep.

A beautiful woman ran toward him with arms outstretched and love glowing in her eyes. His Molly had come to him. As she drew nearer to him, the love changed to surprise and then to horror. Her eyes opened wide and her hand covered her mouth. He spoke to her, called her name, and reached out for her. She backed away with fear and pity replacing the glow once in her eyes.

Stefan jerked awake. His dream had become a nightmare when Molly saw his face. He lifted a gauze-covered hand to his head, where bandages covered the burns on the side of his face. His face would be scarred, no doubt about that, and he'd never let Molly see the scars. She deserved a whole man, not one with half a face and an almost useless hand.

He turned his head to the left on his pillow in an effort to get his bearings as to where he was with his one good eye. It had to be some kind of ward since he could see four other beds besides his between him and the doorway.

Then he remembered. Charity Hospital in New Orleans

was his new home. White walls, white iron beds, and white furniture comprised his new quarters. As to how long he'd be here, he had no idea, but the bed was comfortable, especially after sleeping on a canvas cot so many days.

The door standing open revealed doctors and nurses as they hustled and bustled back and forth in the hallway. The medicinal odors of antiseptic and alcohol permeated the room and caused his nose to wrinkle. He'd better get used to it since he'd probably be here a while.

He started to turn away from the scene in the hallway, but a familiar figure stopped him. Two doctors stood in front of the door with their heads together discussing who-knew-what. Stefan squinted and peered more closely at the younger man. Andrew? It looked just like him. Impossible. Andrew was in Stoney Creek. He couldn't be here in New Orleans. Stefan tried to call out, but his efforts produced only a raspy sound that even he couldn't understand. The two men then proceeded down the hall and out of Stefan's sight. He must be dreaming or hallucinating. He closed his eyes and waited for sleep to overtake him again.

CHAPTER 28

STEFAN AWAKENED TO bright sunlight streaming through the window near his bed. He blinked and gazed at the ceiling. Everything from his waist up hurt. Then he remembered coming to the hospital. How long had he been asleep? Was this a new day or the same one? He raised his head slightly. Men in the other beds on the ward either sat on the edge of the bed or still lay flat. Pain once again throbbed in his face and he lay back on the pillow.

A nurse appeared by his side and smiled. "Good morning, Lieutenant Elliot. How are you this morning?"

He focused his one eye and the kindly face of an older woman became clear. She fluffed the pillow behind his head and straightened his sheets. "What day is this, nurse?"

"It's Friday, July 13. You were brought in yesterday and have been asleep most of the time since then. We gave you quite a bit of medication so you wouldn't feel your pain."

"Morphine?"

"Yes. It does make the pain disappear."

Stefan cringed. That may be true, but too much could be a bad thing. He never wanted to become dependent on it as he'd seen others do. He may hurt, but unless it grew much worse than this, he'd bear it without the drug.

"Your breakfast will be here shortly, and you really need to try and eat as much as you can since you missed supper last night."

As if on cue, Stefan's stomach rumbled and hunger pangs gripped him. "I'd welcome a good breakfast." And a good cup of coffee. A few days had become like years since he'd enjoyed his morning brew.

A young woman entered with a cart loaded with trays. She placed one beside Stefan's bed and then did the same for the others in the ward. His nurse grasped his arms. "Here, let me help you sit up." When he raised his shoulders off the mattress, she arranged the pillows behind him to give him support to sit up and eat.

Pain once again shot through his shoulder and up into his neck then his face, but he fought it off. Stefan grabbed his fork and speared a slice of bacon. He savored the salty pork on his tongue before swallowing then shoveled a forkful of scrambled eggs into his mouth. Not as good as those at home but a little better than a breakfast at the fort. He devoured the remainder of the meal and downed the hot coffee as though it were his last cup.

When the nurse returned, she laughed at his clean plate. "Well, I see your injuries didn't damage your appetite any." She removed the tray. "Do you want to remain sitting or lie back down?"

"I think I'd like to sit up for a while." He'd been lying flat for so long that having his head up so he could look around better was a great relief.

A figure appeared at the door, and Stefan swallowed hard. Not yet, it was too soon. His father strode across to Stefan's bed with his mother right behind him. The shock and dismay in their faces caused Stefan to clench his teeth, but that sent pain to his neck and cheek. He attempted a smile.

"Hello, Father, Mother."

His mother reached out her hand, but couldn't find a place to touch him. She drew it back to her chest. "We came as soon as we could after receiving the wire that you were here." Tears glistened in her eyes.

Exactly what he didn't want, pity. His father's mouth worked in a way that let Stefan know he searched for the words to convey his feelings. Finally he placed a hand on Stefan's head.

"We're proud of you, son. You fought valiantly against overwhelming odds."

The words filled Stefan with hope that there would be no condemnation from his father. "I only did what I was trained to do, but I still lost some good men."

"Yes, and that happens in battle. Your mother and I are thankful you are alive, and we intend to see that you get the best care available. We were shocked to find the extent of your injuries. We've made arrangements for you to be moved to a more private room this morning so true healing can begin."

A smaller room would be nice. Already the coughing, moans, and snores from the other men had begun to irritate him. Then his attitude shamed him. He was fortunate to be in any hospital. "Thank you, but I don't need another room. I'm fine here with these men. Some of them are in much worse condition than I am."

His father frowned, as did Mother, but neither protested or tried to persuade him differently. Mother finally placed her hand over one of his bandaged ones. Tears still filled her eyes.

"Don't cry, Mother. I'll be all right."

"Son, I'm crying because I'm so happy you're alive. Dr. Sutton is one of the best doctors in New Orleans, and he's going to get you up and around before you know it. Then you can come home with us."

His father leaned over and grasped Stefan's shoulder. "We know the extent of your injuries. The doctor told us that your hat protected your head from the heat and flames, but where were your gloves? They would have protected your hands."

Stefan searched his memory for what had happened. "I remember taking them off to get my jacket off to beat the flames in the wagon. I did feel the heat on my face and hands, and flames did hit the side of my face as I fought."

"Taking them off is what caused the injuries on your hands, especially your right hand."

Stefan glanced down at the bandages covering that hand completely. The fingers on his left hand extended from the gauzed wrapped there. If the burns were that bad, what use would his right hand be? The pain in his cheek reminded him of the burns there, and he winced. What kind of scars would be left to endure?

"You do know this is going to end your military career. I'm more than sorry about that, but it's to be expected with the injuries to your hands."

Stefan choked back a sob. Discharge from the army had been inevitable, but no one had spoken of it before he left the fort. To hear it now from his father's lips added to the despair gnawing at his gut. If he didn't have the military, what did he have?

A doctor edged his way to Stefan's bedside. "Hello, Lieutenant. I'm Dr. Sutton, and I am going to get you up and about in no time." He turned to Stefan's parents. "You may want to leave the room for a few moments. I'm going to take off the bandages to check the wounds. The bullet wound is healing well. His chart tells me that only soft tissue was damaged with no major blood vessels, organs, or bones affected. I'll know more after I check it all."

Mother opened her mouth to protest, and Stefan almost laughed when his father clamped his hand on her arm. "Not now, my dear. Let's go into the hall and wait for Dr. Sutton to call us back."

Trust his father to spare his mother any more grief. After they disappeared into the hall, another doctor who had remained to the side, his back to Stefan and his parents, turned around and stood beside Dr. Sutton.

"Hello, Stefan."

Stefan gasped and shook his head. "Andrew? What are you doing here?" He hadn't been an imagination or hallucination after all.

After a cursory glance through the envelopes and finding them all addressed to her father, Molly tossed the mail on the entryway table. It was still too early to expect a letter from Stefan or her mother but she could always hope. She laid her purse and gloves aside and turned toward the kitchen.

Three figures stepped in front of her. Her two youngest sisters stood with hands on hips and frowns rearranging their mouths. Danny stayed behind them, but from his expression, he was none too happy either.

"Now, why all the glum faces? Did I forget something?"

Alice huffed out her breath. "You sure did. You're

supposed to take us out to the ranch. Aunt Hannah and Aunt Ellie said we could go out there and ride horses today."

Danny nodded his head at such a rapid rate, Molly feared it'd come loose. "You sure did, Molly, and it's not fair for you to go running all over town and not take us. Why didn't you get Clara to fetch the mail?"

"I'm sorry, it did slip my mind." She grinned at them and picked up her handbag. "Okay, then let's go. If we hurry, we can be there in time for lunch."

Clara pushed through the door from the kitchen. "I was hoping you'd remember, so I have the wagon all hitched and ready to go."

"Well, aren't you the smart one." She herded her brother and sisters in front of her. "Let's hurry along now and take advantage of Clara's thoughtfulness." Maybe a good ride out to the country would take her mind away from Stefan and the uneasy feeling that something wasn't right.

The girls all chattered away in the back of the wagon, but Danny rode up beside her. He didn't talk all the way to the Gordon home. Molly cut her eyes to gaze at his profile. When had he grown up? He may be only twelve years old, but already he was as tall as Molly and Clara and needed only a few inches to catch up with his brother. His arms had begun to fill out and weren't the scrawny ones of last year. All too soon he'd be a young man and not a little boy any longer.

Molly sighed and glanced over her shoulder. At least the youngest of her sisters still had her childhood. Their innocent giggles and whispers filled her heart with love. If she moved away to be with Stefan, she'd sorely miss them, but then she'd start having babies of her own.

Heat rushed to her cheeks. She shouldn't be thinking

such things. She didn't even know if Stefan still cared about her, much less wanted her for a bride. Best not to get too far ahead of God with her dreams and plans.

When they pulled into her aunt's yard, Grace ran from the house to greet the girls with Joel, Joshua, and Jeremy close behind. That meant Ellie had arrived, and Molly savored the opportunity to visit with her teaching partner.

Grace hugged Molly around her waist. "I'm glad you were so brave and saved Starlight. I couldn't stand the thought of losing him."

Molly hugged her cousin. Bravery had nothing to do with it really, but Grace's gratitude helped with the bad memories. "I'm glad, too. He's a beautiful horse."

Molly led the girls to the barn and the horses there. Clara waved to Molly. "You go ahead and visit with Hannah and Ellie. I'll take care of the others."

Molly laughed and waved back. Not until then had she noticed Clara had worn her split skirt for riding. No wonder she had been anxious to get started. Her sister was almost as crazy as Grace about horses.

Hannah and Ellie waited for Molly on the front porch of the huge ranch house. At two stories high and on a slight hill, it rose with majesty and dignity. Mrs. Gordon joined her daughters-in-law and greeted Molly with a hug.

"How are you doing, my child, with your mother gone?"

"We're getting along fine. Haven't heard yet from Mama, but we should have a letter soon." Molly returned the hug and followed the ladies into the house.

Leather chairs sat on either side of the stone fireplace dominating that side of the room. The stairs to the second floor rose from the center of the expanse, making a nice divider between the parlor and dining area, which had ample room for the ever-growing Gordon clan.

Hannah and Mrs. Gordon headed for the kitchen to finish preparations for lunch. "Shouldn't we go help them? I hate to come out here and then do nothing to help when I brought five extra mouths to feed."

Ellie shook her head. "No, I've already tried. They shooed me out of the way. I did bring dessert, so that will be my contribution."

"I hope it's some of your berry cobbler. I saw an abundance of the berries last week when I was out riding." Ellie had a magic touch when making pastry. Her crusts were so flaky and tender they all but melted in one's mouth.

"It is, and I made plenty. We even have fresh cream for it." Ellie leaned forward, her elbows resting on her knees. "Tell me how you are since that business on the Fourth."

Had it really been only a little over a week since the incident in the livery? "I'm fine, really. In fact better than fine. That little scare made me realize how unrealistic I've been about guns and such. That was what kept me from giving my love completely to Stefan. I couldn't stand the thought of him in the military."

Ellie's eyes sparkled, and she grinned. "And now?"

"I've already written to him and told him of my change of heart and how much I want to be with him no matter where he is or what he does."

"I'm so proud of you. Takes courage to admit you've been so wrong about something like that." Ellie rose and came over to hug Molly.

"We'll see. I haven't heard back from him yet, and it may be that he doesn't care for me that way at all." She had to accept that possibility, but if that last kiss was any indication then he loved her as much as she loved him. The days ahead loomed as eternity. When would she hear from him again?

CHAPTER 29

STEFAN PEERED AT Andrew as Dr. Sutton completed his examination. What was the meaning of Andrew's presence? He hadn't answered Stefan's question, and wouldn't look at him. Instead Andrew concentrated on everything Dr. Sutton did as he removed bandages.

"Andrew, why are you here? Why aren't you in Stoney Creek?" Stefan winced as more bandages came off his burns.

Dr. Sutton stopped and glanced from Stefan to Andrew and back again. "You two know each other?"

Andrew nodded. "Yes, Lieutenant Elliot and his family visited Stoney Creek a few weeks back and we became acquainted then." He glanced down at Stefan. "I'll explain what I'm doing here after Dr. Sutton is done."

"I see." Dr. Sutton continued his examination. "You have what we call second-degree burns on your face and hands from the heat of the flames. You'll have scars, but I'm more concerned with your right hand. It's had more severe burns that have damaged your fingers."

Stefan's heart pounded against his ribs and bile rose in his throat. "Exactly what does that mean?"

Dr. Sutton placed his fingertips on Stefan's chin and turned his face to have a better look at the burns there. "That depends on you, young man." He touched the area around Stefan's right eye. "I'm going to remove this patch from your eye. Tell me what you see."

Stefan braced himself against the removal, but the gentle touch of the doctor lifted the bandage with no pain to Stefan. He blinked his eye and hazy images formed, but no focus. "I see color and shapes, but nothing clearly."

A grin spread across the doctor's face. "Excellent. That means your eye wasn't damaged by the burns. The burns are mainly confined to your right cheek below the eye and down onto your neck."

"But I can't see anything but blurs and haze. How can that be good?" Stefan continued to blink in an attempt to focus.

"Your vision will return. I'll leave the patch off now, and possibly by the end of the day you'll see more clearly." He turned to the nurse who had come back to the bedside. "I need new dressings for the bullet wound."

She nodded and left to fulfill his request. "I'm going to leave the burns on your face uncovered for now and let them heal, but we'll keep a close eye on them to make sure no infection occurs. Your left hand is healing well, but your right hand needs the bandages."

Stefan nodded as the doctor explained. That right hand was the main cause of his discharge from the service. Disappointment and pain clogged his throat. Not a physical pain, but one of failure. Of what use would he be to anyone with a hand that couldn't control a rifle?

While the doctor and nurse tended him, thoughts and images raced across the windows of his soul and collided with such force they scattered like leaves in the wind. Nothing came together except the fact he would no longer wear the uniform of the United States, and could not carry on the legacy of his father and grandfathers before him.

The one image he refused to acknowledge was that

of Molly. He'd be of no use to her now, and the less he thought about her the easier it would be to forget her. What had once been a bright future lay dark and hopeless in the ashes of his injuries. He reminded himself once again that she deserved more than a scarred face and a crippled hand.

As the doctor completed his work, Stefan stared at Andrew, still seeking answers, but Andrew remained silent. Stefan clenched his teeth then relaxed as that action sent needles of torture to his face. "Are you going to tell me why you're in New Orleans? Does Clarissa know?"

Andrew blinked and nodded. "As soon as Dr. Sutton is done, we can talk." He glanced at the doctor. "If that's all right with you?"

"Yes, I'll go out and speak with his parents then you can rejoin me for the remaining rounds." Dr. Sutton turned and headed for the door.

"All right, I guess you do deserve an explanation. I had no idea you were here, and I'm deeply sorry for your injuries."

Stefan opened his mouth to ask again about his presence, but Andrew held up his hand. "No, don't talk. Just listen. We have only a few minutes before your parents return. Neither they nor Clarissa know I'm here. Dr. Whiteman secured permission for me to come here and meet with Dr. Sutton about the possibility of my serving on the staff at Charity. Since I didn't know how it would turn out, I didn't inform your parents or Clarissa. If things do work out, I'm hoping to seek your parents' approval to ask Clarissa to be my wife."

Stefan's eyes widened. If Andrew moved to New Orleans, then his parents shouldn't have any objections to the relationship. "That's splendid, Andrew. When will you tell her?"

"As soon as I know more about my duties and responsibilities here and if it's what God wants me to do." He cocked his head to one side. "Mrs. Whiteman is in St. Francisville with her mother. Does she or her family, more specifically, Molly, know about your injuries?"

"No, and you must not tell them. I can't let Molly see me like this. This is exactly what she worried would happen." He wouldn't be able to stand seeing the expression on her face when she saw him.

"Molly's changed, Stefan. Some things have happened since you left that—" The voices of Stefan's parents rose outside the door. "I have to leave now. I'll keep your secret if you'll keep mine. Agreed?"

Stefan nodded. "But you'll come back later and finish this?"

"Yes, I will." Then he grabbed a chart and strode toward another patient across the room to escape the entrance of Stefan's parents.

His mother gasped and stifled a sob when she saw the burns on his face. "Oh, Stefan, I'm glad you're alive. Things may look bad now, but you'll recover. We've faced hard times before and we'll get through this just as we did then."

"She's right, son. No matter how dark this looks now, life will return. Don't think for one minute we're disappointed in you. You did what you had to do. Yes, it's sad that you won't be able to serve in the military, but you're alive and well. That's the important thing now."

Tears threatened Stefan's composure. The love of his parents filled him with hope that perhaps he had a future after all. He'd been angry with God for the past week, but

God hadn't caused the attack; and even though good men had been lost, He had chosen to spare the lives of others. Something good had to come from that.

His parents then left him to rest. They planned to return home, make arrangements for a longer visit, and then come back to be with him until his release. The only request he made of them was not to tell Mrs. Whiteman of his injuries. He prayed they'd keep that request, especially Clarissa. Keeping secrets was not her forte.

At the soft knock on the door frame, Sallie glanced up from reading the Bible on her lap. "Yes, Flora, what is it?"

"Miss Clarissa Elliot is here to visit with you and your momma."

"Mama's asleep right now. Tell her I'll be right out. We can sit in the parlor, and a pitcher of tea would be nice."

"Yes'm, Miss Sallie. I'll see to it." She turned and shuffled her way to the kitchen.

Sallie bit her lip. Flora had been around as long as Sallie could remember, and she'd been friends with Flora's daughter Lettie since childhood. Flora and George were getting too far along in years to take care of this big house and the land around it. Even though it'd been her mother's childhood home, it had never been home to Sallie. That had been in Mississippi, where Papa had his cotton exchange.

If Tom or Will didn't want to move back here, then they may have to sell it after Mama was gone. That sent an ache to her heart because of her love for her grandmother and the wonderful childhood memories held within these walls.

Aunt Abigail had passed on last year, and her son now lived in Magnolia Hall. Sallie's cousin Peggy had moved to Baton Rouge with her husband, so with Hannah and Sallie in Texas, no one in the family was left for the home.

Sallie sighed and laid her Bible on the table. No need to keep Clarissa waiting. She bent over and kissed her sleeping mother's forehead. "I'll be back in a bit."

Flora met her in the hallway with the tray holding a pitcher of tea and glasses. "Thank you, Flora. If Mama awakens, please let me know. She'll enjoy a visit from Clarissa."

"Yes'm, Miss Sallie." She followed Sallie into the parlor and set the tray on a table by the sofa.

Sallie extended her arms to embrace Clarissa. "How good to see you, child. Is your mother not feeling well?"

Clarissa returned the hug then sat on the sofa when Sallie did. "Mother is fine. She and Father went down to New Orleans yesterday."

"Oh, how nice for them." Sallie smiled, but stopped and tilted her head. No joy shone from Clarissa's eyes. Had something happened to her parents? How she wished to be able to tell Clarissa that Andrew was also in New Orleans, but she had promised to keep quiet.

As if reading her mind, Clarissa leaned over toward Sallie. "Oh, Mrs. Whiteman, have you any word of Andrew? I haven't heard from him but once since my return. I do miss him so."

"I'm sorry you haven't heard from him. I'm sure you will when he has something to say that might interest you." That was not the most brilliant thing she could have said, but anything else would be lying. Best to change the subject.

Sallie poured a glass of tea and handed it to Clarissa.

"Now tell me, have you heard from Molly? She's taken over the household while I'm here."

"No, ma'am, I haven't had a letter from her since July 5. I did send one to her, but she must be terribly busy and not have time to write."

Clarissa's eyes clouded over again. This time Sallie couldn't contain her concern. She set her glass back on the tray and placed her hand on Clarissa's arm. "My dear, something is troubling you. Is there anything I can do to help?"

Tears welled in Clarissa's eyes. "I don't know if I'm supposed to tell you or not, but Mother and Father didn't go to New Orleans for themselves or even business. Stefan was badly injured in a battle with outlaws in Arizona and has been sent home for treatment."

Sallie's heart skipped a beat and her hand flew to her mouth. "Stefan's injured? Oh, my gracious, I'm so sorry." Her heart ached for Clarissa and her family. If he had to be sent home for treatment, his injuries must be serious. Molly! She'd probably sent a letter to Arizona. She'd be devastated by the news.

Then something Clarissa said earlier hit Sallie. "What did you mean when you said you didn't know if you were supposed to tell me?"

"I...I don't think they want anyone to know about it yet. They went down to see how badly he's injured and didn't tell anyone else in the family."

"I see." But Molly should know. It was only right that she be told, but Jenny was Sallie's best friend, and she would not share the news with anyone until given permission to do so.

She grasped Clarissa's hands. "Looks like you and I have a lot of praying to do."

CHAPTER 30

MOLLY RESISTED THE urge to kick and yell. Another week without a letter from Stefan or Clarissa. She sorted through the envelopes in her hands once again. Nothing but stuff for Papa, including one from Mama. She clumped down the steps from the general store that also served as a post office and strode down the street kicking up dust as she did.

She didn't mind Mama being gone so much, especially since Grandma had taken a turn for the worse and Hannah had gone over to join her, but Molly missed her and their long talks. Papa missed her too. The wistful look on his face at dinner each night served as a reminder he was without his strongest helpmate.

Clara met her on the porch with her hands on her hips and shaking her head. "I feel like wringing our sisters' necks like a chicken. What they can get into drives me crazy."

"What have they done now?" With their mother being gone almost two weeks now, Alice and Juliet had begun to miss her, and the past few days had found trouble to be their constant companion.

"Alice decided to fix Juliet's hair, so she found Mama's scissors and did a little cutting." Clara slumped in a chair on the porch. "Oh, Molly, it looks awful. What will Mama say?"

Oh no, Juliet's long curly golden locks were beautiful, and Mama had been so careful about letting them grow.

How could Alice have done such a thing? "I should have been more diligent in watching them. I knew she didn't like the braid I put in, but that was so much easier than trying to keep it curled and looking the way it should. Where are they?"

"Up in their room."

"All right. I'll take care of them. Be sure Papa gets this letter from Mama. That should cheer him up some." She laid the mail on the porch table then marched into the house and up the stairs to the girls' room.

The sound of sobbing stopped her at their door. "I'm so sorry, Juliet. I was just trying to fix it to look nice. I know you didn't like that old braid." The remorse in her sister's voice and the sobs from the other one softened the anger that had risen. Taking a deep breath, Molly shoved the door open.

Two little girls, one holding a pair of scissors and the other with hair half a dozen different lengths turned teary eyes toward her. Alice dropped the scissors to the floor and bawled like a baby. Juliet sniffled and hiccupped, her cheeks wet with tears.

Molly gathered them in her arms. "I guess I should have been paying more attention to you two." She raked her fingers through Juliet's shorn locks and sighed. "Let's see what we can do with this."

She pulled Juliet from the floor and sat her on the bed and glared down at Alice. "Stop that crying and hand me Mama's scissors so I can fix her hair. We'll talk about what you've done later."

Alice blinked her eyes and swiped at her cheeks with fingers before picking up the scissors and handing them to Molly. "I'm sorry. I didn't mean to ruin her." Then she turned and ran from the room.

In half an hour Molly finally had Juliet's hair trimmed to all the same length. Instead of reaching down her back almost to her waist, it now hung straight and limp at her shoulders. The side front sections were shorter, but she didn't want to cut it all that short. After brushing it out, Molly pulled the shorter front sections to the back and fastened them with a clip and added a bow. "There now, it's shorter, but it looks much better than it did a few minutes ago."

Juliet wrapped her arms around Molly's neck. "Thank you." Then she looked down at the pile of hair on the floor and cried again.

"Oh, Juliet, honey, it'll grow back. Why, by the time school starts, it'll be the right length again."

Juliet blinked her eyes then opened them wide. "Papa."

Molly jerked around to find her father standing in the doorway with a most disturbed look in his eyes. "It's all right. I fixed it so it's all one length, and it'll grow back."

"What, oh, yes, her hair. It looks fine. Juliet, would you let Molly and me have a moment alone?"

Molly's heart pounded as her little sister left the room. Something must have happened to Grandma Dyer—or could it be Mama? "Maybe you better sit down." She led him to a chair.

He sat and held up the letter he had in his hand. "Mama writes that Grandma Dyer is in very poor condition, and the doctors don't give her much longer to live."

Molly dropped to her knees beside her father. "Oh, Papa, I'm so sorry. I know Mama is heartbroken, but I'm glad Hannah is there with her."

"That's not all, my child. She also writes that Stefan has been wounded in battle and is in the hospital in New Orleans. Andrew is helping take care of him."

"Stefan…injured…in New Orleans?" Molly fell back. Her heart squeezed tight, and she could barely catch her breath. "How…what…" A sob escaped her throat.

Papa patted Molly's head as he had when he had comforted her in her childhood. "She doesn't go into details, dear, but it was enough of an injury to require hospitalization at Charity. His family didn't want others to know, but Andrew is keeping your mother updated."

Molly lifted her head and pushed herself up from the floor. "Then I must catch the next train and go to Louisiana. I can stay at Grandma Dyer's house with Mama."

"I'm not sure that will be possible right now. We need you here."

His words tore at her heart. Of course she had an obligation to her family, but she loved Stefan and wanted to be near him. "Yes, Papa, I understand." She did, but still she'd think of a way to persuade her father to allow her to go to New Orleans.

Clara appeared at the door. Her eyes glistened with tears and she held a paper in her hands. "This wire just came from Mama. It's for you, Papa." She handed the sheet to Papa then swiped at her eyes with her fingers.

Molly waited as her father read the telegram, her eyes intent on his face. When he frowned and shook his head, he balled the paper in his hand. "Grandma Dyer has passed away. We all must go to St. Francisville for the funeral services." He wrapped his arm around Molly's shoulder. "Looks like you get your wish to be in Louisiana.

I'll go out to the ranch and let Micah know. Then we'll need to secure tickets for tomorrow."

He patted her back then strode from the room muttering about the things he had to take care of before they could leave.

Molly straightened her shoulders and swiped her cheeks. "We have to help get the girls ready to travel. The boys can take care of themselves, and we need to let Lettie and Burt know. They were close to Grandma Dyer when they were younger."

No wonder Stefan hadn't answered her letter. He may not have even received it. As much as she anticipated a trip to Louisiana, she regretted the reason for their going. She wrapped an arm around her sister and led her from the room.

When Stefan's parents finally learned of Andrew's presence at the hospital they didn't express their feelings about his being there, but had questioned him at great length as to why he had come to New Orleans. He had not heard from them since that conversation, but with Mrs. Dyer's death, Andrew had been called back to St. Francisville to help Mrs. Whiteman until her family could arrive. Dr. Sutton had been most understanding.

Only moments before Andrew left, Dr. Sutton informed him that Stefan would be discharged from the hospital and allowed to go home perhaps on Friday or Saturday. Dr. Sutton had asked him to convey that news to Mr. and Mrs. Elliot, who had returned home yesterday to take care of business and so Mrs. Elliot could be with her friend. That instruction gave Andrew a legitimate reason for calling on them.

As soon as he arrived in St. Francisville, he headed for the Elliot home. As he rode up the lane to the main house, he understood why they had named it Oakwood. The tall, stately trees dripped with moss and formed a canopy over the path. The first glimpse of the house brought a gasp from Andrew. Nothing Mrs. Whiteman had said prepared him for the view before him of a magnificent two-story home with stately columns and a second-floor balcony. Rose bushes graced the sides of the broad expanse of steps leading up to the leaded glass double doors.

He halted his horse for a moment to gaze at the beauty of the flowers blooming around the circular drive. Never in his wildest dreams had he pictured Clarissa in a home such as this. No wonder her parents weren't pleased with her attraction to a small-town doctor. Perspiration broke out on his forehead and his throat grew dry. How could he expect her to come live with him in who knew what kind of home in New Orleans?

Clarissa deserved much more than he could offer her. He had a message to deliver, but after that, he'd have to make a decision about his position.

The front doors flew open and Clarissa ran down the steps. "Andrew, you're here. You're really here."

The joy with which she ran toward him melted all resolve. He swung down from his horse and strode toward her with his arms open. She reached him and threw her arms around his neck. As she pressed against him with her head on his chest, all the love he'd held for her these weeks came rushing back and filled him with such happiness he thought his heart might burst.

Andrew cupped his hand on her head and held her tight. "I've missed you so these past weeks."

She leaned her head back and gazed up at him. Her blue eyes had deepened to a violet hue offset by the creamy tone of her skin. She had never been more beautiful or desirable than at this moment. He'd go anywhere in the world so he could be with her.

"I'm disappointed you didn't let us know you were in Louisiana right away, but I'm glad you've been with Stefan. Mother and Father haven't let me see him yet. And I'm sorry about Mrs. Dyer's passing, but it did bring you here."

Before he had a chance to reply, she grabbed his hand and pulled him toward the house. "Come on, Mother is waiting."

When he glanced up at the house, Mrs. Elliot stood in the doorway with her hands clasped in front of her. Her features gave no indication of welcome, and he prayed that would change when she learned of his reason for being here today.

"Good afternoon, Mrs. Elliot." He removed his hat and smiled at her. His ma had taught him that courtesy would get him much farther in the world than intelligence if he practiced it consistently.

"Good afternoon, Dr. Delmont. Come in." She stepped back into the house and the coolness in her voice chilled Andrew to the bone despite the humidity and heat.

The inside of the house awed Andrew even more than the outside had. A circular marbled floor foyer was dominated by a staircase that wound its way to the second floor, its polished wood steps gleaming from the sunlight streaming through the floor-to-ceiling windows on either side of the massive door. Fresh flowers in crystal vases stood on the two tables in the entryway.

Once again the realization of all that Clarissa had and the way she lived choked him. He could never provide her with luxury like this. Then he glanced at the young woman beside him, and the sparkle of her eyes and the warmth of her smile assured him of her love. But would love be enough to leave grandeur such as this?

"I'm sorry Colonel Elliot isn't here, but he's out checking the fields. We haven't had rain in a while and the sugarcane crops are feeling the results."

"No need to apologize, I understand perfectly." He'd prefer to tell both of them the news at the same time, but without knowing when Colonel Elliot would return, that might not be possible.

Clarissa spread the skirt of her dark blue dress across the sofa. Andrew gazed at her and marveled that this beautiful creature could have feelings for him.

Mrs. Elliot snapped her ivory fan open and fanned her face. "It is humid this time of year. Sometimes I wish we didn't live so near the river."

Now was the time to share his news even without Mr. Elliot being here. "Dr. Sutton sent me here to let you know that Stefan will be discharged in a few days to come home."

Clarissa's mouth flew open, but she covered it in a hurry with her hand. Her eyes lit up and danced with excitement.

Mrs. Elliot gasped and set her cup back on the tray with a clatter. "Oh my, I had no idea. That is wonderful news. Do you know the exact day so we can be there?"

"No, ma'am, but Dr. Sutton suggested the weekend as most likely. His wounds have healed sufficiently enough for him to be at home."

Clarissa bounced on the sofa. "Oh, Andrew, that's wonderful. I can't wait to see my big brother, the hero."

Mrs. Elliot sat up taller. "Then we'll make arrangements to return to New Orleans to bring him home. Do you know when Mrs. Whiteman's family will arrive?"

"Yes, Mrs. Whiteman told me they'd be here Monday."

She clasped her hands to her chest. "Being home will be good for Stefan. I just know it."

Stefan's parents had seen and understood the extent of his injuries and the scarring that would be left on his face, neck, and right hand, but they must not have told Clarissa. How would she react when she saw her brother for the first time? And, more to the point, how would Molly?

CHAPTER 31

MOLLY STIRRED RESTLESSLY in her seat, neither the book in her hand nor the passing scenery outside the train held any appeal. Maybe she could talk with her uncle Micah to pass the time. Uncle Micah had secured tickets for the Whiteman and Gordon families to travel to Louisiana on Saturday. His mother had come along to help with Grace and Joel. In another hour they'd be in Baton Rouge, where her mother's two brothers would meet them. Both anticipation and dread whirled in Molly's head as she changed seats, sitting down beside Micah, who stopped reading and smiled at her.

"What's on your mind? I can see the wheels turning."

Molly swallowed hard. Her eyes must have given away her concerns because her uncle never hesitated to ask questions when he saw a need. "I'm thinking about Stefan and Mama and Grandma and my brain is like mush. Mama didn't say what Stefan's injuries are, but they must be bad for them to discharge him from the military. If he's in the hospital at New Orleans, how will I ever get a chance to go and visit him?"

He patted her hand. "I'm sure there will be time after the funeral. Your mother and Hannah will have to stay so they can take care of the estate with their brothers. I'll even take you down there myself if it's that important to you."

Hope brightened Molly's heart. "You would? Oh, Uncle

Micah, I love you." She grabbed him in a hug, and he laughed.

"I can see the young man means a great deal to you. Care to tell me about it?"

Heat filled Molly's cheeks. She'd wanted to share her feelings before, but everyone had seemed too preoccupied with preparations for the trip and dealing with Grandma's death to listen to her. Her uncle's sympathetic gaze touched her soul, and gave her the courage to talk with him.

"I had a liking for Stefan way back when we were children, but he always teased me and played tricks on me, so I thought he didn't like me at all. Then when he came to Stoney Creek with his parents, the old feelings returned. But he was in the military, and you know how I felt about guns and fighting."

At her uncle's nod, she took a deep breath, expelled it, and continued.

"Stefan said he cared about me, and I thought I cared about him, but his plans for the future were nothing like mine. First off I couldn't imagine being married to a soldier, and then he told me that after he retires from the military, he wants to have a ranch and raise horses."

She bit her lip and glanced down at her hands in her lap. "As much as I love visiting with you and Aunt Hannah, I didn't want to live outside of town. I love all the things I'm involved in with school and the church and couldn't imagine leaving."

"I know the encounter at the livery changed your ideas about guns, but what changed your mind about the other?"

From the gleam in his eye, he already knew the answer, but waited for her explanation. "I thought I was going to die, and suddenly I realized I'd never have the chance to be with Stefan. Right then I decided I wanted to be with him wherever he lived. I'm willing to give up everything I know just to be where he is."

Micah chuckled and hugged Molly to his side. "That's what I figured. You've learned a great lesson about love. It's one I learned with Hannah."

"I remember that. I think Aunt Hannah loved you from the beginning, but she was afraid you held only pity for her. I think loving a person means you forget about your-self and know only that you have to be with the one you love no matter what the circumstances."

"You're right about that."

The train whistle sent a warning as their destination approached. Micah reached down to stow his book in his satchel. "I think Stefan will make a fine ranch man, and perhaps that's what he can be now that he won't be in the military. He knows horses and is good at handling them, so I wish you both a bright future."

Molly hugged her uncle again. "Thank you. I'm so glad I talked with you."

"And I'm glad you were willing to share." He stood. "Now let's get everyone and everything ready to get off this train."

Molly scurried back to her seat to help Alice and Juliet with their belongings. With her uncle's help she would find time to go and visit with Stefan. She couldn't wait to see him.

❧

Stefan glanced around the hospital room that had been his home the last several weeks. He'd opted not to be sequestered in a more private room. Instead he'd spent time getting to know the men in the ward. None of them seemed to mind the burns that scarred his face, but then some of them were in a much worse state than he was.

His father and mother entered with Dr. Sutton and Andrew. Andrew's smile must mean good news.

Dr. Sutton held several papers in his hand. "These are your discharge papers. I'm sorry it didn't work out Friday as I'd hoped, but as soon as you're ready we'll wheel you down to the driveway and get you ready for the trip home."

His father clasped his shoulder. "We've asked Andrew to come home with us and take care of you until you are completely healed, and Dr. Sutton has agreed."

Stefan jerked his head toward Andrew. "Is that right? You're coming with us?"

"Yes, I am. However, except for making sure your burns continue to heal properly, I won't have that much to look after. You're fully mobile, and you have no restrictions on your diet, so you should do well. I'll help you with exercises for your hands and get that shoulder fully functional again."

Andrew had become a good friend, and with his help, maybe he would be able to use his hands again. "I'm ready now. Let's go home." He stood then seated himself in the wheelchair provided by an orderly. Once home, he'd be away from the curious stares and looks of pity from visitors.

His mother walked beside the chair, her hand on Stefan's arm. "The army sent all of your belongings to us, so you'll have everything you left behind when you get home."

Everything except the pride and dignity of being an

officer of the United States Cavalry. That hurt as much, and maybe even more than the wounds he'd suffered.

Five minutes later, he sat beside Andrew in the carriage that would take them to the docks for the trip to St. Francisville and to an uncertain future. The only consolation lay in the knowledge he'd be able to ride Warrior across the countryside. He might shut himself off from people, but he'd still be able to work with horses and enjoy the feel of the wind on his face as he rode.

His father cleared his throat. "Hm, there is one thing I need to tell you before we return to Oakwood."

A momentary pause aroused Stefan's curiosity as he peered at his father.

"I've been discussing the sale of Oakwood with Thomas Dyer. He's been interested in adding our land to that he now owns."

Stefan jerked his head, ignoring the pain that shot up his cheek. "Sell Oakwood? What are you talking about?"

"Your mother and I have been considering it for a while. She wants to be in Baton Rouge closer to her mother, and since my parents are there too, it seems like a good move. Our profits have fallen considerably, so it is a good time to do it. When you were in the military, I knew you had no interest in the place. Now that you're to be home, I need to know what your desires are."

Stefan swallowed hard. His desire to work on a ranch with horses had not changed, but his circumstances had. Although he had no desire to run the plantation as his family had for generations, what else could he do? "I don't really have any plans at the moment." He held up his injured hands. "I'm not sure how useful I'd be at anything."

"I see." He glanced out the window. "We're at the docks. We can discuss this further when we arrive home."

His father escorted him up the gangplank onto the steamboat then found them a seat in the enclosed area for first-class passengers. "We can enjoy the view and refreshments on our journey." He glanced around the large room and smiled. "They say the railroads will soon take over all and we won't need these boats anymore. I must say I think I prefer the relaxing ride on a boat."

Stefan nodded his agreement, having no desire for trivial conversation. After refreshments were served, Andrew leaned toward Stefan. "Has anyone told you that Mrs. Dyer passed away? The Whiteman and Gordon families will be arriving today from Texas for Mrs. Dyer's funeral services on Tuesday."

Stefan's heart jumped and his throat closed. Molly here in Louisiana? He'd learned of Mrs. Dyer's death from his mother, but the possibility of Molly coming for the services had never occurred to him. Having her so far away in Texas made his resolve never to see her easy to handle, but with her only a few miles away, how could he bear not being with her?

"I don't want her to see me like this. She had a hard enough time with the idea of my fighting, and she doesn't need to see the results of it."

Andrew shook his head. "She's changed so much in the weeks since you were in Stoney Creek and—"

"I don't want to hear any more about it. Mother and Father and Clarissa may go to the funeral, but I won't. You can't change my mind."

Andrew crossed his arms over his chest and frowned at Stefan. "Are you so vain that you believe your good looks and your military rank are the only important things about you? You're still the same person inside."

"You don't understand. Now leave me alone." Stefan pressed his lips together and turned to gaze out the window to the river so the injured side of his face would be less visible. Already the stares and head-shaking as people saw his wounds humiliated him. All his dreams and hopes for the future had burned up in that fire. Until he decided what to do next, he planned to do a lot of reading and thinking. Since Molly had rejected him in Stoney Creek, and especially since his injuries, she no longer had a place in his future. That crushed his heart but her decision was best for them both.

CHAPTER 32

THE SERVICES ON Tuesday for Grandma Dyer had been beautiful with Reverend Douglas delivering a wonderful eulogy, and the graveside service in Woodville brought back memories of childhood days visiting there and seeing Grandpa Dyer, too. Only one thing marred the entire day, and that was the absence of Stefan. His parents had come, but he remained at home.

Now, in the late afternoon, restlessness and a desire to see Stefan tore at Molly. She slipped out the back way and found George at the carriage house and asked him to hitch one of the buggies for her to ride over to the Elliot plantation.

"Missy, I'm not sure that's a good idea. Does your momma or poppa know you're going?"

Not one to lie, Molly dipped her head and shook her head. "No, they don't." Then she grabbed George's arm. "Please, George, do this for me. I have to go see Stefan."

He scratched his head and glanced at the house. "All right. I can't stand to see the misery in your eyes. Give me a minute and I'll have it all ready for you."

She smiled widely. "Thank you, thank you." Then she stepped back and let him go about the business of hitching a black horse to the buggy. In a few minutes, he led the horse out to the drive and helped her up to the seat.

George handed her the reins. "I don't know why I'm a doing this, but you be careful, Missy. Be sure you leave Oakwood to get home before dark."

She promised she would and headed out to the road leading to Oakwood. All the way there she rehearsed what she wanted to tell Stefan. Andrew had said he hadn't had the opportunity to tell Stefan about what had happened to her, and he'd also warned her about Stefan not wanting to see her.

That was nonsense. As soon as Stefan heard about her experience and what she had learned, he'd welcome her with open arms. Andrew had even warned her that Stefan's injuries were ugly, but then any injury that discharged one from the army must be ugly. She'd deal with that when the time came.

The oak-tree-lined path to the house brought back memories of playing with Clarissa when Molly and her family came back to visit. With all the family around for the services, she and Clarissa had found no time to visit, but they would soon.

Molly climbed down from the buggy and dropped the lead weight on the ground. Before she reached the porch, Clarissa opened the door and ran out and wrapped her arms around Molly.

"Oh, I'm so glad to see you. I have so much to tell you, and I'm sure you have as much to tell me."

"Yes, I do, but I came to see Stefan. I have to tell him how much I love him."

A shadow crossed Clarissa's eyes, and she bit her lip. Tears welled in her eyes as she grabbed Molly's hand. "He won't see you. He won't see anybody. He doesn't even want Mother or Father around. All he wants is to be alone." Then a sob escaped. "Oh, Molly, his face is burned and looks so bad, and his right hand is crippled."

Molly's heart skipped a beat and a lump rose in her

throat, threatening tears in her eyes. She blinked them away. No, Stefan would not see her crying. She loved him no matter what. "Where is he?"

"He's in the library. That's where he spends all his time, except when he goes up to his room at night or out to ride Warrior."

Molly squared her shoulders and walked to the double doors. He had to see her. She had so much to tell him.

Molly's voice echoed in the entryway and jarred Stefan from his reading. What was she doing here? He'd told everyone he didn't want to see her. Stubborn as she was, of course Molly wouldn't listen, and now he'd have to deal with it.

He laid aside his book and strode to the door. Moments later her knock sounded.

"Stefan, it's Molly. May I come in?"

Her voice squeezed his heart with remorse and his throat tightened. He had to be strong. "No, Molly, go back to your grandmother's house. You don't need to see me now or ever again."

"Oh, but I do, Stefan. I love you, and I don't care what you look like or what you do with your life. I just want to be a part of it and do it with you."

She loved him. The words hit his chest with a hammer blow that sent him a step backward. No, she couldn't, she mustn't. He had nothing to offer her now. Regret for what could have been filled him with overwhelming sadness.

"Stefan, please let me in."

Her sobs from the other side almost broke his resolve,

but he steeled himself and hardened his heart. "No, Molly. Not now. Not ever. I'm done talking. Go home."

The hardest words he'd ever spoken, but the most necessary. He turned from the door and strode to the window overlooking the driveway where her buggy sat waiting. If he could see her for a moment, he'd be satisfied. Then she'd be out of his life forever.

Her footsteps clicked across the tile and then the front door slammed. She ran to the buggy and hefted the lead weight onto the floor and climbed up to the seat. She snapped the reins with a fierce jerk that must have startled her horse. He reared back, front hoofs pawing the air, then came down with a thud and raced up the road.

Molly! She couldn't control the horse. Without hesitation he raced through the French doors to the outside and to the stables. He grabbed a bridle and reins from the wall and burst into Warrior's stall. No time for a saddle, he had to get to Molly now.

With the bridle and reins in place he hoisted himself up onto Warrior's back and dug his heels into the horse's flanks. "Let's go. We have a rescue to do."

Once on the path to the main road, Molly's buggy came into view, still careening at a high speed. Stefan flipped the reins from side to side to spur Warrior even faster and gained on the buggy. They'd be at the gate in moments, and if the horse didn't slow down for the turn, they'd be in the fields and rough terrain, and there was no telling what would happen then.

Warrior gained speed and shortened the distance in a flash. At the same moment Stefan reached the runaway's side and stretched out his good hand to grab the reins. Pain shot up his arm, but he held tight as the horse snorted and bolted sideways. Molly screamed and the buggy swayed then toppled to the side, throwing Molly headfirst to the ground.

Stefan pulled Warrior to a halt and scrambled to where Molly lay quiet and still on the side of the road. He gathered her in his arms and held her close. "Oh, please, God, she has to be all right."

He rocked back and forth on the ground and looked around to figure how to get her back to the house. A figure on horseback neared, and soon his father pulled to a stop and dismounted. "I saw her buggy at a distance as I was riding home, and I could tell it was going dangerously fast, so I followed." He touched the side of Molly's neck. "She has a pulse." He then ran his hands over her arms and legs and checked her neck. "No broken bones either. Still, we have to get her back to the house and send for her father."

His father pulled the buggy upright. Thankfully the horse had stopped running once the buggy tipped over.

After his father had the horse under control he knelt beside Stefan again. "Let's put her on the buggy then you can lead it back to the house."

They laid Molly on the buggy seat. After tying Warrior behind them, Stefan pulled himself up to sit beside her and took up the reins despite the pain gripping his arms and shoulder. His father mounted and rode beside them. Isaac, a stable hand, met them halfway back, riding an old nag. "I figured you might need help."

"Yes, Miss Dyer is injured. Ride to the Dyer home and bring her father here."

"Yes, sir, Mr. Elliot." He nodded to Stefan as he passed and galloped down the road to the Dyer home.

Once back at the house, Stefan and his father carried

Molly to the large front parlor and laid her on the sofa. Mother grabbed Clarissa's arm. "Run, tell Delfina we need water and some cloth to clean the wound on Molly's head."

Clarissa spun around to run her errand, and Mother knelt beside Stefan while his father went to the porch to watch for Dr. Whiteman.

Stefan grasped Molly's hand. "I didn't get to her in time to stop that horse. If I hadn't been so cruel to her, she wouldn't have been so upset. None of this would have happened."

His mother wrapped her arm around his shoulders. "Stefan, please don't blame yourself. It was an accident, and by being there, you prevented a greater tragedy."

Maybe so, but his own selfish pride had sent her away in tears and if she was badly injured, he'd never forgive himself.

Delfina returned with the water and a cloth. His mother dipped the cloth in water then wrung it out. With gentle strokes, she wiped the blood from Molly's forehead. "The cut is deep, but I think I've stopped the blood. She may need stitches, but I don't know. We'll wait for her father to get here."

Molly's ashen face sent tentacles of fear around his heart. Her dress skirt was torn and a sleeve had ripped. He placed his mouth next to her ear. "Molly, I do love you, and I am so sorry for driving you away."

Molly's lashes fluttered against her cheeks, and her eyes opened. Their green depths swallowed him, and he wanted to drown in their beauty. Her eyes focused on him and she smiled.

"Stefan, I love you more than you could ever imagine." Then she frowned and lifted her fingers to his burned cheek. "Oh, Stefan, how terrible for you. What pain you must have felt."

Stefan flinched and sat back on his heels. Not able to stand the pity and the pain in her eyes as she looked at him, he jumped up and fled to the safety of the library. Now that she'd seen his ugliness, she'd understand why there was no future for them.

He slammed the door shut and dropped to his knees. "Why, God? Why?" God may have a purpose for all that happened, but why did His purpose have to include this?

CHAPTER 33

WHERE IS STEFAN? Please, I must see him." Molly tried to sit up, but Papa's hand restrained her. He knelt beside her and examined the cut on her head.

"He's not here right now. Lie still so I can see about your injuries."

"But he saved my life. He chased down the horse and he was there when I overturned. I have to see him." The memory of his burned face surfaced and squeezed her heart. Tears welled, but she blinked them back.

Papa stood and rolled down his sleeves. "As far as I can tell, your shoulder is sprained and will be sore for a few days. The cut on your head is to the bone, but with such a thin layer of skin there, I think it will be all right without stitches. The bandage and tape I applied should keep the edges together and allow them to heal."

He turned to Colonel Elliot. "Now tell me about Stefan's injuries."

Molly concentrated on the information Stefan's father shared. "The burns on Stefan's right hand were deep but didn't do serious damage to the underlying tissue. However, his hand will be scarred with some restriction in movement. The burns on his face will leave scars as well."

That was why he hadn't wanted to see her earlier, but he said he loved her. None of it made sense. If he loved her, then what difference did it make if his face was scarred? He was alive and that's all that mattered.

"Colonel Elliot, where is Stefan? He was here right before Papa came." As soon as she had touched his face, he'd jumped up and run from her.

"He's in the library and says he doesn't want to see anyone."

Mrs. Elliot grasped Molly's hand, tears sliding from the corners of her eyes. "My dear child, Stefan is hurting. Not just from the wounds, but from the pain of leaving the military. He feels that he is no longer of use to anyone for anything. I heard him say he loves you, and I know he does, but I'm afraid he doesn't think he's worthy of your love now."

Love for Stefan flooded her soul and formed a lump in her throat she couldn't swallow. Her shoulder and head ached, but the ache in her heart from Stefan's rejection hurt far more than any injury to her body.

"Mrs. Elliot, I love him with all my heart. I don't care what he can or can't do or how he looks now. He's alive and he's here. That's all I care about, and I need to tell him that."

No answer came from either Mrs. Elliot or the colonel. Clarissa stood to the side wringing her hands and crying. Movement behind her father caught her attention. Her uncle Micah turned and strode from the room. Molly frowned. "Why is Uncle Micah here?"

"We didn't know what to expect so he came with me to repair the buggy if it needed it. One of the wheels was loose and Isaac is having it taken care of now. We'll be ready to take you home when it's done."

"But I don't want to leave without seeing Stefan again. I have to talk to him, and he has to listen." She couldn't bear the idea of going back without trying to make Stefan believe she loved him.

"I understand, but your mother and sisters are very worried about you. Your mother wanted to come with me, but since we came on horseback, she decided to stay and wait."

Molly worried her bottom lip. She didn't want to upset Mama, but seeing Stefan had become urgent. She grabbed Papa's arm and her nails dug into the flesh through his sleeve. "I won't leave without seeing Stefan or at least talking to him, whether it's face-to-face or with a door between us."

Papa glanced down at her hand on his arm, and with his gentle touch pried her hand loose. "If you're this determined, we'll see what we can do." He glanced up at Mrs. Elliot.

"I don't know. I think Micah went in to see him. I'll check." Her skirts swished as she spun around and left the room.

Stefan jumped up when Micah strode into the room without being invited or even knocking. "I don't want to see you or anyone else." He retreated to the wingback chair near the fireplace, now as cold and barren as his life.

"I don't care whether you want to see me or not. You don't have to look at me and I don't have to see you for you to listen to what I have to say."

He pulled a chair up close to Stefan. "First, I want to thank you for saving Molly. She could have been more seriously hurt if you hadn't been there to tend to her immediately."

"No thanks are needed. I'm the reason she ran out of the house so distraught in the first place. That caused her to startle the horse." No matter how he tried to justify the reasons for sending her away, he was the cause for her injuries. He was no good for her, and the sooner they took her home, the better for her.

Micah cleared his throat and braced his elbows on his knees. "Anybody with half a brain can see how much you love that girl in there, and she loves you just as much. If you let what has happened to you prevent you from embracing that love, you're a bigger idiot than I thought you were."

That was a laugh. They may think him a fool for not accepting her love, but he'd be a bigger one if he did and then couldn't take care of her. "And how do you think she'll feel about me when I can't provide for her or take care of her? I don't want or need her pity. It's best if she leaves and forgets ever having met me."

"Son, if you ask me, you are making trouble for yourself. Whether she wants to stay with you or leave because of your injuries is her choice, not yours, and you must give her the opportunity to make it."

"I don't want her to have to make the choice. This way is better. There's nothing I can do for her the way I am now." Why couldn't people leave him alone?

"There's plenty you can do if you want to do it. Molly told me that your dream after the military was to own a ranch and raise horses."

"Some dream that was." Without savings from his time in the military he had no hopes of owning a ranch or doing much of anything else. He could work here raising sugarcane, but it was the last thing he'd wanted to do with his life.

"It can still come to pass. I saw how good you are with horses when you were out at our ranch. You chose one of my finest for yourself in Warrior, and he took to you right away because he recognized you're a horseman."

"What good does that do now? I still have a crippled hand. And look at my face. Who'd want to hire me or work with me with these scars?"

Micah rubbed his chin and shook his head. "They don't look all that bad to me. Let me tell you one thing. If you think no one will care about you or work with you, you underestimate the people around you."

He leaned forward. "Look at me, Stefan."

Stefan steeled his jaw and clenched his teeth but he turned to the man beside him. The look in his eyes was not one of pity, but of true concern. Maybe it didn't bother Micah, and he'd been through some hard times himself so perhaps it would be wise to listen to him.

"When I first met Hannah, her crippled leg created a great deal of pity, but as I grew to know her all her other qualities overshadowed that. But I didn't want to be saddled with a cripple so I ignored those qualities. Then all those things with my pa's death, the mortgage on the ranch, the fight with Levi, and then the mine discovery changed my perspective on life and what is important. Hannah's love and faith in me never wavered. That's when I decided God was pretty good after all, and I wanted Hannah for my bride because I loved her too much to let her handicap stand in the way. Molly is just like her aunt and her mother. They care about people and what's inside, not what looks pretty on the outside."

"So you're saying I should let Molly see me like this." Stefan shook his head. "I don't think so. I don't need her pity."

"It won't be pity you see, but her love and God's love for you shining through. God's love will never fail you, son, and the sooner you realize that and accept Molly's love, the sooner you can get on with life."

Dare he hope Micah's words were true? "But even if she still wants me, what can I do to take care of her and provide for her? I can't use these hands for much." He held out his hands, healing from their burns.

Micah tilted his head to one side. "When you were riding after the runaway and then stopping the horse, did you use your hands? Did they hurt? Did they keep you from helping Molly?"

Stefan gazed at his hands. He didn't remember if they hurt or not while he was chasing after Molly. His eyes opened wide and he raised his head to smile at Micah. "I used them like I always have when I was riding."

A wide grin spread across Micah's face. "I thought so. You can do anything you set your mind to doing. And here's what I propose. When you've completely healed and are ready to work, come to Texas. Levi and I could use a good man with horses like you. There's a piece of land that can be yours one day if you want it. If the three of us pool our knowledge and work together, we can have one of the best spreads in all of Texas."

Stefan sat with his heart thudding in his chest. "I don't know what to say. I never expected something like this. You're not taking pity on me because my mother and your wife's family are close friends, are you?"

"Not hardly. I'm doing it for you and Molly to have a chance at the happiness you two deserve."

"I'll have to discuss it with Father in light of what will happen to the land here. He told me of plans to sell to Thomas Dyer. If that goes through, then I'll think about Texas."

"I understand, and my offer is there whenever you do decide."

Before Stefan could absorb all that Micah proposed, his mother's voice called from the hallway. "Stefan, please come and speak with Molly. She refuses to go home until you do."

Stefan turned to Micah. "I'll talk to her. If she rejects me, then I must reject your offer. If this is God's answer for me, I'll know when I look into her eyes."

"Good enough." Micah slapped him on the back then stood. "Let's go talk to the young lady."

CHAPTER 34

STEFAN'S HANDS TREMBLED when he entered the parlor, the fear of rejection coursing through his veins. Molly sat on the sofa where he had laid her. A bandage covered the wound on her head and a triangle of fabric supported her left arm. Even with the torn dress and smudges on her chin she was the prettiest sight in the room. Her gaze locked with his as he approached her with a prayer in his heart.

Stefan sat then grasped her hand in his least injured one. "You asked to see me and here I am, but before you speak let me have my say."

She gazed back at him without a flinch or flicker of her eyes. At her nod, he continued. "Now that you've seen the damage done by my injuries you understand why I didn't want to see you. My life has changed completely since the last time we met, and I can no longer offer you the life I had hoped for us. I understand if you'd rather not pursue a relationship now, but know I do love you with all my heart."

Her hands were like ice, and a shiver shook her shoulders. Everyone had left the room to give them privacy, and Stefan swallowed hard, waiting for her response.

She threw her arm around his neck. "Oh, Stefan, those are the most wonderful words I've ever heard. I love you so much I'm afraid my heart will burst. Where we live or what you do won't matter because we'll be together. I'm so sorry that your injuries cost you your army career, but you have so much more to offer this world."

He held her shoulders and pushed her back to gaze into her eyes, unable to believe the words she'd spoken. "You really mean that, don't you? Despite what you see, you still love me."

"Of course I do. What I see is the same man who came to Stoney Creek back in June and won my heart with his caring ways." She pointed a finger to his chest. "It's what's in here that counts, not what's on the outside."

Never had words been so sweet to his ear. This was God's answer, and he accepted it with joy and thanksgiving. He raised his hands to cup her face in his palms. "Molly Whiteman, you are the most wonderful woman I've ever met."

When his lips touched hers, every nerve in his body jumped to attention. This was the woman he loved, and she loved him despite everything. The pressure from her lips deepened, and she wrapped her arms around him and leaned into the kiss.

He wanted the kiss to never end, but after a moment he pulled back and breathed deeply.

Molly sighed. "What is it, Stefan?"

"I'm medically discharged from the army, but it hasn't changed my ideas about guns and the military."

She placed her fingers on his lips. "Ssh. That doesn't matter. I was held hostage by some horse thieves at the livery on July Fourth and it changed my attitude because, at that particular moment, I wanted a gun more than anything to defend myself."

His heart lurched first with shock then with concern and then relief. "You were held hostage? Were you hurt?"

If he'd been there, whoever had her would have been dead before he knew what hit him.

"Not physically. My uncles and the sheriff came to rescue me. I was a little shaken up, but it sure cleared my head and my heart. I wrote to you and told you all about it, but you must have already left the fort by then."

He wrapped his arms around her again. He could have lost her, but God had spared her and shown her the reality of life and brought her here. Stefan almost choked with the realization of what he'd nearly turned away. "If anything had happened to you...I can't even bear to think about it. God took care of us both in those few days."

Then he released her and they sat facing each other on the sofa. "There's one other matter we have to consider. I remember how much you love living in town and being around people and visiting and socializing. I can't give you all of that if I'm working a ranch."

"Working a ranch? Where? I told you I'd go anywhere with you. I don't care if you move to the great northwest or to the mountains or stay in Louisiana, I want to be there too."

Delight filled him, and he couldn't stop the grin from turning up one corner of his mouth. "Then how about Texas? On your Uncle Micah's ranch? He's offered me a job there."

Molly's mouth dropped open. Had she heard him correctly? Back to Texas and to the Gordon ranch? "Oh, my, that's even better than I ever dreamed." She stood and reached for his hand. "Maybe I could even keep teaching, like Ellie."

He lifted her free hand to his lips. "Then, Miss Molly Whiteman, will you be my wife and work with me to raise the best horses Texas has ever seen?"

Molly's heart jumped and beat faster than the flutter of hummingbird wings. Stefan's blue eyes penetrated her very soul and beyond to depths she didn't know existed. He loved her and that's all that mattered.

"Oh, Stefan, yes, yes, and yes and yes again!" She planted her lips on his to seal her answer. This moment would live forever in her memory.

Hands clapping and laughter broke them apart. Heat filled Molly's face, but this was the happiest moment in her life, and she was glad to share it.

Papa strode to her and held out his arms for a hug. "This will make your mother very happy. This is what she's been praying for."

Colonel Elliot stepped to his son's side. "Micah Gordon has told me of his offer. The ranch in Texas is a long way from here, but not as far as Arizona, so I'm happy for you." He reached out and hugged his son.

Stefan stepped back. "Thank you, but what about the plantation?"

Mr. Elliot grinned and stepped back. "I am pretty sure the deal I made with Thomas Dyer will go through. He'll add Oakwood to his land, keep all our workers, and move in here. Mother and I will then move to Baton Rouge to be closer to your grandmother."

Stefan grasped his father's hand. "I'm sorry to see Oakwood leave the family, but happy it will be in such good hands. And with me being a part of his family, it won't seem as much of a loss."

Molly's heart soared at this new revelation. Nothing could keep Stefan and her from going back to Stoney Creek now.

Clarissa tugged Molly's arm and pulled her aside to a corner of the room. "Andrew and I have committed to each other too. He's decided to stay in New Orleans with Dr. Sutton, and he's going back there tomorrow to make all the arrangements. I wanted to be near you, but think of all the fun we can have when you come to visit. And I know we'll want to come out to Texas and visit with his family, too."

"What do your parents think about that?" Concern for how they'd previously acted toward Andrew prevented her from sharing Clarissa's happiness.

"Since Andrew has been helping with the medical care of Stefan, Mother and Father have come to know him better. Now with the plantation being sold and Andrew staying in Louisiana, Father won't be as reluctant to see me married and living in New Orleans."

Papa joined the conversation. "I don't mean to interrupt, but Molly, I think you'll be happy to know that I'm going to suggest to your mother that we allow you to stay here while she settles Grandma Dyer's estate."

Molly squealed and hugged her father then winced. She'd forgotten about the sore shoulder, but she ignored the pain in the joy of the moment. "Oh, Papa, that would be wonderful. Then I can see Stefan every day and help him get better."

"I thought that might please you. My retired friend, Dr. Sanger, is at home now taking care of my patients, and when I return he will remain in Stoney Creek and help me until I find a replacement for Andrew."

"That's perfect." She grabbed Clarissa's hand. "Yours is the next best news I've had in a long time, the best being Stefan of course."

"We've talked about an early fall wedding here at Oakwood, but it'll most likely be at Grace Church. So, it looks like I'll be Andrew's bride by Thanksgiving."

Molly squeezed Clarissa's hand. "I can hardly wait. It'll be so good to have you close by while I'm here with Mama." Tears welled in Molly's eyes, but these were tears of pure joy. She'd spend the rest of her life with the man she loved. And her two best friends were going to be married, too.

Stefan reached for her and pulled her against him. "Are you sure you want to be tied to me the rest of your life?"

Her heart filled to the bursting point and beyond. "As sure as I could ever possibly be. Just try and get out of it now that everyone here has heard you declare your love."

His laughter rang in her soul. "I don't think that's about to happen." Then he sobered and held her hands. "Your Uncle Micah talked to me about God's unfailing love. He seems to have proven that beyond a doubt with all He's done in the past few weeks."

Molly nodded in agreement. "My uncle is a wise man." She stepped closer to enter Stefan's willing embrace. God had worked in mysterious and even painful ways to bring them to this moment. But she had no regrets. He had brought them together, in His timing, in His way. No matter what they faced in the future they could stand on the assurance that God's love had never failed them—and never would.

OTHER BOOKS BY MARTHA ROGERS

Winds Across the Prairie

WINDS ACROSS THE PRAIRIE SERIES

The Winds Across the Prairie series brings you back to the town of Barton Creek in Oklahoma Territory, providing a glimpse into everyday life at a time when Oklahoma was drawing homesteaders to its territory before the days of statehood.

Amelia's Journey

Ben Haynes and Amelia Carlyle were childhood friends before Amelia's family moved to Boston. After they run into each other at her sister's wedding, Ben calls on Amelia several times. As he leaves for Kansas, they promise to write. Although Ben captured Amelia's heart, her parents discourage the relationship and forbid her to correspond with him. She promises to wait for him, but will the love and loss they experience along the way draw them closer or tear them apart? Can a Boston socialite find true happiness with a Kansas cowboy?

Becoming Lucy

After the deaths of her parents, seventeen-year-old Lucinda Bishop is sent to Oklahoma to live with her aunt and uncle. Oklahoma ranch life brings more than this heiress bargained for when she meets Jake Starnes, a ranch hand running from his past. As her friendship with Jake grows, Lucy faces emotions she's never experienced before. With Lucy's help, will he get his life together and face the consequences of his past? Or will he lose the girl he loves before he gets a chance?

Morning for Dove

Love knows no boundaries of race or culture when it is rooted in God's love for His people. When Luke Anderson falls in love with Dove Morris, he is aware of her Native American heritage. He does not, however, expect the sudden prejudice his mother exhibits toward Dove. When a wildfire threatens Morris Ranch and Luke risks his life for Dove, will his parents see how rooted the love between Luke and Dove is? Or will Luke's parents try to tear them apart? Can love overcome the intolerance in the Oklahoma Territory?

Finding Becky

Becky Haynes returns to Barton Creek as a new college graduate with a strong independent spirit and Geoff Kensington, a recent acquaintance who shows more than just a passing interest in her. Rob Frankston waited four years for her return and is puzzled by the new Becky. When strange accidents start happening around the town, Rob becomes suspicious. Is it just jealousy? Or will he be able to convince the old Becky to return before it's too late?

Caroline's Choice

Caroline Frankston longs for more than her provincial life in Barton Creek. When her feelings for Matthew

Haynes appear unrequited, she moves to Oklahoma City for a fresh start. Matthew realizes his feelings for her after she is gone and decides to tell her when she returns to Barton Creek for a visit. When Caroline goes missing after her train is in an accident, Matt sets out in search of her. Will he find her, or has any chance of spending his life with Caroline disappeared?

Christmas at Holly Hill

When Clayton Barlow returns home after a prison sentence, he is determined to make a new start and prove he is trustworthy. Merry Lee Warner was his childhood friend and is now a schoolteacher. When Clayton's feelings for her resurface, he doubts he could get a woman like Merry to love him. Will the trust of an unlikely new friend be enough to restore Clayton's relationships with the town and reunite him with God and Merry?

SEASONS OF THE HEART

Set in the late 1800s the Seasons of the Heart series weaves together the stories of four women whose great faith make a difference in the lives of the men they love. The series moves from Connecticut to Texas as it follows the lives of these women and their families as they find true love and bond in friendship only God could orchestrate.

Summer Dream

Rachel Winston is tired of being known as the minister's daughter in her small town. When she starts making plans to visit her aunt in Boston for the social season, Nathan Reed arrives. Rachel can't help but wonder if he's the one. Nathan has no desire to experience life with Christians after his experiences with his own family; not that he even had a chance to court Rachel until he resolves his anger with God and his family. When Nathan is caught in a blizzard and lies near death in the Winston home, Rachel and her mother give him a lesson in love and forgiveness while nursing him back to health. Will Nathan make peace with his family and return before Rachel chooses a path that will take her away from him?

Autumn Song

Kathleen Muldoon left her family's ranch to live with her aunt Mae, who runs a boardinghouse, and study medicine under Old Doc Jensen in Porterfield, Texas. Daniel Monroe moved to Porterfield to set up his law practice and is introduced to Kate at the boardinghouse. Sparks fly, and then turn to ashes as the two begin arguing. Will Daniel accept Kate's independent nature and dreams of becoming a nurse? Will Daniel's law practice destroy her father's land? Can they both overcome their pride and become everything God wants them to be?

Winter Promise

Abigail Monroe is almost twenty-five. She is educated, beautiful, and single, and she fears she'll become a spinster if she stays in Briar Ridge, Connecticut. She decides she needs a fresh start and joins her brother and his wife in Porterfield, Texas. A sprained ankle sends her to the new town doctor, Elliot Jensen. Elliot, however smitten he feels by Abigail, is frozen by his emotions due to his painful past. Will he wait too long to share his feelings? Or will Christmas bring them both the gift they seek?

Spring Hope

Libby Cantrell arrives in Porterfield, Texas, in the middle of a cold winter night. She is exhausted, ill, hungry, and trying to run away from her past. Sheriff Cory Muldoon finds her behind a barn and takes her to the doctor. Cory is determined to know the truth about her even though he is attracted to the young woman. Libby escaped her abusive father and is trying to create a better future for herself. As winter becomes spring, will Cory be able to accept Libby for who she is now and forgive her sordid past?

 THE HOMEWARD JOURNEY

THE HOMEWARD JOURNEY

Love Stays True

Sallie Dyer fell in love when she was just a young girl. Manfred McDaniel Whiteman and his brother, Edward, left Bayou Sara, Louisiana, to join the war and were taken prisoners. Now Sallie has grown into a caring young woman and is still waiting word of her beloved Manfred—despite her father's worries that he may never come home. Following the surrender at Appomattox in April 1865, Manfred and Edward are released and begin their journey home. Along the way they encounter storms and thieves, and are thrown in prison. Will Manfred return home before someone else claims Sallie's hand? Can the two of them overcome the distance that the war put between them?

Love Finds Faith

Hannah Dyer is a successful nurse who moved to Texas to help her brother-in-law's medical practice. Despite her success, Hannah fears she is not good enough due to her birth defect of having one leg much shorter than the other. When Micah Gordon returns home, his father hopes he will finally settle down to ranch life. Hannah is smitten with Micah but believes she has no hope of attracting him because of her leg. Micah is determined to not settle down, no matter how attracted he is to Hannah. After Micah suffers a tragic loss, he loses his faith and almost loses his ranch. Can Hannah's care and faith help him recover and find new hope, faith, and love?